READY
OR NOT

THE HUNTER'S CLUB

ALINA MAY

The story, all names, characters, and incidents portrayed in this production are fictitious. No identification with actual persons (living or deceased), places, buildings, and products is intended or should be inferred. This story is not meant to be used as a guide to sexual expression.

Ebook ISBN: 978-1-964979-02-1

Paperback ISBN: 978-1-964979-03-8

Hardcover ISBN: 978-1-964979-04-5

Paperback Black Pages ISBN: 978-1-964979-05-2

Book Cover Occult Goddess

Formatting by Occult Goddess

Illustrations by Lulybot

Editing by Deliciously Dark Editing

Page Edge Design (hardcover) Painted Wing's Publishing

This content only suitable for 18+

TO ALL MY GIRLIES WHO LOVE HALLOWEEN, BEING CHASED BY MASKED PEOPLE, AND WANT TO GET EATEN OUT IN A CORN MAZE.

Welcome to the debauchery.

AUTHOR'S NOTE

Please be aware that this book is extremely dark. In most scenes, the characters do not consent. Some of the characters have had horrible things happen to them as children, and the characters do not interact with each other in healthy ways. If that made you cringe, put the book down because it gets worse.

Manson and Riley are both diagnosed with Antisocial Personality Disorder or, as it's commonly referred to as, psychopathy. People with this diagnosis do not feel emotions the same way most people do. In addition, Rachel is diagnosed with Autism, so she does not express emotions in the way most people expect. I really wanted to explore the concept of "love" amongst people who are unable to feel it or have a difficult time expressing it. Romance to these three means something very different than to most people. And (because they are all traumatized) the way their love is expressed is very dark and very illegal.

In real life, doing anything without consent is NEVER sexy.

You should be running for the hills at this point. Still here? LOL you're my kind of person. Now that you're as prepared as a few paragraphs can get you (left intentionally vague so Amazon doesn't boot me), are you ready for a really fucked up game of hide and seek? Now's your chance to back out. Cause if you keep reading, ready or not, here they come.

List of warnings:

PLAYLIST

(Can also be found on website)

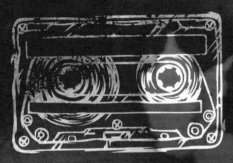

Awkward – ChewieCatt, Chewie
Somebody's Watching Me – Rockwell
The Hide and Seek Song – Headquarters Music
Cute Girl – Diggy Graves
I Don't Care – Single Version – Fall Out Boy
Mind Games – Sickick
Who Am I? – Kode
Invincible – Adelitas Way
Identity – grandson
Formaldehyde Footsteps – Houndrel
Hero Killer – PierceTheSkies
Past The Past – New Medicine
BITE BACK – n9neful
LALALAND – Kami Kehoe
HOLOGRAM – Poe the Passenger
Better With – Friday Pilots Club
Enemies – The Score Dirt
Nap – Diggy Graves
Trick or Cheat – Diggy Graves
Evil People – Set It O!
Look Down On Me – Kode
Bring Me To Life – Evanescence
Therapy – VIOLA
Grave Half Empty – Diggy Graves
Whos a good girl? – Manic Kazzy
Something To Hide – grandson
Side E!ect – FKA Rayne
Dark Room – Foreign Figures, Jonny T
Take What You Want (feat. Ozzy Osbourne, Travis
Scott) – Post Malone, Ozzy Osbourne, Travis Scott

TRIALS – SCARSET
When The Darkness Comes – Jeris Johnson
Harder To Breathe – Letdown
i feel lost – Aaron Hibell
Hole In Your Head – Ekoh
IF IT DOESN'T HURT – NOTHING MORE
Love Is Madness (feat. Halsey) – Thirty Seconds To Mars, Halsey
Antisocialist – Asking Alexandria
Loathe – FKA Rayne
Slumber Party (feat. Princess Nokia) – Ashnikko, Princess Nokia
Monster Made of Memories – Citizen Soldier
Let it Go (with Lo Spirit) – Chandler Leighton, Lo Spirit
HEATHEN – n9neful
EAT SPIT! (feat. Royal & the Serpent) – Slush Puppy, Royal & the
Serpent
She Keeps Me UP – Nickelback
WOOF – FKA Rayne
Dangerous State of Mind – Chri$tian Gate$
Cold – Crossfade
I Wish A Bitch Would – Delilah Bon
Cacao and Cocaine – SOFIA ISELLA
A GOOD DAY TO D13 – Arankai
deathwish (feat. nothing,nowhere) – Stand Atlantic, nothing,nowhere
sorry im a haunted house – Savage Ga$p, KAMAARA
Heavenly Bodies – Arankai
Barbie & Ken – Scene Queen, Set It Off
Pull the Plug – VIOLA
Wicked Game – Witchz
Alkaline – Sleep Token
Halloween (feat. Nicolle Galyon) – Walker Hayes, Nicolle Galyon

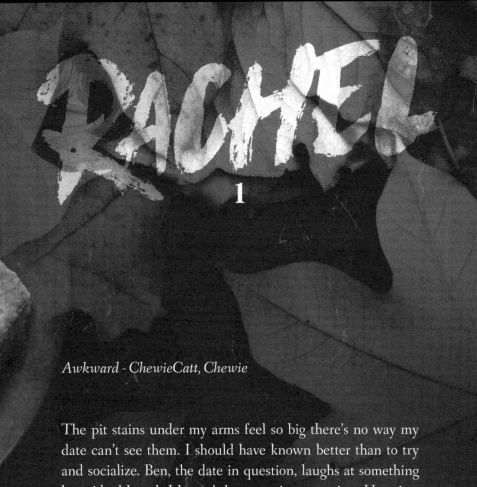

RACHEL

1

Awkward - ChewieCatt, Chewie

The pit stains under my arms feel so big there's no way my date can't see them. I should have known better than to try and socialize. Ben, the date in question, laughs at something he said, although I haven't been paying attention. He raises his eyebrows at me and continues laughing, so I assume he told a joke.

I force a laugh.

"You should have seen their faces." Ben slaps the bar countertop next to his third empty glass, making me jump. He waves two fingers at the bartender. "Another."

Hell, no. I hate every second of this, and I pick at the sticky countertop. I want to go home. Home where the music isn't blaring so loud, my clothes don't stick to my skin, and the furniture doesn't feel like it has years of sticky beer all over it.

I suck in a breath. But I can't go home. I owe it to Cali. She disappeared a week ago, and I can't get any information on her. The cops won't talk to me, her family won't talk to me, and there's just...nothing. Nothing except her final phone call to me saying she was in trouble. She asked me to meet her, then just...poof. Gone.

The bartender slides another drink to Ben.

Ben, aka Cali's ex-boyfriend. The one who was wildly suspicious at the time of her disappearance.

I haven't slept in a week.

So I did something stupid.

Something utterly idiotic, given that I fit into society like a two-by-four in a pack of colored pencils. Also, given the fact that I hate people and make either aggressive eye contact or none at all.

I invited Ben on a date.

Yeah, the Ben who has anger issues and the Ben who Cali broke up with a week before she disappeared.

Everyone is telling me it's nothing, that Cali's just taking a break after her breakup, but after her frantic call to me, I'm sure there's foul play.

Cali used to work with me at the hair salon and was always nice to me despite the fact I never really seemed to fit in. She had wild, curly hair, a loud mouth, and a massive fucking attitude. She cussed out many customers who gave me shit and stood up for me to our boss. I fucking loved her.

The bartender sweeps back over our way like a breath of fresh air. Ben's saying something about the sports game on the TV, but I lock on the woman in front of me like a lifeline. She has on a crop top with ghosts and the word "boo-bies." The shirt barely contains her breasts, and they damn near spill out of the top. I wish my tits looked like that. If they did, I'm pretty sure I could navigate all social situations with a shimmy of the titties and a smile. No pit stains anywhere in sight.

Something nudges my arm, and I jump. It's Ben. "You've barely had any." He motions at my glass of wine.

I try to pretend like I'm loving this and plaster on a smile, taking another drink.

"So..." Ben takes another look at me, and I realize he keeps staring at the blue streaks in my dark hair. "You live alone?"

"Yep," I respond, popping the p. As soon as the word is out of my mouth, I realize he probably asked for something other than a factual answer. I glance over at him.

"Good, 'cause I'm crashing with my parents right now." Ben's face is flushed red, and his hair is pale blonde. It looks sweaty. He wiggles his eyebrows at me. "Wanna get out of here?"

Jesus. Dread washes through me, but I struggle to keep it off my face. This is exactly what I wanted to happen. If I can get him drunk and comfortable, maybe he'll talk. And if not, at least at home I have a block of kitchen knives. If it came to it, I wonder how hard it would be to push a knife through his skin? I suppose that would entirely depend on the sharpness of my knives.

"Uh, hello?" Ben waves a hand in my face.

Fuck. I must be doing that thing again where my face goes blank while I'm thinking. I plaster on a smile and drop off my stool, "Yeah, let's go."

"Hold up," Ben slaps his hand down on the counter. "Need my card."

The bartender glances over at me, and I imagine all she's seeing is a girl falling out of her chair to go home with a mediocre frat guy. Just another Wednesday.

I wince.

"Let's go." Ben grabs my elbow, and I yank it away from him. Immediately, I laugh awkwardly, skirting away from him and picking at the skin around my nails. I don't want him to touch me again.

As soon as we get to the parking lot and are surrounded by the hot, dry air, I realize that Ben's drunk, and we drove separately. And he's gonna have to come to my house.

No. *No, no, no.*

He already reeks of stale beer and sweat. If I'm stuck in a car with that smell, I will throw up. I dig my nails into the skin around my thumb, the sharp bite of pain keeping me from spiraling more.

"I'll drive," I offer weakly.

Ben laughs harshly, "No way, buttercup. I'm the gentleman here."

My skin prickles. "I need my car."

"As do I."

I lock eyes with his watery blue ones. "You follow me?"

He shrugs. "Fine."

On the drive back, I keep worrying that Ben will crash and I won't get the information I need. I keep checking in the mirror, but Ben doesn't swerve. Cali hinted he might be a habitual drinker.

I bite the skin around my index finger. What in the actual hell am I doing? Somehow, I didn't think we would actually get this far. I haven't done anything like this in...well, like ever. I mostly keep to myself, and I like it that way.

We get back to my house, and for a second, I just sit there and think about driving away, hiding at the grocery store or the corner gas station, and pretending like this never happened. It would be so much easier.

But Cali can't do that. She's missing, and no one is helping her. And for that reason, I get out. Ben's waiting, and when I walk up the steps, he palms my ass. It makes all my muscles lock up, and fire shoots through me. I want to run and fight, but that would ruin everything I have going. Instead, I just let us in the house and resist the urge to bite my nails.

My house is modest, a one-story ranch, but I've made it my own. I've thrifted and shopped estate sales for most of the furniture and decor, including my orange couch and dark wood furniture. The Halloween decorations I got from the dollar store actually fit well with my witchy decor.

Ben runs his hand along the Halloween ghosts I have set up, and I glare at him. He's knocking them out of the careful lines I've set them up in.

"Want a drink?" I ask, mostly to get him away from my things, and then I move to the kitchen.

As I feel Ben's presence in my house, my brain screams *stupid.* So stupid. So fucking stupid. I'm alone with a man in my home. I mean, I told my mom I had a date and sent her Ben's picture, but what's my mom gonna do? Beat him over the head with her TV remote? Then, in the next minute, forget she met him and ask his name?

I turn on the video on my phone, put it in my back pocket, and pull a beer out of the fridge. My shirt is still soaked under my arms, although I tried to get the AC to air it out on the way over. It may be fall in Oklahoma, but it's still hot as balls.

Ben takes the beer from me. I duck back into the fridge for one for myself, saying, "Cali liked Miller Lite, too."

Ben's face flushes as he cracks it open. "You heard from her?"

"I was kinda hoping you had." I lean against my sink. Just talk about this, and then he can go. It'll be over soon.

Ben runs his hand through his hair. "Not a word."

That better not be because she's dead.

I plaster a smile on. "Did you see her on the 6th?"

5

Ben guzzles his beer, glancing around. "Wanna give me a tour?"

I tighten my fingers on my beer. "I haven't cleaned up."

Ben snorts. "I don't care." He saunters closer to me. "As long as you're cleaned up downstairs, I don't care a bit." He winks, a grin on his face.

My cheeks flame, and for a second, I'm speechless. How dare he? How fucking dare he? He just had the hottest girl around on his arm, then she disappeared, and he's hitting on *me?*

Putting my beer on the counter, I move to the side to get away from him. Ben steps into me, pinning me against the marble. His body is hot, and his beer breath brushes across my face. "You're pretty, you know that?"

I hold my breath and try to scoot away, shoving against him. "I..."

Suddenly, Ben's big hands are all over my breasts. He's fondling them, gripping and gently pinching. "These are cute. I like small things."

I cry out, shoving hard against him. In his inebriated state, Ben takes a stuttering step back.

"Hey, baby." Ben immediately comes back, pinning me against the counter. "What's wrong?"

"Get off me." His body is damp with sweat, and I feel it on every inch of my skin. It makes panic race through me. His slightly sticky shirt makes me want to scratch all my skin off.

"What?" Ben grabs my chin, forcing me to look at him. His grip is soft, with just enough pressure that I can't get away. "Chill, baby. I'll make you feel good."

I suck in a breath.

Suddenly, Ben's hand is down my pants.

I cry out, struggling to get away. Ben fumbles around, his fingers brushing my pussy over my panties.

"I'll be gentle." The smell of old beer and bad breath wraps around my skin, and I can feel it all over my face.

It's not the first time I've heard those words, and they make my whole body lock up. I want to throw up. I can't move.

"C'mon, it'll feel good."

For a moment, I'm locked in the past. I can't move my arms. I can't move my face. Can't even blink.

A fresh burst of beer breath wakes me up. I reach back, fumbling for a knife out of the knife block.

"What a good girl." Ben presses me against the counter just hard enough that I can't leave. My arm hurts craning it back, but then I grip a knife and brandish it in his face.

"Whoa." His eyes widen, and he takes a step back

I suck in a breath. "Where is Cali?"

"Girl, chill." Ben has his hands up.

I wave the knife at him, my hand shaking. "Where the fuck is Cali?"

"Cali?" Ben looks confused.

"Yes! Your girlfriend?" The adrenaline rushes through me, and my voice comes out high and uncontrolled.

"She's not my girlfriend; she dumped me two weeks ago!"

"Where is she? Don't pretend like you don't know."

Ben throws his hands in the air and backs up a step. "Not you, too! First the cops, then you?"

"Tell me where she is," I demand. My arm is fully shaking, and my hand is numb as the adrenaline courses through me. Nothing is going right, and I'm ruining this whole thing. I've fucked it up so massively.

"Is this why you invited me over?" Ben glares at me.

I don't answer. I suddenly realize how big Ben is and how I might very well become his next target.

I brandish the knife again. "Get out."

Ben's face is red. "You can't fucking threaten me!"

"Get the fuck out!"

He stumbles back again, "I'll call the cops!"

I follow him with the knife, a slew of emotions running through me so fast I can't keep track of them.

I ruined this whole thing.

Ruined.

Ben backs out of the house, stepping onto my front porch. "Fucking cunt! Crazy ass bi–"

I slam the door, locking it. I drop my head against the cool door, sucking in deep breaths.

I was stupid to even try.

I should have killed him. Fuck, I should have killed him!

I grip the knife tighter. What the hell kind of thought was that? I don't want to go to prison. I wouldn't last a week.

I tried and got nothing. No answers. I thought I'd at least get something. A hint, a clue, *something.*

I stand there. My face feels hot. My whole body feels hot. I can feel the heat along every inch, up and down my neck, and in my hair.

I'm alone. A mixture of comfort and vast emptiness rushes through me. I'm always alone. I kicked my ex out years ago when he started having the kid talk, and since then, I've kinda been a loner. Until I met Cali. And now she's gone, too.

I still feel Ben's hands all over my breasts. Breaking for the bathroom, I throw on the water and splash it on my face. It's not enough. I need more.

I turn on the shower and get in, clothes and shoes still on. I realize my phone is recording in my pocket, and I turn it off and throw it across the bathroom. I stand there, soaking in the cold water.

I can still hear *his* voice.

More.

Ready or Not

I throw on the bath. Before it's even full, I drop down into it, letting the water lap around me and wrap my feet and legs in a warm hug. It touches me all over with a consistent pressure, soothing away my irritation. I rip my clothes off, and as the water rises, my tension eases.

I drop my head on my knees.

I feel a blemish on my forehead and touch it with my fingers. Fuck, did I get a pimple, too?

I glance around, wishing I hadn't thrown my phone so I could use the camera to look at it. Still, I pick at it. I pick and pick and pick, locked in a cycle until I get it out of me.

Cali was the one person who understood me, and now she's gone. She's gone, and I just ruined the one way to get her back.

Maybe. Unless she's dead.

I close my eyes. I don't have anyone left who understands.

And that is the loneliest thought I've ever had.

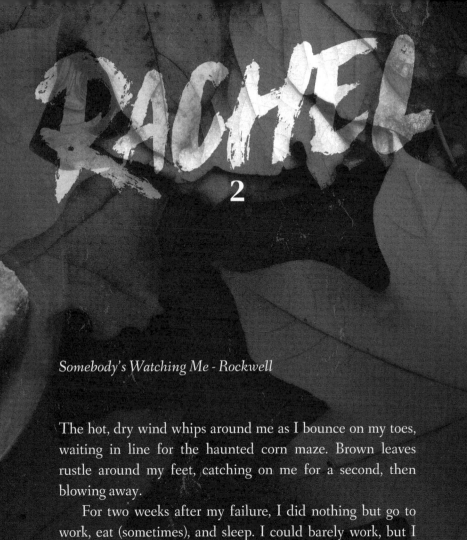

RACHEL

2

Somebody's Watching Me - Rockwell

The hot, dry wind whips around me as I bounce on my toes, waiting in line for the haunted corn maze. Brown leaves rustle around my feet, catching on me for a second, then blowing away.

For two weeks after my failure, I did nothing but go to work, eat (sometimes), and sleep. I could barely work, but I needed the money and the routine. It kept me from picking all the skin around my fingers completely off. Coincidentally, I also had the worst customers call in, yell at me, and complain to the shop because I didn't cut their hair just right, even though they were happy with it when they left the store.

As Halloween approaches, I get more antsy. Cali made me promise I'd go to the corn maze with her since we both loved them, and I couldn't get that promise out of my head as much as I tried. What was the point? She's not here anyway.

But I made a promise. It got to the point where it was

either taking a bubble bath with the toaster or going to the corn maze.

Unfortunately, here I am.

A scream comes from the maze, and the girls ahead of me titter and laugh. As they chatter, one backs up and bumps into me.

"Oh, sorry!" She giggles.

Her arm is sweaty, leaving a wet swipe on my shoulder. Immediately, I want to claw my skin off. The girl is probably in her early twenties, with an odd expression on her face. I blink, trying to look chill.

The girl's eyebrow quirks up. I still can't tell what she's feeling, so I laugh awkwardly. "It's okay."

Immediately, her other eyebrow goes up, making me laugh more uncomfortably.

The girl continues giving me a look, then turns back around with her friends. They laugh again, and shame heats my face.

I laugh when I'm uncomfortable. People tell me it's not the proper reaction, but it's compulsive in social situations—I can't stop. I laughed when Karen made a complaint about me today, and my boss yelled at me.

I wish Cali was here.

Give me nature and animals any day of the week. Or monsters. It's easy to tell what a monster wants from you. There's no guesswork. Which makes my life so much easier. It's probably why I've always found comfort in Halloween. That, and I've always loved the costumes.

I realize I've wrapped my arms around myself, and the pit stains are back. I force myself to unwrap my arms and, instead, pick the skin around my nails.

I heard this place has absolutely no contact. Which is perfect.

Ready or Not

Halloween music plays over the speakers as I get closer to the entrance. It grounds me and sends a wave of nostalgia through me. There's a scarecrow at the beginning of the maze with tattered clothes and an angry, white mask. It glowers at me as I wait. The electronic tones, the recorded screams, and the smell of sun-baked straw makes me suck in a deep breath.

The group ahead of me laughs. It sounds mean, and I catch one of the girls looking at me.

Despite myself, my face flushes. Thank god their group is next to go.

As I scan over the maze, I catch sight of someone in the corn maze staring at me.

It's a woman in the last row of corn. She's in a full law enforcement uniform, with a half mask pulled up over her nose. She's tall as fuck, I would guess almost six feet, and holds her vest with both hands, staring at me.

I swallow.

The woman's dark eyes burn into mine. A tingle runs through me. I've never seen a scare actor with this kind of costume on. She looks like a real cop. Wait, maybe she is?

I glance around for a cruiser or another cop, then back at her. Only, she's gone. There are just empty rows of corn.

Goosebumps prickle down my neck, and suddenly, I'm up next. I didn't even realize the other girls had gone through. The person manning the line tries to bunch the people in line behind me with me.

"No," I clear my throat. "I'm alone."

Please let me go alone. I need to go alone.

I don't know those other people. I don't want them touching me. Crowding me.

The employee rolls his eyes but motions at the other group to wait.

The maze is dark. Occasionally, lights flash, and there are

13

distant screams. I suck in a breath, pulling in the energy of the air around me. I wish I could take my shoes off and run through this barefoot. I want to feel the hard, dry dirt and ground myself. But I don't. People would yell at me.

The man jerks his head at me to go.

I move forward on my toes, too jacked up to fully touch the ground. The corn grew tall this year, and the stalks tower over my head, dry leaves rattling in the wind. Smoke hisses on my right, and I jump. An automated voice cackles: "Ready or not, here I come."

As I round the bend, a clown jumps out at me. I can't help a scream as tingles wash across my skin.

The clown leers down at me, laughing. "Lost, pretty girl?"

I skirt past him, flying down the path and immediately being forced to take another turn. A chainsaw starts up with its loud rumbling. I whirl, trying to spot it, when the sound gets louder behind me. I dart away.

As I round the bend, something reaches out and snatches my arm, yanking me to a halt.

"No running," a rich voice demands.

I whirl on the person and suck in a breath. The masked woman towers over me. It's the cop from earlier. She's stunning up close, her dark eyes rimmed in dark lashes, her skin creamy, and her gaze arresting. The rest of her face is covered in a black mask, but her brown hair is in two long braids down the sides.

The woman's hand shoots tingles down my arm.

What the fuck? They aren't supposed to touch us. I try to yank away from her.

A dark, manicured eyebrow arches up. The woman's eyes are expressionless. It makes the skin on the back of my neck prickle.

She lets me go.

I back away, and immediately, the woman's posture changes from bored to predatory.

"Sorry," I stammer. I inch back, and she just watches me. When I hit corn, I turn and speed walk away. My body floods with adrenaline.

The next actor to jump out at me really makes me scream, and I bolt before they can also grab me. The deeper I go, the louder the music starts thumping and screeching from all sides of the maze. I can feel it in my chest, the pound, pound, pound.

As I turn a corner, the maze gets dark, and smoke fills the air. As it settles on my skin, I realize it's mist. It wraps around me like a wet blanket.

There are so many sensations going on at once, and suddenly, I don't want to be here anymore. I want to curl into a ball on the ground. Want to dig my nails into the dirt to feel just one thing other than *everything*. Why did I even come in the first place?

A form appears at the end of the row I'm moving down.

My stomach clenches, and I stop.

The form cocks its head. It's the woman.

How is she everywhere? I shrink closer to the corn. Maybe I'll blend into the darkness and the fog. The water in the air goes from ticklish to drowning. It's everywhere. It's in my eyes and hair, on my clothes, and it's hard to breathe.

"Scared?" The woman's voice is rich and...toneless. Uninterested, almost. It gets caught up in the mist.

Is she talking to me?

She's standing still. I think she's facing me, but it's hard to see in the darkness.

I say nothing.

Her head shakes.

"I'll give you a five-second head start. Then you're mine, little deer."

Alarm bells start ringing in my head. Something isn't right.

"Five."

I take a step back into the corn.

"Four."

Fuck this. Something is weird about this maze, and I'm not sticking around for it. They can ban me for running through their corn if they want to. I turn and dart from the path and down a row of corn.

An empty laugh follows me.

"Three-two-one. Ready or not, here I come."

I run. Dry leaves whip me in the face, and I hold my arms out in front of me to try and brush the leaves out of the way. I sprint as fast as I can, putting distance between myself and the maze, then dart to my left. I crack through stalks and slow down to reevaluate. Surely, she won't follow me.

I slow, panting for breath. The music is quieter over here, so my pushing through the corn is louder. I duck down, trying to see through the thin bottom stalks. My heart is racing, and I put my hand on the dry dirt to ground myself.

I try to control my breathing.

This is just a weird moment. Maybe I'm making it up. She was just a scare actor, and I overreacted.

As usual.

Something rustles behind me.

Instinctually, I stand, but as I do, my vision is disrupted by the leaves. I brush them aggressively out of the way, only to be met with a masked face.

But it's not the woman.

A man in a full cloth mask with the eyes cut out, a

helmet, and full soldier attire stands there. He looks cold. Lethal.

A scream bubbles up in my throat, but it gets trapped there.

The man stares at me.

Say something! The words feel trapped in my chest. I stammer, "Uh s-sorry. I got lost."

Instead of responding, the man just cocks his head. It's eerie. He looks like a hawk, sizing up a rodent.

Nope. I need to go. But I stand frozen. My legs won't move.

There's a dark chuckle, and then the man's voice comes out raspy and mocking. "Boo."

That breaks whatever spell I'm under, and I turn on my heel and run—smack into a warm body.

RACHEL

3

The Hide and Seek Song - Headquarters Music

I reel back. It's the woman.

"I...I'm sorry." I gasp for breath. "I'll get back on the main path." I whirl to keep both of them in my vision.

Neither responds. Their presence is stifling, and I feel like I have to say something, but I don't know what.

"I didn't mean to!" I bite out. "You weren't supposed to touch me. It's against the rules."

Emotions bubble up in me, but I can't tell which ones. All I know is my body is buzzing, and my chest feels like it's in my throat, and I hate it. I hate it, I hate it.

I take a step back, trying to get a breath.

The woman chuckles. "You hear that? I broke the rules."

The man says nothing.

I have to get out of here. "I'm going."

"Rules, rules, rules." The woman follows me calmly. "Don't you get bored following the rules all the time?"

All the emotions bubble in my throat. I want to laugh. I need the feelings to get out.

"Run, pretty little thing."

I do. This time, I don't make it far. The man heads me off. As I move to get away from him, arms wrap around me from behind, and suddenly, I'm flying towards the ground. I try to catch myself but land on the ground, my whole right side skidding against the dirt.

The woman is on top of me in an instant, pinning my arms above my head. She fixes her eyes on mine, and this time, they look dead. "Shhh. You know you can't get away from me, right?"

I buck up, trying to knock her off. Her eyes crinkle at the edges. She's...smiling.

"What are you doing?" I gasp.

The woman pins both of my wrists in one of hers and traces the other hand down my face.

"Get off me!"

The woman's voice is husky now. "Bet a cute little thing like you would look so good coming around my fingers."

I freeze, then panic runs through me. Oh fuck. Fuck, fuck, fuck.

"No, I'm not gay." I struggle for real, but the woman's weight on me is solid. She presses me into the dirt, her ass sitting over my crotch, then runs her nose along my neck. "Mmmm." She darts her tongue out, licking up my sweat. "You taste so good when you're afraid." Her vest rubs against my chest.

The man stands, watching us. He does nothing.

"Please, help," I plea.

"Help!" The woman laughs. The sound is rich and settles around us like a blanket. "What do you need help with, darling? I'm right here."

With one clean yank, the woman rips my top off. Immediately, I'm bared to her. I don't wear bras, and I regret it now.

"Stop," I whisper.

The woman locks her gaze on me. I can't tell what she's thinking. She just hovers over me, with her toned body poised to strike.

Silent. Expressionless.

All of the emotions in my throat bubble over, and a tear slips out of my eye.

The woman watches it trace down my cheek. When she looks at me again, she cocks her head. "Crying?"

"I don't...please, let me go."

She blinks slowly. "I love bringing people to their knees."

I can't stop the second tear. It rolls down my face, all of the fear and panic escaping in an overwhelming little drop of liquid.

The woman makes a frustrated sound, then pinches my nipple.

Immediately, the sensation shoots through my body. I arch my back, trying to get away from it. She rolls the bud in her fingers, more gently, soothing.

My cheeks burn as a forbidden sensation runs through me. A stranger is touching my nipples. A *woman*. This is wrong. So wrong.

I squirm again.

The woman tsks, reaching back to her belt and pulling out something that clinks. Before I can get a good look, she whips them up to my hands, and I feel something cool lock around my wrist.

Handcuffs.

I want to scream, but I can't. The words are locked in my

body. The woman has my other wrist locked quickly. I yank back, but they're stuck around the corn stalks.

"You going to beg, little deer?" The woman throws me a dark look, then untucks the bottom of her mask. She dives down, and I feel a wet mouth on my nipple. She bites me, making me cry out. Immediately, her tongue soothes the sting, making lapping motions.

"Such pretty tits. You should show them off more."

"I—please, I'm not gay."

My nipples are hard as stone. All I can see is the top of the woman's stunning face. When she turns her dark eyes up on me, I look away.

My pants are yanked down, and I squeeze my eyes shut.

The woman sucks in a breath. I feel the air on my wet pussy.

"Look at me."

I don't.

A painful shock radiates from my pussy, and I snap my eyes open. Her hand is poised over me like she just hit me.

The woman watches me. "Obey."

No! No, no, no. I struggle again, kicking out at her. But she's between my legs, and getting any power to my kicks is hard. She's so close.

The woman's eyes crinkle. She's smiling again. Then she lifts her mask from the bottom, and a hot mouth closes over my pussy.

I cry out, arching my back. The flat of her tongue lands on my clit, softly moving up and down, up and down.

"No, please." The handcuffs cut into my wrists, shooting pain through me.

The woman's hands grip my asscheeks, yanking me up into her mouth.

Goosebumps run across my body against my will.

The woman continues her steady assault on my clit, not pressing too hard, just enough to flick a steady sensation into me. She watches me the whole time, pupils blown, dark lashes swooping. I can't look at her.

Pleasure fills me, but I try to fight it down. This is wrong. This is so wrong.

I struggle weakly.

The woman moves her chin up just enough to slip a finger inside me. Despite myself, I let out a gasp. She slips inside me so easily. My cheeks burn. Softly, she moves that finger up and down, hitting a spot in me that makes pleasure course through me.

This time, I can't keep a full moan from escaping my mouth. I throw my head back, clenching my teeth.

Suddenly, the woman eats me enthusiastically, licking and slurping like she's starving for me. Immediate sensation washes through me, and she continues to play with her finger. The pleasure is building higher.

Then, the woman stops.

I pant, looking down.

The man is behind the woman. He has his hands on her hips and is looking at us with dark voids for eyes.

The woman glances behind her as the man grips something on the woman's thigh.

Her gun.

She stiffens as the man holds the gun up to the faint light.

"Don't you dare," the woman growls.

The man just chuckles, racking the slide back with a mean snick. Something hard falls into the dirt by my face.

Oh fuck. It's a bullet. A real bullet.

It's a real gun.

I struggle for real, kicking and fighting and bucking with everything I have.

The woman pins down my hips. "I'm not done with you yet. You haven't prayed to your goddess."

Immediately, she puts her mouth back on my pussy.

Fear and adrenaline radiate through me. My hands are stuck, my hips are stuck, and that horrible, awful pleasure is back.

The woman grunts into me, and I snap my gaze to the man behind her. He makes eye contact with me and then winks. I'm shifted enough that I can see he's messing with her. With the other hand, he runs the gun up and down her back, pointing it at me.

The woman groans again, her eyes glazed over. She glances at me, then her eyes darken. "No." She yanks her hand out of my pussy to slap it.

I cry out.

"Don't fucking look at him. Look at me while I make you come."

Pain shoots through me, but the woman immediately laps it away. She eats me like she owns me. Like my body was meant for her mouth and fingers, and she'll wring every ounce of pleasure from me that I have.

I feel my orgasm building. The feeling is so powerful and compelling. I fight with it, with her, but there's nowhere for me to go. It's like the woman can sense that I'm getting close, too. She maintains the same pressure and rhythm, fucking the hell out of my clit until I'm wound tight.

The woman's face slams into me with a little extra power as she's shoved from behind, and that pushes me over the edge. My orgasm slams into me with blinding intensity and washes over my entire body. My muscles lock up, my toes curl, and all the pressure from earlier comes rushing out of me.

I want to scream, but I'm silent. I'm locked there, everything forced out of my muscles as the woman continues her assault on my clit.

My world grows fuzzy as I come down off the high. I can feel the dopamine flooding my system as it mixes with the stress. My muscles go limp.

Vaguely, I hear the woman moan and cuss. I blink slowly. A shadow moves above me.

"Such a good thing for me." A tickle of hair brushes the side of my face, and I look over. The woman is leaning over me, and one of her braids has fallen down. And past her, I see dark roots and dirt and...

I focus closer.

A tiny little mouse skull. It's weathered and dirty from the elements, but the brown and white bone peeks out at me all alone.

"There. Be free, bambi."

Suddenly, my hands are loose. I yank them down over my head. They're numb.

I watch the woman, who turns to the silent man. "Give me my gun."

He says nothing.

Her voice lowers. "I'll kill you, Manson, and I'll get off doing it. Wouldn't want me to get off without you, now would you?"

I scoot up, feeling flooding back into my arms. I'm still overwhelmed with the looseness from the orgasm, but I know I need to move.

I inch back, seeing if either one will pay attention to me. They're still facing each other. Now's my chance.

I grab the mouse skull and run.

RILEY

4

Cute Girl - Diggy Graves

The woman I picked is a fascinating creature. She has those big brown eyes, a perfect body, and a pussy that tastes like heaven. When she was standing in line, she looked at me with an expression much like a deer's. Like she was frozen and didn't know what to do. And she was quiet. Not loud like the rest of the fools who come here.

Hunting her down and eating her until she came was fascinating. She hardly reacted. Just a few tears, some apologies, and then quiet. She's nothing like most normies who make a huge dramatic show.

So naturally, I followed her home.

I meant to scare this woman tonight. Meant to get under her skin, literally and figuratively. To feed on the power she gave me. But she was so expressionless, besides those few tears. They leaked out of her eyes without all the gross slobbering that most people do. Instead, they made her eyes shine even brighter with an unreadable expression.

She reminds me of me.

And that hasn't happened since...Manson.

Right now, the woman is sitting in her driveway in her little Toyota. I know she's thinking about me. I bet she's wondering what my pussy tastes like.

Most women do. Not that I ever let them taste it.

Maybe she's crying again? It's possible I read her wrong, although it's rare—if ever—that I'm wrong.

Bambi's car door pops open, her dome light turns on, and she gets out. I'm leaning against the neighbor's house, watching her. If she sees me, it'll be round two.

But she doesn't, and there are no tears on her face.

My mouth kicks up in a grin. What a fascinating little creature.

I wait until she goes inside, moves around, flips what I assume is the bedroom light on, and then, finally, it goes off again.

Fuck. I need a cigarette. They're in my saddlebags on my bike—a Ducati Panigale—but I can't step away from her house, not even for a minute.

What is my little deer like? The little deer who gives nothing away?

My phone vibrates. I pull it out, expecting a message from Manson. Instead, it's a message from a rando I've been conning.

User1995: I'm in for 500

I roll my eyes. I saw this coming a mile away. The man did a shit job of pretending he wasn't interested in the mounted deer head I said I had. Sure, he didn't know it was me he was talking to. He thought it was Wesley, the deer-hunting YouTube sensation. But I hunt, too, and I'm a hell of a lot better than Wesley.

Anger prickles over my skin, and I message back.

> Me: Great! I can deliver if that makes it easier.

> User1995: That would be awesome.

He gives me his address, and I smile while rage boils in my chest. Nothing makes me angrier than posers—people who want to mount an animal on their wall and pretend like they hunted it, brag to their friends, and make up stories about things they didn't do.

No poser deserves that attention, and no animal deserves to be dead on the walls of those shits.

I shake it off. I'll take care of him later.

I glance at my doe's window and wait longer. After I've waited as long as I can, I break in.

Not that I care if she's awake to call the cops, but people have less opportunity to lie about who they are when they're unconscious. And I find lying inconvenient.

Unless I'm the one doing it, of course.

Bambi's house is a small ranch. I'm guessing three small

bedrooms, a bath, and no garage. As soon as I kick the front door open, the faint smell of old person fills my nose.

Well fuck. Old people are inconvenient. Much like children. Is she stuck taking care of one?

The living room is silent. Is she a hard sleeper? Probably, after I fucked her good. She exploded in my mouth, her pussy gripping me so tight I was shocked.

I grin.

My doe's living room is decorated in 1970s decor and Halloween accents. She has multicolored flower-print chairs, oranges and yellows all over everything, and an extravagant chandelier over the dining room table. She also has pumpkin decor and ghosts and witches everywhere. It's kinda ugly.

I frown. Is this her choice, or does someone else live here?

I sort through the mail she has on the dining room table.

Rachel. I don't see anyone else's name. So, my bambi's name is Rachel.

I lick my lips. I can still taste her pussy.

Stalking down the hall, I head directly to the room where I saw her light on. Sure enough, when I crack the door open, Rachel's there in bed. She's curled up, with her wrists tucked under her chin, snoring lightly. Her pretty little lips are parted, and I see the swell of her hips under the sheet.

My mouth waters.

I should see how much I can do to her while she's asleep.

I force myself to pause. Not until I'm done snooping. I need to know more about her so I can...motivate her to do what I want. This is just the beginning, and I won't fuck it up by not preparing correctly. As Manson likes to get all over my ass for.

I check the room opposite the bedroom. Most of it is storage for miscellaneous items. When I check the last bedroom and flip on the light, I suck in a breath.

There are skulls. Hundreds of them. All over tables, on shelves, and in display cases.

A strange feeling twists my gut. I look over all those dead animals, and the greed of humanity hits me.

They'd rob an animal of its life just for this? Trophies?

Rage filters over my vision.

No animal deserves this.

My phone buzzes again. I rip it out of my pocket.

> Manson: Where you at, sis?

I almost throw my phone at the wall. He knows I hate it when he calls me that. Instead, I stomp out of the house, blindly typing.

> Me: Fuck off.

Normally, I wouldn't give him such ammo. He latches onto any weakness like a bloodhound, but when I'm mad, I can't stop.

> Manson: Why you in such a bad mood?

I can practically hear his smirk.

Manson: Did stalking your prey not get your jollies off?

I grip my phone so hard my fingers hurt and throw it violently into the saddle bags. Of course Manson knows I'm here. I forgot to check my bike for trackers before I left. Not only is my step-brother obsessive about me, he's obsessive about the people I fuck. "Obsessive," meaning he usually kills them and leaves the bodies in my cornfield. The killing doesn't bother me. I never stick around for longer than a fuck, but it's the principle of it. Manson thinks he's in charge of my life, and he makes me clean up his messes.

Arrogant prick. I'd put him at the top of my list to kill, but that would only go to his head.

I suck in a deep breath and start the bike. I wasn't expecting the animals. I shouldn't be disappointed because I shouldn't have gotten interested in the first place. I need to get myself back together so Manson doesn't rip me to shreds. I snatch up my phone.

Me: Kill this one, too, I don't care.

Then I turn my phone off and peel away from the curb.

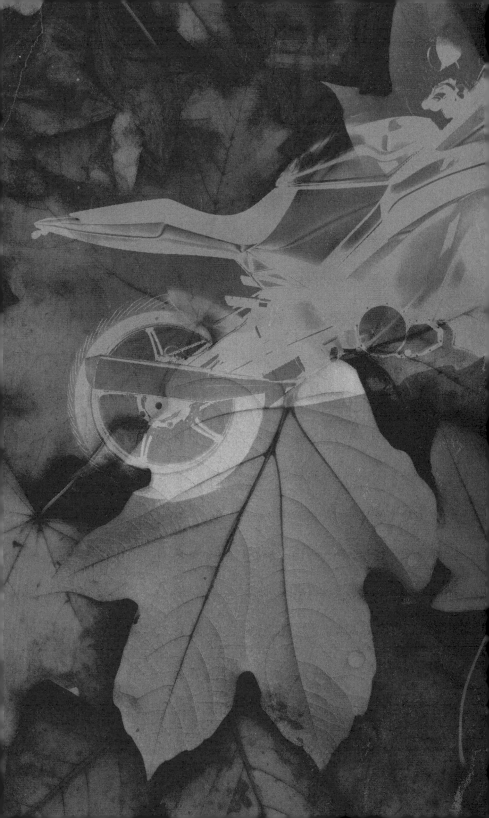

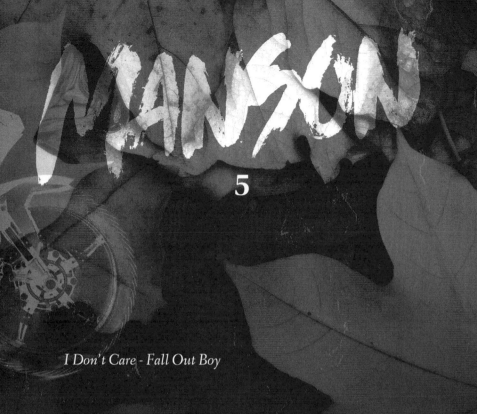

MANSON

5

I Don't Care - Fall Out Boy

I stare at the text on my phone.

Riley never talks like this. In fact, she's never openly acknowledged that I kill her one-night stands. She just buries them in her fields and is extra salty at me for the next few days.

What's gotten into her?

A slow scowl creeps across my face. Is she trying to keep this one alive? That could be the only reason she's giving me permission—to try and throw me off the scent.

Jealousy rips through me, and I glare at where I saw Riley's bike tear off down the street. I followed her here, of course, intent on doing the very thing she told me to do.

But now, I'm interested.

And that's what has me walking up to the small house Riley was just in. When I see the front door ajar and the splintered doorframe, something hot closes around my chest.

Reckless. This girl is so fucking reckless. She's going to get herself caught. She didn't even wear gloves.

I step over the splintered wood. The house is silent, and the walkthrough indicates one occupant, the same female from earlier, in her bed. How she's slept through two break-ins is beyond me and actually pisses me off.

I spot something on the bedside table. Pulling on the latex gloves I always keep with me, I check the bottle and find sleeping meds prescribed to Rachel Hiebert. That would explain why she didn't wake.

Rachel, hmmm? What about you has caught the eye of my Riley?

Sure, she's stunning. She has a nice body, a pretty face, and blue-streaked hair. But it's not unusual for Riley to find lookers.

I sweep the house more carefully, looking for answers, then unlock Rachel's phone using her face ID. I start with her messages, but I don't see any between her and Riley. Although, I know Riley posts online as almost everyone but herself, so her real name wouldn't pop up. But nothing looks like anything Riley would be remotely interested in. In fact, there isn't much of anything. The person Rachel talked to most, some Cali chick, cut off contact about a month ago.

I check Rachel's search history.

Oh. Cali went missing a month ago. Rachel is obsessed with finding information about her, or obsessed with finding information *others* know about her. It appears Cali was in trouble, and then she disappeared. The disappearance looks clean. Nothing sloppy, not like most murders done by emotional people.

Much like a job I would pull.

I stare down at the sleeping woman and narrow my eyes.

She doesn't seem capable of killing anyone. So if not her, then do I have a rival running my streets?

My fingers clench on the phone. I know it wasn't Riley. I keep close tabs on her. I will not allow Riley to kill anyone until she's less sloppy and impulsive. I've spent years teaching her how to be, but she fights me at every turn.

My chest is tight again. I rarely feel anger, but of all people, Riley pulls it out of me easily. She's stubborn and refuses to be taught. She also is damn near impossible to manipulate. The woman is cold. Ruthless.

And so very interesting.

I drop the phone on the bed and check out Rachel's bookshelf. Riley has never been interested in a woman like she has Rachel. So, I check Rachel's books. I find there's plenty of information to be used against women on their bookshelf. They keep all their hopes, dreams, and fears all prettily bound up in printed words. Perfect for me, or anyone with half a brain, to exploit.

I sift through Rachel's selection, finding much less romance than I thought. Most of her books are thrillers, splatterpunk, or horror. I find a few self-help books on Autism and one on how to talk to people.

I cock my head. I have the same one at home. Why does Rachel need to learn how to talk to people?

Riley's text still burns in my mind.

Kill this one, too, I don't care.

Oh, Riley, but I think you do care.

I don't think I'll kill this one just yet. I think there's a few more miles I can get out of her.

I turn back to the bed and check her pill bottle. Rachel's prescription was just refilled, and she hardly has any left. She must have damn near overdosed herself on the pills. Convenient for me.

Unless she dies, of course.

Fucking hell. I'm going to have to do something I haven't done for anyone except Riley—keep someone alive.

I haul Riley's obsession over my shoulder. She shifts and groans slightly but otherwise remains unconscious.

Well, my little intrigue. You're going to have to stay breathing for a while. You're not done being useful.

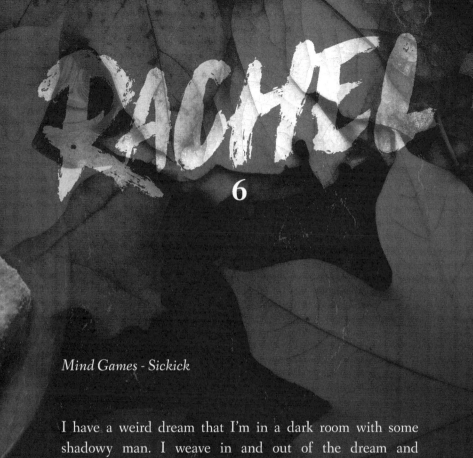

RACHEL

6

Mind Games - Sickick

I have a weird dream that I'm in a dark room with some shadowy man. I weave in and out of the dream and consciousness. I can't keep my eyes open. Or closed? I'm so confused.

The first real thing I feel is cold. It starts at my fingertips, and I focus on the feeling as hard as I can. This is awake. I know this isn't a dream.

It takes a while to be able to move my hands and even longer to sit up. When I do, I realize I'm lying on a couch. The room is dark and open. It looks like...I'm in someone's dining room? There's no table, only the couch I'm on and a small coffee table. Beside me looks like a shadowy living room, in front is a kitchen, and on the other side is the...front door?

What is going on? Have I not woken up? This isn't my

house. My brain feels sluggish. My body is covered in sweat, but I'm freezing.

Fuck. The sleeping pills. I took too many before I went to bed. I rub my eyes.

The cornfield comes back to me in horrifying reality, and my stomach clenches. All the emotions I tried to escape come roaring back in confusing noise. That woman fucked me against my will, and then I ran home, took pills in an attempt to forget, and passed out.

Where the fuck am I?

I stand, and my legs are shaky. How could I be so fucking stupid? I stumble to the front door, feeling queasy. The knob is cool in my hands, and I twist, but the door doesn't open. I rattle it, then glance up.

It's padlocked—from the inside.

I stare at the lock for a second.

Oh fuck. I think I'm going to be sick.

I make it to the edge of the door frame before I hurl onto the floor. There's not much to puke up, but my body expels everything I have. I need to puke up the horrible feeling in my gut, but as soon as I'm done vomiting, it's still there.

I need it to get out. Get out, get out, get out. I try to puke again, but the fear remains.

Slowly, I straighten. There has to be another way out. As I glance around, I notice the short dresser by the front door with a mirror above it. By the side of the mirror is a collage of printed faces. All of them have different expressions. And above each expression is written a word. Happy, sad, scared, angry, and on and on.

They're all emotions. Someone has been studying emotions.

I'm going to be sick again.

I latch onto one face and realize it's the same one I'm

making: fear. I scramble back the way I came, only to hear the creaking of the floor above me.

Footsteps.

I'm not alone.

I dart to the kitchen, intent on opening the window and scrambling out. All I can see is a porch and a big front yard. This is someone's home in the country.

"Going somewhere?" a deep, soothing voice rumbles.

I whirl and suck in a gasp. A man stands in the entryway to the kitchen, leaning casually against the wall. He fixes startling green eyes on me. His face is handsome, his cheeks carved, and his jaw sharp. He's in a tank, and his arms, hands, and neck are covered in tattoos. In fact, the only area not covered is his face. The man offers a small smile.

I can't tell if he's smiling at me or laughing at me.

The man raises his hand in a placating way. "You're sick. Let me help."

I grip the counter behind me so hard I feel the edges cutting into my fingers.

The man smiles wider, and it's dazzling. His teeth are all white and straight. "I'm not going to hurt you."

"I want to go home."

"Of course." The man gestures at the couch. "I need you to be able to walk, though."

I narrow my eyes. This is not right. None of this is right.

The man steps out of the entryway so I have space. I glance around the kitchen.

"No knives." The man chuckles, and then his voice becomes demanding. "Rachel, come."

My gaze snaps to his, and that feeling rushes back into my stomach. "How do you know my name?"

"I think you'll find there's a lot of things I know." He

winks at me. I feel like I'm looking at an animatronic. Something is off. I just can't tell what.

I swallow. "Let me go."

The man just laughs, moving to the couch and dropping down on it. "Sit."

I walk stiffly to the entryway but don't sit.

The mood instantly shifts, and the man's eyes go dark. He stills.

The danger is instantly tangible in the room.

I didn't obey.

The man blinks slowly.

It's clear that if I don't sit, I'll piss him off more, and that's not what I need. So I force myself to walk stiffly to the couch.

The man's eyes track me. Sitting is the hardest thing I've had to do, but I force my knees to bend.

As soon as my ass hits the cushion, all the tension immediately melts away, and the man smiles again. "Good girl. I want to make sure you're alright before we leave."

I just stare at him. No way he locked me up here just to let me leave.

"Scared?" He watches me.

I shake my head. All kinds of emotions course through me, and I can't put a name on one. It feels like they're all happening at the same time.

"How long have you known Riley?"

I blink. Who the hell is Riley?

The man shakes his head. "The woman you fucked in the corn maze."

I suck in a breath through my teeth, a wave of emotions crashing over me at once. This must be the man in the mask who watched us. Who pointed a gun at me. My breathing picks up, and my chest gets tight. What was his name? I search my brain. *Manson.*

"Rachel. I asked you a question." The man, Manson, cocks an eyebrow. It's both menacing and friendly, and I can't sort out how he means it.

First of all, I didn't fuck her. She fucked me. But what I say is, "I don't know her." I want to get sick again. Not from the pills but from the emotions trapped inside my body. Emotions I don't know how to put a label on.

Suddenly, all expression is wiped from Manson's face. He just stares at me, and all of my focus is on his face. His blank face.

Manson blinks twice, then reaches to the back of his pants and pulls out a gun.

The gun.

He doesn't point it at me, just puts it on his knee. And his expression doesn't change. "I'm sure you don't want to be stuck here longer than you have to."

What the hell does that mean?

Manson continues staring at me. "So, tell me about your relationship with Riley."

"I have none!" Heat flares across my skin. "The first time I met her was in the maze!" I'm not a liar. In fact, it goes against my very nature. I pride myself on my absolute honesty.

Manson blinks slowly. The lack of emotions on his face is both comforting and disconcerting. It's impossible to guess what he's feeling.

"Why is she obsessed with you?"

I have no idea what he's talking about. That woman is fucking horrible. Why the hell does he think I have a relationship with her? But instead of those words, what comes out is a soft, "Hard to be obsessed with someone you just met."

Manson eyes me. "That is incorrect."

I scoff out a breath. Is this some kind of quiz? Why is he

wasting time with me? "If you already know the answers, why are you asking?"

Manson's eyebrows shoot up for a fraction of a second. "If you don't want to end up like Cali, you'll start working with me."

Ice fills my veins. For a second, all I see is my friend's face. The friend I've been trying so desperately to find.

I shoot forward. "You know where she is?"

There's a blank expression on his handsome face.

"Please," I plead. I'm not touching him, but I'm close enough to. I look into his blank, green eyes. "Please tell me she's alive."

"Rachel. I asked why Riley is so obsessed with you."

Frustration bubbles in my throat, and I clench my fists. "I don't know! I don't even know who Riley is. I don't lie. I know you don't know me, but I don't lie."

Manson eyes me, and my eyes dart to the gun. He still isn't pointing it at me.

He sees me looking at it. "All right, I believe you."

I open and close my mouth. I'm not sure what to say to that.

Manson leans forward and smiles. "Let's play."

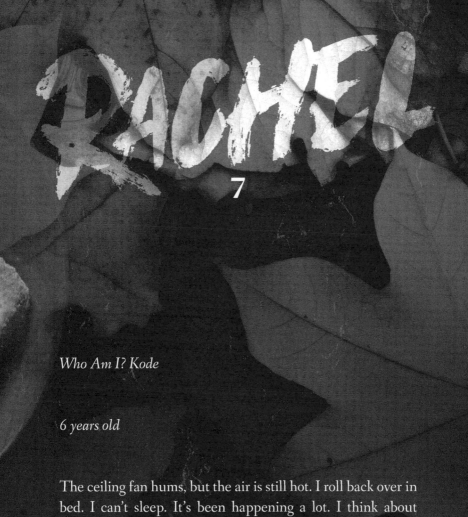

RACHEL

7

Who Am I? Kode

6 years old

The ceiling fan hums, but the air is still hot. I roll back over in bed. I can't sleep. It's been happening a lot. I think about getting up to organize my Barbie clothes again, but I don't want Papa to see the light under my door.

Thinking about getting caught makes a twisty feeling fill my belly. I already don't feel good tonight. My head hurts, and it feels like everything is touching me all at once. The sheets stick to my skin, and it's all sweaty, sweaty, sweaty.

I roll again. The night drags on. I don't want to get up, but my head hurts, and I want medicine, but Mommy is in there with Papa. He'll wake up if I get her.

I wait for what feels like hours until I feel like jumping out of my own head. Maybe it won't happen tonight.

I creep out of my bed and open my door slowly. The light under my parent's door is off. Well, Papa isn't my actual dad, but he's been living with us for a few years.

I pad to the kitchen, looking for the bottle of medicine Mom keeps above the sink.

"Rachel?"

I jump. Papa is sitting in his green armchair in the living room. It's dark, except for the light from his phone.

"Papa," I gasp.

"What are you doing up?" His voice is full of softness. I've learned that he makes his voice that way when he wants to sound like he cares.

I swallow. I feel my cheeks get hot, like I did something wrong. "My head hurts."

Maybe he won't do it. Maybe if he knows I'm hurting, he won't do anything.

"Awww baby, come here."

I stand, frozen. Every time I go there, he makes me feel good, but I feel like I did something wrong.

"Rachel," Papa says with that soft voice. "It's not nice to disobey. You'll hurt my feelings."

I clench my fingers. I want to tell him that I don't care if I hurt his feelings. But I don't.

"I'm going to count to three. If you don't come here, I'll tell your mom what a bad girl you're being."

I swallow. I don't want to be a bad girl. I always try so hard to be good. Slowly, I creep over to his armchair.

"Come here, sweet girl." Papa reaches out his hands. As soon as his hand closes over my arm, I feel the touch every-where. It's overwhelming, and it hurts, even though he isn't squeezing.

"Show me where it hurts." Papa brushes his other hand down my hair. His hands are rough and calloused. He says it's from all the hunting and skinning he does. Momma likes it, says we have to go grocery shopping less, but I hate it. I hate seeing the dead carcasses left in our backfield to rot. The poor animals are stripped of their life so cruelly. Sometimes, I keep and clean the skulls, then line them up along the back of the house. Feels better than to let them rot.

"Rachel." Papa's voice is soft, and he tips my chin up to look at him. I squeeze my eyes shut. I can feel the green corduroy of the chair against my legs, and it makes me want to scratch my skin off.

"Tell me where." His hands roam down my arms.

"My head." I still don't open my eyes.

"Poor baby." He scoots forward, pulling me up on his lap. I go stiff, hating the smell of old smoke. Hating how gentle he is. He's always gentle, but everything still feels wrong.

"Let Papa make it better." His hands start roaming softly.

"Medicine," I choke out.

"What do you feel?" Papa's hands roam lower, and he kisses the top of my head softly.

My tummy hurts. I dig my fingertips into my palms. The little bit of pain helps me. Helps when I'm confused.

"Tell me what you feel," Papa demands.

"Sad."

"Poor baby. I'll kiss it better."

When his hands brush down under my PJ bottoms, I dig my fingers in deeper. He always makes it feel better. But then I feel worse.

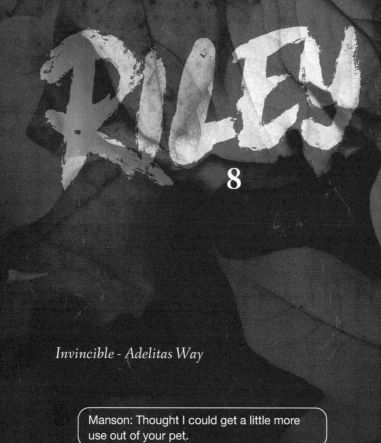

8

Invincible - Adelitas Way

> Manson: Thought I could get a little more use out of your pet.

The text is sent with a picture of Manson pointing a gun at Rachel. She's looking with those big doe eyes at the camera.

I shoot up from my chair. "What in the ever-loving fuck?" What is Manson doing? Before I can think, I throw my chair across my garage, and it clatters into the wall with a crack.

Manson is messing with my toy. *My* toy. I told him to kill her, not fuck with her.

Rage—the only true emotion I feel—flows through me. I don't feel most things. Haven't since I was a kid. According to society, that's made me do some fucked up things. Fuck society. They're a bunch of group-thinking morons. The things I've done have always had a purpose. Even if that purpose was to kill my never-ending boredom.

But Manson? Manson is another beast entirely. He's extreme, even to my standards. Especially when it comes to me.

Me: You're pathetic.

My hands shake. Always. He always has to butt his way into every single part of my life. If there's one emotion I feel every day, it's hatred for Manson Kennedy.

Manson: Awfully emotional. Did something upset you?

I throw my phone down on my workbench. I know better than to respond to his needling. The attention is what he wants. Craves. And it pisses him off more when he doesn't get it.

Instead, I pace.

When I saw the animals, I stopped being interested in Rachel. People who hurt animals for personal gain are the worst of the worst scum to me. I'm careful about every animal product I consume. I hunt, but I use every bit of the animal. So it's not the fact that he has *Rachel*, but the fact that he thinks he can take what was mine. Like he's been doing ever since I met him when we were teens.

Fuck! I grab my butcher knife and hurl it across the room. It sticks into the wall and quivers there.

I'm gonna kill him, and I'm going to enjoy every minute of it.

RILEY

9

Identity - Grandson

16 years old

"Fucker!" I hiss as I accidentally drop the dead wasp. Pup whines beside me, and I scoop the carcass off my bedroom floor and drop it into my spell jar.

Pup dances anxiously, and I ruffle the top of his head. "You worry too much." The dog just drops his head on my leg and rests it there.

I use the term dog loosely. I'm still not sure this isn't some sort of coyote mix. He started coming to the back door for the past few months. At first, Pup was an annoyance, but he became obsessed with me, following me everywhere, and eventually, I couldn't say no to those adoring yellow-brown eyes. So, I snuck him inside occasionally. What started as occasionally became all the time. Manson hated it, so my loyalty to Pup only grew.

I throw some rusted barbed wire and the goofer dust I stole my mom's credit card to buy into my jar. Then, I reach to grab the paper with one name on it. I only remember one, but I feel like there's more, which bothers me.

Pup whimpers under me.

"It's okay, boy." I rub his head again and drop the card into my jar. Dumping rubbing alcohol in, I light it all on fire. I watch the flame lap at the man's name and say, "I hope you suffer."

Pup licks my hand. I glance down at him, and he buries his long snout under my hand.

"Riley!" There's a harsh knock at my door, then the door opens.

Jesus. That's mom, and she's already in a bad mood. I turn to the door, bored. Mom steps inside and then sucks in a horrified gasp.

"Fire!"

"Yeah. I made it."

"What the fuck are you doing?" Mom rushes over, then stops, searching. Probably just realized she can't put it out with her hands. I can't help but smirk at her frantic energy. Pup gives a low growl.

"Do something, Riley!" Mom gasps.

I push back in my desk chair. "It's contained." In fact, the fire is already starting to go out, having burned up the few things that were flammable in my spell jar. I'm not entirely convinced that witchy things are real, but I also can't disprove they aren't. So I do them, fuck the consequences.

"Riley." Mom whirls on me and snaps her hand across my face. Pain lances across my skin, and then there's a growl and a flash of movement. Pup leaps past me, biting onto my mom's arm.

Crying out, my mom shoves back against my dog. I scramble up to see her aiming a blow at him.

I lunge, bowling into Mom and shoving her backward, and we all stumble back into my bed. I spring back, yanking Pup away to check him for injuries. Fuck. No one has ever stood up for me like that before.

"Nasty mut." Mom gasps for breath, using the bed to steady herself. "Fucking hell, he bit me!"

Pup is still growling at her, all the hair on the back of his neck raised. Mom stands there trembling. I see it a second before she moves. She's going for Pup.

The pure rage that flashes through my system over-whelms every other sense. I scream, launching at my mother and pummeling my fists into every part of her body that I can.

"Fuck you!" I scream, hitting and scratching at her. "You fucking coward!"

"Psychopath!" Mom screams, trying to hit back at me.

"And?" I almost laugh, seeing how frantic she is, while energy runs through my body. I pull back for a second, enough to stand over her and gloat.

Mom uses the bed to get up. She stands, but she's not as tall as me anymore.

Pup growls again.

"I'll kill him," Mom mutters.

Pure hatred runs through me, and I launch myself at her with a scream. I throw punch after punch, wanting her to feel the pain before I snap her neck.

Vaguely, I see motion beside me, and I'm yanked off my mother. I turn on whoever dared to touch me and lunge at them.

It's Manson. He ducks close to me and slams me into the wall. "Enough."

"I'll fucking kill her!" I growl, scrambling to get away.

"No, you won't." Manson's voice is sneering, and his grip is rock solid.

"I'm calling Jim!" Mom gasps.

"Oh sure, running to yet another man. You're pathetic." My rage knows no bounds. I've never been this angry before. Not when Mom jumped from boyfriend to boyfriend, not when I was forced to move from school to school, and not even when Mom did the things to me that she did. But now? Now I'm going to kill her.

Manson presses his arm into my neck as Mom storms out of the room.

"Get yourself together," he hisses at me.

"Get off me!" I shove at him, but he only fixes his dark eyes on mine. His pupils are huge.

"Manson, fuck off." I try to knee him, then stomp on his foot. His pupils only grow wider. I can't see Pup, but I feel him brush against my leg.

"Get him, Pup," I demand.

But he doesn't.

Manson just smirks at me. "You done?"

I heave for breath, stopping my struggles. Clearly, I can't outmuscle him. So, I just need to outsmart him.

Manson watches me for a beat longer, then steps back. We just stare at each other. I've disliked Manson since I moved here. He's too quiet. Too perceptive. Even now, he watches me like he knows me.

He doesn't know shit.

Finally, Manson smirks. He reaches down to pet Pup, who lets him.

I glare at the dog, who just pants and looks at me.

"You've been feeding him." That's the only reason Pup wouldn't go after him.

Manson ignores my comment. "My name better not have been in that jar."

"Don't flatter yourself," I spit out as he walks to the door. Before he walks out, Manson pauses. "Riley. Don't kill your mother."

Rage filters through me again. I'll do whatever the hell I want.

Before I can say anything, Manson shuts the door.

Later that night, I try to poison my mom. I move to the kitchen to prep her dinner, but as soon as I reach into my backpack to grab the rat poison I lifted from the local store, Manson's hand closes over my wrist.

He gives me a cold stare.

"Fuck you, Manson Kennedy," I hiss.

His gaze doesn't change. "Fuck *you*, Riley Kennedy."

"That's not my name." I try to yank away from him.

"It will be, one day." And with that, Manson jerks me to him, kisses my lips, then snatches the poison. "I said no. And one day, you'll learn to obey me. Until then, I'll have fun punishing you."

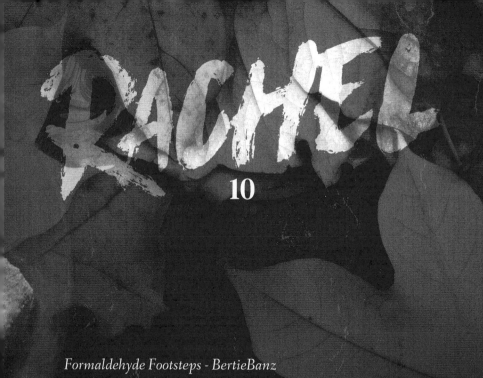

RACHEL

10

Formaldehyde Footsteps - BertieBanz

"Please. Just let me go home." I stare at Manson moving around in the kitchen. He took a picture of me at gunpoint, messed around on his phone, and then got up to make us drinks like he didn't have a care in the world.

I eye the area of the house Manson originally came from. It looks like there's a living room with stairs going up, but it's dark.

"You said you'd let me go."

Manson doesn't even glance back.

I stand. My legs are still shaky, and I still feel sick from the pills I took. I curse myself again for taking them.

Manson turns back around, three solo cups in his hands.

I freeze.

Manson merely raises an eyebrow. "Wouldn't suggest running. You'll puke all over my floors. Again."

I glare at him. "Let me go."

"We're gonna play a game." He puts the cups down on the coffee table. They're full of some sort of red liquid.

I take a step back.

"It's fruit punch." Manson shakes his head. "I don't want you getting sick and making more of a mess. Drink it. You need the sugar."

The man's eyes are eerily blank. There's no expression in them at all.

I narrow my eyes. "What's the game?"

A corner of Manson's mouth quirks up in a smirk. "Russian roulette."

"Fuck no." Adrenaline runs through me. I need to get out of here. I know he has a gun, and I have to go. Running is less dangerous than staying here.

Just as I dart up, there's the sound of a door slamming back in the house.

Manson smirks.

A shadowy figure in a biker helmet stalks to the living room. She yanks the helmet off her head and snaps, "Rachel, come here."

It's Riley.

I'm frozen. Which is the lesser of two evils?

"Rachel," Riley snaps.

Stiffly, I move her way without taking my eyes off Manson. He just watches Riley.

"Riley." His voice sounds bored.

"Enough, Manson." Riley reaches into her waistband and pulls out a gun.

Quick as a flash, Manson has his gun out, and it's pointed at me.

I scream, automatically scrambling to get away.

Riley steps in front of me, grabbing me and shoving me behind her. "Go ahead. Shoot me, Manson."

"Get out of the way."

"Make me."

There's a growl.

I yank on my arm as hard as I can. It rips out of Riley's grip, and I fall on my hip. Quickly, I scramble up, and a gunshot explodes through the house.

Wood splinters by my right leg, cutting into me. The force of it causes my leg to buckle, and I drop to my hands.

"Next one goes into her skull. Come here."

My ears ring, and everything feels fuzzy.

"You won't kill me, Riley. I know where Pup went."

More ringing.

"He's dead. That was ten years ago," Riley bites.

My leg feels hot. I glance down at it. It's red. There's a lot of red.

"Guess you won't know unless you both come here."

There's a harsh curse, then I'm yanked up by my armpits. Everything feels like it's moving in slow motion. Is this shock? I'm placed back on the couch, in the middle between Manson and Riley.

He throws us a brilliant grin, flashing his white teeth. "You're back, little intrigue."

"Don't talk about my fucking toy like that," Riley snaps.

Manson's grin only grows wider. I shiver. I see the smile lines around his eyes.

"Tell me about Pup."

"Only if you play my game." Manson reaches to the coffee table, where the drinks are still laid out. "Drink, Rachel."

"Fuck you," I grit. My leg is pounding.

Manson just laughs. "Your life means nothing to me. Drink, or I'll kill you."

The only thing that comes to mind is the image of my

brain all over the walls. I open my mouth, "That would make more of a mess than puke."

Manson shakes his head. "Naive girl. Drink."

I look at Riley. She raises an eyebrow at me, then glances at Manson.

"You're gonna play the same game with her that I play with you," Manson demands.

Silence.

"We'll play, then I'll tell you about Pup."

Riley reaches for the coffee table and snatches up a drink for herself. "There's nothing to know. He disappeared. End of story."

Manson leans back, something flashing in his eyes. "But it'll kill you that I'm the only one who knows."

Riley glares at him, then chugs the drink.

Manson fixes a dead stare on me. "Drink."

I feel the powerful bodies on both sides of me. Both are people with guns who seem to hate me for no reason.

"Here." Riley grabs a drink from the table, then throws a leg over me, mounting me. I gasp as Riley looks down at me with a grin on her beautiful face. "Open up."

"Fuck you." Adrenaline races through me. If I'm going to die, I'll die fighting.

Riley smirks, running a finger up the side of my neck. The mock gentleness makes me shiver. "Be a good pet, and obey."

I search Riley's dark eyes. They bore into mine with intoxicating intensity. Her face looks soft and feminine, with pretty cheekbones and a flush on her cheeks, but her eyes are harsh. Riley's pupils grow wider, and she leans down to my ear. Her delicate breath brushes the shell of my ear. "I'd love to make you choke on it."

She pulls back enough for me to meet her gaze again. I

narrow my eyes, then snatch the cup out of her hand. I down it, the sugary drink immediately making me want to vomit.

Victory lights in Riley's eyes. She lowers her forehead to mine, her eyes hooded, whispering, "That's my good girl."

My heart races. Riley pulls back enough to continue to look into my eyes. I become deeply aware that she's still straddling my lap, her soft tits right in my line of vision. My cheeks burn.

"Manson," Riley says. Manson reaches to grab the last cup, then also shoots it down.

"You dosed all of them." Riley says it like a statement.

Manson's eyes glint. "Gotta keep things interesting, Riley Kennedy."

Riley leans over, grabbing Manson's jaw. His smirk just grows.

"That's not my name. I'd rather die than marry you."

Manson groans. "Keep talking dirty, Mrs. Kennedy."

"Fuck you." Riley spits on Manson.

He grunts, snapping his hand out to her throat and yanking her off me.

I scoot back. The pain in my leg comes shooting back. I glance down. There's a piece of wood the size of a pencil sticking out of it.

Shit. I can't pull it out, or it'll start bleeding heavier.

"Let's play hide and seek." Manson grabs Riley's hips. "Whoever finds the toy first, fucks her."

"Stop playing and tell me what I want to know. I took your stupid drink."

I stand in confusion. How dare they treat me like just a game? Is this what happened to Cali? Is this how she died?

Rage rushes through me. I refuse to be just a game to them.

"You have till the count of zero, Rachel."

I jump. Why are they talking to me? Why can't they play their own stupid game and keep me far, far out of it?

"Thirty. Twenty-nine."

I jump up. As I dart past the coffee table, Manson lunges at me and grabs at the wood in my leg. I scream, my body numb with adrenaline.

"Twenty-eight."

I dart to the back door, but Riley chases after me, putting herself between me and the door. "Stay inside, bambi," Riley demands.

I backpedal away, then go the only place I can—up the stairs.

Manson's monotone counting continues. The second floor is just as dark as downstairs. I dart into the room at the top, hoping there's a porch roof or something to jump out on.

The bedroom is virtually empty, just a bed and a night-stand. And outside the window, there's no porch. Just a straight drop to the hard ground below.

I yank on the window latches anyway. They're stuck.

"Ready or not...here we come."

Fuck! That was way faster than 30 seconds. I dart to the closet. There are some clothes and shoes, but it's mostly empty. Shutting the door behind me, I tuck myself into the corner and grab a shoe, anything to use as a weapon. I immediately try to slow my breathing. It comes hard and fast, and my heart is beating so quickly I feel it squeeze with every pump.

As I still, fire races up my leg. It hurts more now, and it feels wet. I reach my fingers down. Fuck, the stick is gone, and warm, heavy blood soaks my sock.

Footsteps sound up the stairs in a heavy cadence.

"Where are you, little intrigue?"

"She's mine, so fuck off."

I grip the shoe harder. As I do, a rush of bright light rushes through my head. What the hell? I suck in a breath, squeezing my eyes shut.

Something scratches outside the closet, and I snap my eyes open, trying to see in the pitch-black.

"Bambiii."

More scratching. Are they scratching the walls? It makes shivers run down my arms. Fuzziness fills my brain, and for a second, overwhelming sensations wrap me in bursts of color and goosebumps. I suck in a breath to stop my spiral. What is going on?

"Oh, bambi. You left such a perfect bloody trail."

The closet door rips open, and Riley grins down at me.

I scream, launching myself at her.

Riley ducks into me, grabbing me around the waist. I slam the shoe into her head, clawing at her.

She laughs, "Yes, feisty thing. Fight me so good."

Suddenly, I'm flying through the air. I bounce on something soft, realizing I've landed on the bed. Riley crawls up over me, grinning. "Keep going. Make me stop, Rachel."

I twist over, trying to get up on my hands and knees, but Riley just drops onto my back. Her grip is harsh and painful.

"Need some help?" Manson's voice deadpans. The deep sound of his voice wraps around me in a warm hug. My brain is fuzzy again. I struggle weakly.

You can't feel sounds. Why am I feeling sounds?

I jerk my elbow back, crashing it into something.

"Jesus."

The pain cracks down my arm, shooting into my mouth and exploding out of it in a burst of color. I watch the splatters of blue drop onto the bed.

What the actual fuck? What the hell was in that drink?

There's a laugh, and then I'm flipped back over.

"Damn. It's pretty."

I glance down. Both of them are looking at my leg. In the dim light of the room, I see the red smeared all over the light bedspread. It looks like it's fucking glowing.

Fuck! I scramble back, only to be stopped by Riley's grip on my hips.

"Yes," she chuckles. "Keep painting your pretty blood all over Manson's bed." She jumps up on the bed and sits on my legs.

"Get off me!" I kick, but my limbs feel fuzzy.

"Does it hurt?" Riley turns her blank eyes on me.

I swallow. I don't know what she's talking about. Something is wrong with my head; the colors are so much brighter.

They watch me with predatory stillness. Then, slow grins creep over their faces.

"Good," Riley coos. "Show me just how much it hurts." She ducks down, holding my leg down, then licks her hot tongue across my skin.

An explosion of heat, goosebumps, and pain runs up my leg. Riley lifts her face, her mouth and chin covered in blood, and grins at Manson.

He grabs her chin and smashes his lips to hers, kissing her heavily.

I watch them, entranced. The glowing red reflects on their skin, making them look luminescent. Manson's powerful body looms over Riley, but she gives it just as good as she gets, shoving back into him.

With a snarl, Manson lets go of Riley and dips his head to my leg. He licks my wound in an aggressive swipe, ripping his tongue along the edges. White hot pain flashes in the room, and I close my eyes from the brightness. The warmth of the blood and his tongue set my leg on fire, and suddenly, my mouth fills with the taste of copper. All the sensations overwhelm me, and I thrash back and forth.

"Good girl. Give me that pain." Riley groans and reaches her hand down to her cunt, rubbing herself over her pants.

Too much. It's too much. Every time I'm touched, lights flash across my vision. Bright whites streak back and forth as pain flashes through my leg. The whole room looks brighter, and the shadows move and dance.

"Shhh."

I don't realize I'm screaming until Manson claps his hand over my mouth.

"You ever been on a trip before?" Riley cocks her head at me.

I blink. It looks like light is shooting out of her eyes. They're so big and bright and expressive. How did I not notice how expressive they are?

The corners crinkle, and she smiles. "Oh, this'll be fun." She ducks down, and I feel hot fingers on my hips before my shorts are yanked down.

"No," I groan into Manson's hand. He laughs, the sound rich and deep. It fills the air with actual warmth and sends a bolt of heat straight to my clit.

Riley bites down on my pussy, and I scream, the sound coming out muffled. The pain shoots through me in bursts of color.

I think I pass out for a second because everything is peaceful and quiet one second, and then suddenly, it's all loud again. Sensation rushes over my entire body, but I feel something on my pussy. I snap my eyes open and see Riley's fingers press down on my clit. She rubs it firmly. Despite everything, pleasure shoots through me. She's not gentle, and I buck up into her.

"Good girl. Be my pretty little slut," she says. "Let Manson watch something he can't have."

Immediately, there's a growl, and Riley's hand is snatched off my pussy. I snap my eyes open to see Manson's head duck between my legs. He latches onto my clit and sucks aggressively.

My back bows, and I let out a scream. The pleasure tastes warm, like honey.

Tastes? Fuck, something is messed up.

Manson eats me firmly and consistently until I feel the orgasm approaching. All the sensations are heightened, and the wave of pleasure hits me startlingly fast. I come, my muscles locked up, lights dancing around the room, and honey on my tongue.

Riley watches me with a smirk. Her face and mouth still glow red.

Manson pulls back. "I got her to come faster than you did."

Riley arches an eyebrow. "You looked good bowing when I told you to eat."

Manson's eyes narrow. "I took your toy, little sister."

Riley smiles. "You're so easy to manipulate, you know that Manson?"

I see the aggression before he moves. It's like a wave of heat rolls off Manson, and he lunges at Riley.

I struggle to roll away, but my muscles are like liquid gold. Manson wrestles Riley until she's lying next to me and looks down at both of us with a feral smile. "There. Both of my pretty toys are under me. Just how I like it."

11

Hero Killer - PierceTheSkies

One week ago

I survey the sex club in front of me, the heavy beat of the base pounding into my chest. The music used to make me feel a little something other than the endless boredom. But now, I feel nothing.

I didn't plan on coming tonight, but the void is so empty I wandered in here, hoping it would help.

I stare out onto the dancefloor from my reserved corner. My dad used to always bring me here, but now I've taken over most of the family business, and I'm too busy for it. I'm one of the major drug distributors in the region, and at first, I found it stimulating. I used to love working relations between us and the cartel, weeding out moles and doling out punishments with my fists. Anything to keep my mind off the infuri-

77

ating woman my father brought into our lives. I've tried everything possible to get her to bow to me, but she won't. She's impossible to manipulate, aggressive, and damn near as smart as me.

Which I never find.

I look over the club again, feeling a hint of annoyance thinking about Riley. The woman I still haven't tamed.

Nearly naked men and women dance on the dance floor, and some fuck openly on the couches arranged around the area.

The Hunter's Club looks like a swinger's club. It's where the rich, bored, and famous come to get their rocks off, at least on paper. The real reason people come here is to be noticed by Wyatt, the owner. If he likes you, he'll invite you to his private island to play his little annual hunting game.

I've gone every year since I was seventeen. Besides messing with Riley, it's been the greatest thrill I've ever felt.

I shift, thinking about her again. She hasn't talked to me in days. Which usually means she's mad at me or up to something and doesn't want me to know about it.

I check my phone again. We aren't supposed to bring our phones in here, but I could care less right now. There's nothing from Riley.

I grip my phone hard, looking up at the room again. My gaze immediately catches on a tall, lithe woman who's just walked in. She's in a short, sparkly black dress that grips her body. I cock my head in interest. Not many women are as tall as Riley.

As the woman turns, I catch a glimpse of her face.

My whole body locks up. It *is* Riley.

What the hell is she doing here? This club is full of pieces of shit who will eat her alive.

Rage rushes through me, and I jump to my feet. Riley is

mine. No one else gets to touch her. Stalking to where Riley leans against the bar, I come up behind her and drop my arm around her shoulders. She turns a dazzling grin to me that instantly disappears as soon as she sees me.

"Long time no see, sis." I grip her tightly.

"Manson," she smiles, but it's fake. As is everything about her tonight. She hates dresses, and her hair is even out of her favorite braids.

"What are you doing here?" I can't keep the slight quiver out of my muscles. Adrenaline is flooding my system.

Riley turns away from me. "Just looking for a good fuck."

I laugh, although nothing is funny about this. Riley knows just how to fuck with me. I yank her back from the bar. "Join me, sis."

Riley tries to yank away from me, but I pull her back toward one of the private rooms. No one even bats an eye as she fights me. Around here, discretion is more valuable than anything. People have been killed for less.

I yank Riley into a private room and slam the door.

"Let go." She shrugs out of my grip.

"Riley," I growl. "What the fuck are you doing here?" I know she's not just looking for another fuck. Riley can get whoever she wants at a normal bar. She came here for a reason.

The stunning woman in front of me fixes her dress, intentionally drawing my eyes to her ample breasts. She smirks a little when she sees me looking.

I lunge forward, pinning her against the wall. The whole room rattles with the force of it.

"Easy, brother," Riley puffs out a breath. "Jealous much?"

I narrow my eyes at her. She does make me jealous. Every time she takes someone home from the bar. She knows it, and

I know it. But still, she refuses to be in a relationship with me. It's infuriating and aggravating.

And endlessly fascinating.

"Tell me," I demand.

"Fuck you." Riley has fire in her eyes. "Let me do this one thing, Manson. Stop getting in my fucking way!"

I don't let off the pressure I have on her neck. "You know what this place is," I say it as a statement, not a question.

She doesn't flinch.

My stomach knots. I know why she's here. Riley is the most bloodthirsty woman I've ever met. Bloodthirsty and *reckless*.

"How did you even get in here?"

She bats those long, dark eyelashes. "You weren't supposed to be here."

I close my eyes. "Did you tell them you knew me?"

"Your dad, actually." She shoves against me. "Don't flatter yourself."

As usual, whenever I'm around her, I feel a mix of hatred and electricity. "You can't be here."

"Why? Because it's against the rules?" Riley's tone is mocking. "Since when did you ever care about rules?"

It's true. No women have ever been allowed to join the club as hunters. Wyatt's orders. So, my little pain has done her research.

I watch her, enjoying the pulse of her heartbeat under my arm. She feels so fragile and warm. I could kill her so easily. How dare she give other men the chance to do that? I run my thumb along her pulse point, and goosebumps break out across her skin.

"You haven't killed anyone." Proving yourself is a rule to joining the club as a hunter. Riley should know that, having done her research.

Her eyes immediately light up with rage. "And who's fault is that?" she hisses at me.

I shake my head, immediately stepping back. If she still blames me for that, then she isn't ready.

"No," I say.

Riley's hand rears back for a blow. I watch her, staying still. She slaps her hand against my face in a sharp crack. The stinging pain radiates across my face, but I don't move.

"Fuck you, Manson Kennedy," Riley hisses, looking more beautiful and breakable than ever before. I just want to squeeze that pretty little neck until it turns purple.

I take a step closer to her. She stands her ground, seething. I trace my finger along her jaw. "Too impulsive, little sister. Learn how to kill correctly, or don't do it at all."

"How can I learn if you won't let me?" Her creamy skin is flushed and angry. I want to bite it. To make it red and irritated. To leave my marks all over it.

Despite the fact I'm mad, I smirk. I like seeing her so angry. It makes my dick hard. If it gets me this reaction, I'll never let her kill.

I turn away and head for the door.

"Wait," Riley says.

I stop. I could get her kicked out of this club permanently, and she knows it.

"I'll marry you if you get me in."

Everything around me freezes, and the thudding of the base grows distant. The world stops.

This is the first time Riley hasn't thrown the idea back in my face with hatred.

I turn and stare at her, soaking in her face. It's a beautiful mask of indifference. She's lying to get something that she wants. But I don't care. This is the first step in breaking her down. The idea of her on my arm and my ring around her finger is something I've dreamed about for a long time.

Riley stares at me with her brilliant jewels of eyes. We stand there silently.

I know marrying your step-sibling is frowned upon by the rest of society. But I couldn't care less. *That's* not the issue. The issue is that she isn't bowing at my feet, begging to be mine.

I look down at her. "You haven't proven yourself, Riley. I can't always be around to protect you."

"I never asked you to." Her eyes glint.

I shake my head. Riley never asked me to, but she's needed it. As much as I want her on my arm willingly, it's not something I'd sacrifice her safety for.

"Prove yourself to me, Riley. Do it the right way, don't get caught, and for the love of Satan." I snatch her up under her chin. "Don't ever come here alone again."

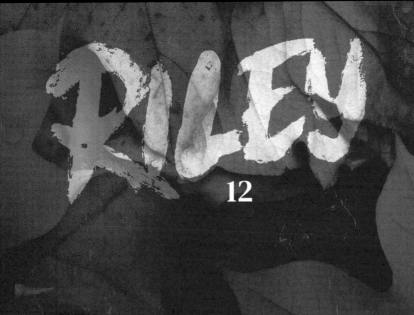

12

Past the Past - New Medicine

Rachel is fully tripping out, her little chest rising and falling rapidly. I'm not surprised that my little deer hasn't taken acid before, but seeing her so out of it makes me feel a strange sense of protectiveness.

Manson still towers over both of us. He's stunningly handsome, and I hate to admit that. He's always been the hottest man I've ever seen.

Manson looks between both of us, and then his gaze locks on Rachel. I look over to see what he's looking at.

"Prove yourself," Manson says softly.

"What?" I blink at him.

He turns his green eyes on me. "Prove. Yourself."

Our conversation from the club comes rushing back to me.

Manson pulls back, and I sit up. "Oh, that's not how this works."

"Isn't it?" He folds his heavily tattooed arms.

"No." The old bitterness and resentment washes over me. "You don't get to push me around and pick who I get to kill and who I don't."

"If you can't do it, just say so."

I jump to my feet and get in Manson's face. My voice comes out low, "You know damn well I can do it."

"Then do it." He lifts an eyebrow.

You know what? I take it back. He may have the jawline of the century, but Manson is the most infuriating prick I've ever met. I seethe, "I was going to. With my mom. And then with you. And then with every mother fucker who crossed me." Every single time, Manson has intervened. He told me if I killed anyone, he'd get me thrown in prison for the rest of my life. I've seen his connections, and he wasn't kidding.

"It's okay if you're scared."

It takes everything I have not to deck him. But he would *love* that. Instead, I grit, "You think you're God and can just use me to kill off anyone you want?"

A small dimple forms on Manson's right cheek.

Of course he does.

"Not happening." Forget the fact I was okay with him killing Rachel just hours ago. Now, I'm going to make her outlive both of us just to spite him.

How inconvenient.

"Let's go, bambi." I grab her arm. "I think we've wasted enough time here."

She struggles lightly, but she's too far gone. I hardly even feel the effects. I've needed more and more doses to get me to feel anything recently.

"You can't leave." Manson steps in my way. "Not while high."

"Rachel, did you hear something? Must be an annoying

fly in here." I grab her under her arms and lift her up. She's so delicate and light, and it's easy to make her do whatever I want. It makes my pussy throb.

"Riley–"

"If you don't tell me about Pup, I swear I'll never talk to you again." The words slip out of my mouth before I can stop them. I shouldn't care about Pup. I'm not sad that he's probably dead. All creatures die. But I never knew what happened to him. And that part eats at me.

Manson's voice lowers dangerously. "I wouldn't suggest that, Riley."

I shoulder Rachel into the hall, beyond pissed. "I swear, Manson. Not another word."

He follows us down the stairs. "You can't ride your bike with her. She's tripping. She'll jump right off the back, and you'll wreck."

I ignore him. We make it to the back door and out.

"Riley," Manson growls.

Instead of my bike, I head to his truck. I pop the passenger side open, dump Rachel in, and then go to the other side.

"You can't leave without—"

I fish the keys I stole from his pocket out and dangle them in the air.

There's a beat of silence.

I don't wait. I open the door and get in.

"Pup is buried by the tree in my dad's backyard."

I freeze. Something uncomfortable grips my chest and hurts. I turn back to Manson.

He just looks at me.

"You killed him?"

Manson doesn't answer.

Alina May

He killed him. Some part of me cracks.
I slam the car door and peel away.

13

BITE BACK - n9neful

17 years old

It's been three days since I kept Riley from killing her mom.
She hasn't spoken a single word to me since.

I pace my room, and an odd feeling runs through me.

I check my phone again. The tracker I put on Pup hasn't
moved in hours. I let him outside to keep my dad from killing
him. I don't care, but Riley cares.

And that means everything.

Despite the fact he's a fucking coyote, I've been feeding
him every day and keeping an eye on him. The fact he hasn't
moved has me concerned.

Unsure what to do with my restless energy, I throw on
my shoes, grab my pistol, and head outside. Tracking through

the summer heat sucks ass, but it beats the stifling silence from Riley.

She hates me for keeping her from killing her mom. But I followed her to the appliance store she got her poison from. They had recordings from all angles. She was fully recorded during the whole transaction, and in her rage, she didn't notice.

But I did. As would every cop in the area.

It's not like the cops can't be bought out. But it's the principle of it. Do it right, or you don't deserve to do it at all.

I only allow the best for Riley.

When I come close to the spot my tracker indicates, I shake the bag of treats.

Nothing.

It takes only a few minutes of searching to find the body. Pup was shot.

I stare at his form, calculating. My dad wouldn't do this. Pup was out of the house, so he didn't care. So, who else?

I glance around at the surroundings. We're close to the neighbor's property. I don't know his name, but I do know he has chickens.

I bet Pup was after the chickens, they shot him, and he drug himself out here to die.

I clench my jaw. How dare they touch something that belonged to my little pain?

I planned everything out for the next hour. Calm. Calculated. The only way to be when you're planning something of this nature. I need Riley to understand this.

I shoot her a text.

Me: Meet me in the backyard. 10 mins

. . .

I stare at my phone but get no response, even after ten minutes have passed—then twenty.

I stuff my phone into my pocket. Fine.

It takes only ten minutes to get the neighbor—still don't know his name—into the back field where Pup lay. It was easy. The man had no cameras, and his wife was at the store.

"You did this." I point my gun at him. The man is old, in his 60s, and he trembles. "Did what?"

"The dog."

The man looks down. "The coyote?"

"No, that's my woman's dog." I shake my head at him.

"I'm sorry! I had no idea." The man's eyes are confused. I guess to him, the charming neighbor he once knew is now pointing a gun at his head.

I shrug, then fire a round into the man's head.

He crumples. As I watch the blood pool into the ground near Pup, I feel my dick get hard.

I growl, "*I'm sorry* doesn't fix things for Riley."

By the time I drag Pup back to the house, it's dark. I'm hot and sweaty, but I get to work digging a hole under the tree. The grass is rough and sunbaked, and getting the spade in is hard.

This is ridiculous. Animals are leeches of energy, and the only purpose of a burial is not to get caught.

But, for some reason, this creature meant something to my little pain.

So I dig.

When I'm done, I go to dispose of the neighbor the right way.

Riley could have learned a lot. I'll teach her to ignore me.

And in the future, I'll never give her another chance. If she ignores me, I'll take everything that she cares about until it's only me that she sees.

RILEY

14

LALALAND - Kami Kehoe

I take Rachel to my place, which is just around the corner from Manson's. Almost all the cars from the corn maze are gone, and the sky is just turning gray.

I get Rachel out to my barn, which I've transformed into a workshop. I've even installed an old garage door where the main doors rotted out. The barn is full of junk and empty stalls, but I mostly stay in the front, where I've cleared out a space. I wave my hand at the old couch I keep in here, complete with a blanket. "Sleep."

Rachel is stuck staring at my setup, her eyes wide. Probably tasting colors at this point.

I shake my head and guide her to the couch. "Sleep it off, girlfriend. You'll feel better in the morning."

"Why do you have a bed in your shop?" She looks around at my workbenches, buckets, hoses, tubes, and tools. "Wait, I'm not your girlfriend."

"It's not a bed; it's a couch, bambi. It's for sleeping. And sometimes fucking."

Rachel's face turns red, which makes me smirk. As much as she pretends not to like it, she loves it when I touch her.

And I love it, too. That pretty little body is so responsive. So tense and hungry. It makes me wonder how long it's been since someone has touched her.

At that thought, a strange anger fills me. Who else has touched my little deer?

Loud chirping outside the barn doors breaks me out of my haze. It's morning already, but I'm not tired. I'm wound up. I need to work with my hands. Go hunting. Do something. But I can't leave her. Now that Rachel's on Manson's radar, he'll do anything he can to fuck with her. Which just puts me in a mood.

How dare he mess with me, and what's mine after killing Pup? I'll kill him for what he did.

Rachel wanders to the couch, but she just stands there, staring at it.

"It's green," she says softly.

"Yep. Gold star for you." I move up behind her, pick her up, and toss her gently on the couch. She screams softly, then hisses.

I glance down. Her leg has clotted up, but it looks nasty. Fuck.

Gathering the first aid kit, I drop it on the couch. Rachel scoots back and eyes me like...well, like a wounded animal.

I sigh. "Please don't make this hard for me."

She blinks slowly. I could tie her down, and I might, but that could turn her trip bad, and I don't want to deal with a screaming woman for the next few hours.

I hold my hands up. "I'll be gentle."

Something flashes in Rachel's eyes. All her muscles lock up, and her breathing picks up.

I softly grab her leg and hold it down. Her skin is so soft. "Easy. It'll hurt, but I'll be careful."

"No." Rachel panics, backing up against the back of the couch. Her leg shakes under me.

"It's just pain, bambi." I'm getting annoyed.

"No," Rachel gasps again. "Don't be gentle."

I look up at her, confusion running through me.

Rachel sucks in a breath. "Please. Don't be gentle."

I arch an eyebrow, then shrug. However the princess wants it.

I don't want to break open the scab, but I do pour a generous amount of rubbing alcohol over Rachel's leg. She hisses, and I have to hold her down to keep her from scrambling away from me. Once I've blotted up most of the area, I wrap a bandage around it. As far as I could tell, the splinter only went in an inch or two. If there are any little wood pieces left, they'll get infected, and she'll have to go to the hospital.

It bled pretty good. Manson has blood all over his house. Her blood. I smirk. It almost tempts me to kill her just so I can frame him.

When I'm done, Rachel's eyes grow heavy. Finally, under the effects of the drug, she passes out, half-splayed across the couch. I stare at her for a second, wishing I could sleep that deeply. But I don't sleep. Not much, anyway, and not heavily.

I work for a few hours, setting up supplies, defrosting my meat freezer, and cleaning my tools.

Anything to forget.

Pup was the last time I remember feeling any sort of affection. His death marked the death of my humanity, and I kind of like it that way. There's less pain when you have no emotions. No anxiety, no fear, no...nothing.

I'm numb.

Unless Manson's around. Then, that blessed rage courses through me, and for a minute, I feel alive.

When Rachel wakes again, I'm just starting to feel fatigued.

Rachel groans, rubbing her eyes. "Where am I?"

"My barn." I continue sharpening my favorite hunting knife. I use it mostly to get the hides off small game.

Rachel squints her eyes and groans. "Water?"

I jerk my head at the side of the couch. I've left some water bottles, a thing of painkillers, and an apple.

I don't deal with whining well.

Rachel looks around at the hides I have strung up to dry on the walls. We sit in silence for a while while Rachel takes the pills and some water. She doesn't whine, or beg, or cry.

Which is fucking intriguing.

Finally, Rachel asks, "You're a hunter?"

I just grunt. I've hunted ever since I moved out on my own. I can't stand mass animal farms. Those animals have no quality of life. They live in crowded pens, some of them never seeing the light of day until they're killed. Then, parts of their bodies were wasted. If not in the process of gutting them, then when they're eaten and scraped from the plates of the ungrateful to the trash. The entitlement of human beings drives me insane. Other humans are the worst thing to happen to my planet.

So I hunt my own meat. I get the thrill of a good hunt, and I take care of my world so it'll keep producing for me. Plus, Manson keeps fucking up my plans to do this to people, so here we are.

Rachel looks uncomfortable.

"Don't pretend you have a bleeding heart." I snort. "I saw the collection you have at home." At the mention of that, I get pissed again.

Rachel's eyebrows shoot up. "You were in my house?"

I shake my head. "Don't change the subject." I don't care about her opinion of me breaking and entering. Actually, I don't care about anyone's opinion, period.

"I don't have a bleeding heart," Rachel huffs. "But even if I did, that wouldn't be a bad thing."

I snort. "Spoken like a true bleeding heart."

"I'm going home." Rachel jumps off the couch.

I continue sharpening my knife, the sound of the grinder filling the barn.

"It's your death wish," I say over the grinder as Rachel stomps to the door.

Out of the corner of my eye, I see her pause. I won't let her leave, but I want to see what she'll do.

"Where's Manson?"

Oh, so she does have some brains.

"Out looking for you."

Lie. He knows exactly where she is—with me.

Rachel pauses. "Can you take me back home?"

"Take you back to the place he's looking?" I snort. "I gave you more credit than that."

Rachel looks torn.

I shrug.

Finally, she says, "Let me call someone."

I just turn and raise an eyebrow at her. "Do you know who Manson is?"

Rachel glares at me. She still doesn't get it.

"Manson has hired guns all over this damn region. You think just staying with a family member will get you out of his reach? Use your brain, bambi. You saw him; you know what he's capable of."

Rachel is still frozen, like a deer in the headlights. Probably knows she can't trust me, but Manson is even less trustworthy. She's stuck. Because the more I use her emotions against her, the more I seem like the best option. Humans fear the unknown much more than they fear the known.

"Stay with me. I'll keep you safe from him." Ironically, I've told her more truths than lies in this conversation.

What an interesting predicament.

I hold my hand out to her.

Still, nothing.

Okay, so she's a lot smarter than I gave her credit for.

"Let me rephrase this." I stare at her. "I won't let you risk your life running right into Manson's hands. You have no choice. You're staying with me."

Rachel's eyes flash with defiance a second before she darts out of the barn.

"Jesus," I groan. Who knew having a toy would be such work?

I jog after her, only to find her puking her guts out at the edge of the corn maze. She sees me and starts running again, only to double over. She half-jogs, doubled over and hurling.

"Are you quite done?"

She waves me off. I wait until she's done. Nothing but bile is coming up.

I need to feed her something real.

"Whenever you're finished, I have things to do." I tap my foot.

"You drugged me!" she yells.

I blink. "Yeah."

"It was awful!" She whirls on me. "You can't keep me prisoner."

"Why not?" I cock my head.

"Because!" Rachel's face is pale. "It's not right!"

"It must be quite hard trying to live with what's right and what isn't." I blink at her. I don't understand why people would want to live that way. Emotions and morality put so many rules on an already boring life.

Rachel just stares at me, her face a curious void of emotion. It's not the first time I've seen her go blank. The first time I saw her, I thought she might be one of us. Her face was empty, and every time she showed an emotion, it seemed rehearsed. But now I know she can't be. She doesn't seem to have a manipulative bone in her body.

"What are you looking at?" Rachel's face gets red. She's embarrassed.

Okay, definitely not one of us.

"You done puking?"

Rachel squares her shoulders.

"Good." I snatch her up and throw her over my shoulder. "If you run from me again, I won't be this nice."

I don't normally sleep in the house, but I might need to today. I drag Rachel inside, ignoring her cute attempts to claw my eyes out, and push her into the master bedroom. I don't want to share a room with her, but given our circumstances, it's the best way I can protect her. Manson will expect us in the barn, and this place is much easier to protect.

I handcuff Rachel to the headboard. She acts quite unhappy about the whole thing, but I don't care. I cuff her so both arms are stretched above her head but leave the cuffs loose enough that they aren't biting into her skin. While I enjoy pain, I want Rachel to relax enough that I can get some sleep.

Once she's secured, I move around the first floor, setting up mouse trap trip wire alarms. I position them around the doors and windows and use fishing line so Manson can't see. I also pull the blinds down so he can't see where we are in the house.

I don't have cameras set up in my place. I learned the hard way when Manson hacked them and used them to spy on me. So this will have to work. This way, if someone walks against the fishing line, it triggers the trap to snap, hitting on some bullet primer. It's loud as fuck. And I've never used these, so Manson shouldn't be expecting them.

I bring some pillows up to the room and settle myself against the door. Rachel stares at me from the bed. She's stopped babbling, and I can see her calculating from here. "You're not sleeping on the bed?"

I shake my head. I don't like beds. Too many shitty memories. Plus, I'm pretty sure Rachel's calculating how to kill me. So I settle onto the floor with my pillows.

It's kind of a pain in the ass to have a prisoner. This must be why Manson doesn't keep people alive for long.

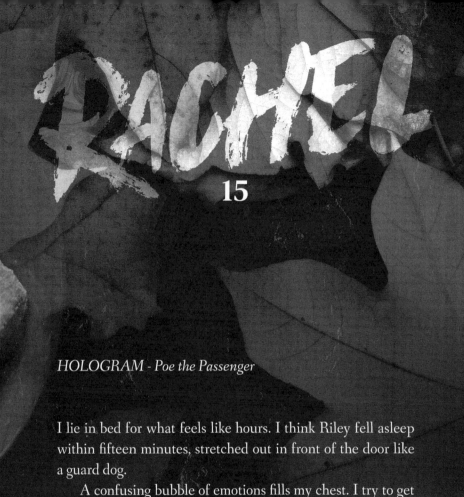

RACHEL

15

HOLOGRAM - Poe the Passenger

I lie in bed for what feels like hours. I think Riley fell asleep within fifteen minutes, stretched out in front of the door like a guard dog.

A confusing bubble of emotions fills my chest. I try to get out of my cuffs, wiggling them back and forth quietly, so much so that the edges of my hands get bruised and ripped. On top of that, my leg hurts.

My skin feels gross. I feel sweaty, and I can *feel* the gunk in my skin. I hated every minute of that trip. I finally feel back in control, but even though I'm in control of my mind, I'm so far out of control it's not even funny.

I shimmy up so I can run my fingers along the pimple on my forehead. It hurts, so I pick at it while I think.

There is something really wrong with both Manson and Riley. One minute, they're like robots; the next, they switch on emotion on a dime. They do it so effortlessly, too, and it just confuses me more. I already have a hard time reading people, but this? This is like an Olympic sport.

I want to go home. I'm fucking starving, I stink, and I want to lose myself in my bones. Even just sitting in the room looking at them helps. They're the only friends I have that don't judge. Plus, everything is simple and orderly when I'm in that room. I have a system for everything. The skulls are ordered by species and height. They're all labeled with the type and the month I found them. Everything has a place.

I need a routine. If I don't have my favorite food (currently chicken nuggets, preferably the frozen ones from Tyson), my comfy sweats, and my skulls, everything else starts to fall away, too.

Having a routine makes sense. It's predictable. But now, all my emotions are out of place, and my gut twists.

I need Riley to let me go, but I'm not sure how to accomplish that. I doubt I'll be able to pull on her heartstrings. I don't think she has them, and even if she did, I've never been good with that kind of thing. I'm going to have to outsmart her. And Manson.

I study every inch of Riley's room, trying to stave off a panic attack. It looks basic. Impersonal. She doesn't even have any family pictures. Her dresser is dusty and looks unused.

My breathing picks up. If they know where I live, how can I go home?

Riley groans.

I stiffen.

She moans, picking herself off the floor, shaking the sleep from her head.

"Wow. Forgot how much the floor sucks." She stretches. "Gotta pee?"

I flush, and as I do, my stomach growls.

"Oh fuck. I've gotta feed you too, don't I?" Riley runs her hand down her face. "Fuck. Well, alright then, up you go."

Riley uncuffs me and accompanies me to the bathroom. She keeps the door open while I pee, so I can't even look for any potential weapons, then switches spots with me.

As she sits down, she mutters, "Don't run off; the house is trapped."

I glance at the hall, considering it anyway. My heart is pounding.

Riley sighs. "Rachel, please. Have I ever lied to you?"

I stand there, frozen. How am I supposed to know the answer to that? I have no way to prove either answer.

Riley finishes, washes her hands, then moves past me to the top of the stairs. She brushes past me, and I realize again how tall she is. A shiver goes up my skin from where she touched me. Riley fiddles with something on the wall. It looks like...a mousetrap glued to the wall?

Shit. So she wasn't lying.

"Come." Riley grabs my hand and pulls me downstairs. Her hand is surprisingly soft and shoots a bolt of electricity through me.

It feels weird. I pull away from her as soon as I can.

The downstairs is basic, too. There are only two couches, no coffee table, a dining room table, and some chairs. It's an open floor plan, all surrounding the stairs. There are dusty parts and clear wood floors all around the place. Almost like furniture was moved out, and it was never cleaned. All the curtains are drawn. It feels eerie. Like this place used to be a home, but now it's just a shell.

Riley opens the freezer. "Want steak?"

I swallow, looking around. The mousetraps are all over the house.

Riley just looks at me. "If you're planning on running, you'll need more food in your system."

I square my shoulders. "Wouldn't make sense to run with you right here."

Riley lifts an eyebrow. We stare at each other for a second, then she laughs. "You know, you're alright, Rachel." She goes back to the freezer, grabbing a bag of something.

Riley pan-fries some meat, and I watch silently. I note everything I can about her. She's much stronger than me and has a patchwork of tattoos along her arms. Her hair is still in those two braids, and she doesn't wear makeup. What's her story?

Riley puts a plate of steak down in front of me. She hands me a fork and a sharp knife, then gets some of her own and sits across from me.

We eat in silence. Or, I try to eat. The steak tastes...off. I try to pretend like I'm eating to appease her. I didn't see her put anything in it, but it definitely doesn't taste right.

Riley watches me push a piece of meat around the plate. I glance at her, and her face switches from blank to friendly in an instant. "Don't like venison?"

Venison? That's why it tastes off. "It's fine."

"You suck at lying, you know that?" Riley slowly puts another bite in her mouth.

My face burns, and anger runs through me. I lean back in my seat. I've always sucked at lying, and Riley seems exceptionally good at picking up lies. Which is fucking unfair. But clearly, she's onto me right now. I need to take another route.

I pick at the skin around my nails. "You took me to piss off Manson."

Riley eyes me, her gaze dead. She just watches me for a while. For a second, I feel like crawling out of my skin. How am I supposed to respond to a stare like that? I know what expression to show around angry people, sad people, happy people. But this? This is nothing.

So I suck in a breath and, finally, let my face fall into the expression I always make while thinking.

I stop trying.

A hint of something enters Riley's eyes. She waves her knife at me. "You know killing you would make my life easier, right?"

I do know that. The question that has been burning in my mind is: why hasn't she? I narrow my eyes at her.

Riley stares at me, and then a smirk creeps up her face. "Do you want me to kill you, bambi?"

"No." The word slips out before I realize what I'm saying. But when I say it, I realize how much I mean it. I want to be in control of the way I go. I don't want it to be at the hands of some fucking crazy woman.

Riley smiles at me. It's a brilliant kind of smile where she shows all her teeth. "Well then. Let's go get some groceries."

I blink. This is a trick. No one goes from blank to friendly that quickly.

"Listen, I don't like a mopey, whiney prisoner. You're not useful to me if you're starving." Riley shoves the last bites into her mouth. "Plus, I'm bored."

I cross my arms. She's...bored? I'm having the worst twenty-four hours of my life, and she's *bored*?

Riley cocks her head. "Want to, or not?"

I consider stabbing her with my knife, but I know she'd just kill me. "Yes." I get up.

"Good. Leave the knife. If you stab me on the way over, it'll kill both of us." Riley moves to the back door, unsets the trap, and opens the door.

I follow slowly. Instead of walking outside, Riley turns. "Loud noise. Cover your ears."

I stare at her, watching her whip a pistol out of the back of her pants. Things move in slow motion as Riley points the gun at something outside, and an explosion fills the room.

I scream, clapping my hands over my ears. My whole body buzzes.

"Sorry," comes a muffled voice, then a hand clamps down over my elbow.

"What the hell?" I yank back.

"Come on." Riley motions outside. The gun is back in her waistband, and she's acting like nothing happened.

I try to calm my racing heart. The noise made my blood heat and race, and I can feel it everywhere.

"Why?" I demand, not even able to pretend I'm not rattled. I follow Riley across the yard to the barn. The sun is blazing hot, and it looks like it is the middle of the afternoon.

"Manson had one last trail cam up to watch me."

"What?"

Riley holds the barn door open for me. "You're like a broken record. What? Why?" She rolls her eyes. "I found most of the others, but he thought I missed that one."

So she found cameras and just left the last one? "Why?" I step inside, wincing as I realize I repeated the question.

Riley laughs. "You're really naive, aren't you?"

Anger floods me. "What's that supposed to mean?"

"It means," Riley disappears into a stall for a second. There's a rattling and shuffling, and then she wheels out a motorcycle. It looks sporty and fast, not that I know much about bikes, "That you need to get a little more street-smart if you want to survive."

All I can do is stare at her.

Riley fiddles with the bike. "Rachel, Manson is like a cat with its prey. He plays with it before he kills it. He'll probably have you eating out of his hand before he slices your throat."

I look over my shoulder. "I thought you were trying to stay away from him."

"Trying," she hisses.

"Why? Is he trying to kill you?" Their relationship seems extremely complicated.

The barn is silent for a bit. Riley looks like she's examining the paint on the bike for scratches.

I stand around, waiting.

"No, he's not trying to kill me." Riley tinkers around for a bit again.

I shift, wanting to ask why again, but before I can, Riley speaks up, "So, what's *your* story?" She flashes me a smile before getting back to the bike. "Hot girl, lives alone, super weird, buddies up with serial killers."

I blink, and my stomach turns to ice. Serial killers? Suddenly, I'm more than aware of the gun she has stuck in her waistband.

"Answer the question, Rachel."

I rub the back of my neck. "What do you want to know?"

"Why are you living alone? You're what, late twenties?"

I try to keep my face looking normal, but the comment stings. "Twenty-nine."

"So?" She stops for a second and fixes her piercing eyes on me. "What gives?"

I shift. My face feels hot. "I just never found the right one, alright?" Why does she want to know this? My last boyfriend was a gamer who wanted more from me than I could give—kids and a steady stream of affection. I don't do affection. I prefer to sit quietly in the same room as my partner while we each work on our respective projects.

Riley arches an eyebrow. "Could it have anything to do with the collection of dead things?"

"No," I snap.

Riley chuckles, then holds up a small metal piece. "Here's one."

"One what?" I'm getting so over not knowing anything that's going on.

"Tracker."

I suck in a breath. Riley throws it on the ground and keeps going.

Something bothers me about the fact that she doesn't like my collection. "You can't judge me." I motion at the barn, which she clearly uses to butcher animals.

I catch the tiniest hint of a smirk, then it's gone. "Yeah. I eat them, Rachel."

I cross my arms. "All of my bones are ethically sourced, so you can get off your high horse."

"I'm not worried about a thing," Riley says. "It's just weird. You collect dead things. Sounds like something Manson would do."

"It's not weird." I pick at the skin around my nails again. It's not weird at all. Everyone hates on collectors like me, judging and thinking it's weird. "Bones are the map to what's underneath. Often, what something looks like on the outside isn't what they're really like on the inside." They're like hidden puzzles.

"Like people?" Riley holds up another metal piece.

"Exactly." I narrow my eyes.

"People are snakes." Riley nods as if we're in a perfectly agreeable conversation.

"No, snakes are way better than people," I snap. I always know why a snake does what they do. Plus, their bones are prettier. I have a few in my collection, and they're some of my most prized pieces. I have to be incredibly careful with them, as the bones are extremely delicate.

Riley lifts an eyebrow. Other than the eyebrow, her face is blank. Then she smirks again. "You're something, aren't you?"

I try to react to that the way she'd expect me to. The problem is, I'm not sure how she wants me to take that.

Riley throws another tracker on the floor. "Where there's one, there's bound to be another. And another. It's the oldest trick in the book. Stick with me, Rachel, and I'll teach you some things."

"How are we going to get groceries with a bike?"

Riley hands me a helmet. It has a bunch of sharp, white teeth painted along the front in a creepy smile. "Saddlebags, babe. We'll only get a few. Put it on."

I look at the helmet. "There's only one."

Riley throws me a smile and winks. "Gotta protect my precious cargo." She throws on a pair of sunglasses, tucks the gun into the front of her waistband, and says, "Now get on, bambi. We got places to be."

16

Better With - Friday Pilots Club

"It's about Riley," Seb's voice demands into the phone. Seb is my right-hand man. I go to him for most of the day-to-day stuff I don't want to do. The stuff that used to be my job. Until I took over when my dad was killed.

My tone remains even, but immediately, I'm on alert. "What about her?" I roll myself out of bed. I slept off the acid, and Seb's call woke me up.

"I have something to show you."

He's never mentioned Riley. I thought I'd made it very clear she was off limits. To everyone. Why did he feel the need to call me? With Riley, anything could have popped up. I've tried to keep Riley out of trouble, but maybe I missed something. She's been getting more and more out of hand.

Seb rambles on about something, and I grip the phone until it digs little grooves into my fingers. I drop my head while my voice lowers, "If you don't tell me right now what's wrong with Riley, I'll hang up the phone, ride to your place, and put a bullet in your head. I'll replace you with Jeremy. I'm sure he'd love your spot."

"It's one of the rental properties." Seb sputters out an address. Riley's address. "Someone approved the eviction of the last tenants."

Yes, I did. Riley forged the papers to look like my family's business name. When they came through the office, I handled them, and then I handled the complaint they filed.

They must have filed another.

"And?" I ask, my voice low.

"And that was part of the Henson family. This has Riley all over it. She's out of control, and now the Hensons are pissed and coming after us."

The Hensons are small potatoes, and I couldn't care less. If Seb had any balls, he wouldn't either. He's clearly not cut out for this.

"I also have collections up my ass."

I frown. I was taking care of the bills. What the hell did Riley charge to our business? And why does Seb care?

Seb's voice lowers. "She's distracting you. I don't like to see you distracted."

Tick. Tick. Tick. The muscle in my jaw does a little dance.

"I'll handle it," I say.

"Manson, you know I care. I think she's just...you'd be better off without her dragging you down."

An instant flash of heat and anger fills me. I see what he's doing. He's going to try and paint me as distracted. As the one making bad decisions because of my wife. He's going to try and take over my spot, using Riley as an excuse.

I hang up the phone, stuff my pistol into my pants, then stalk downstairs. Grabbing my bike keys, I pause.

I should check on her. Just to make sure.

Opening my tracker app, I check Riley's second bike. It's still showing at her place.

See. Still home.

But still, I open my app to the trail cam I have on her house.

There's an error code.

What the fuck?

I watch the last footage I have. It's from an hour ago, and it looks like the camera just shuts off. I watch it again. There's a slight movement from the back door and the flash of something.

Slowly, my blood boils. She took out my camera.

That little bitch.

I can't help the thrill that runs through me. Oh, I'll have fun punishing her for this little stunt.

This better be worth it, Mrs. Kennedy, 'cause I'm about to make you regret ever defying me.

I send a message off to Jeremy to put a bullet through Seb's skull, then jump on my bike to get my wife and the pretty little side piece she's claimed.

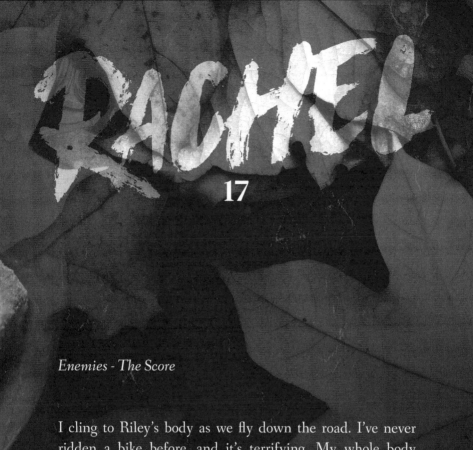

RACHEL

17

Enemies - The Score

I cling to Riley's body as we fly down the road. I've never ridden a bike before, and it's terrifying. My whole body vibrates with the power of the engine. Riley tried to explain the leaning and counterbalancing to me, but eventually, she just told me to hold her and not to touch the "fucking gun," or she'll "send us both to hell." She said that part with a smirk.

Riley guns the engine, and I'm forced to hold her tighter. My arms are wrapped around her simultaneously toned and soft stomach while trying to keep them off the pistol. We're easily doing a hundred down the empty roads.

I'm so close to her. Pressed into her. I know she can feel every inch of my tits against her back. I try to move so she doesn't feel them, but she just swerves, making me grab hold of her tighter. She repeatedly reaches back and squeezes my thigh, and when we slow for a turn, she yells at me to hold tighter. She doesn't want a bump to make me fly off.

As the scrub trees whip by, for a tiny second, I feel exhilarated. We're *flying*.

Touch it, my intrusive thoughts whisper. *Touch the gun.* It's like standing on the edge of a cliff when your mind says to jump.

I inch my hands higher on Riley's torso so I don't even brush it. But that pushes my hands into her soft and plump tits, which makes a surprising jolt of heat run through me.

Touch it, touch it, touch it. The words repeat in a pretty cadence in my head.

No. I'll run when we get to town. There will be people there to help.

I find myself grateful for the helmet 'cause Riley's hair is whipping back in my visor constantly. I look over to my left to try to lean out of it. Riley finally starts slowing while we're still in the country. Slowly, I unplaster myself, and she immediately whips to the left.

I squeal, gripping onto her. When I unpeel my eyes, we've pulled into a driveway to a small but fancy house.

Riley stops.

"Where are we?"

Riley giggles. "No need to shout. I can hear you."

I flush. Everything in this helmet sounds muffled.

"Get off."

I look around in confusion. How am I supposed to get down?

Riley nudges my leg and takes off her sunglasses.

I take a tentative step down. She follows, gripping the helmet and forcing me to look at her. "You look cute all flustered."

I try to pull away. "Fuck you."

"Nah, stone-cold top for the ladies." Riley reaches under my chin and undoes the strap. "Take it off."

I do, yanking it off my head. My hair is knotted and sweaty underneath, and I suck in a breath of hot air. "Where are we?"

Riley just winks at me and starts walking up the steps. "Come."

"Whose house is this?" I hiss, feeling like I'm the one doing something wrong.

Riley knocks on the door and shoots me a dark look. I look over my shoulder. There's nothing but dead grass and an empty road. There's nowhere to run, and I'd be an easy target to shoot. I move up beside her on the porch.

Riley knocks again, and the door jerks open. A man in his twenties stands there. He has a wrinkled shirt and a headset on. He blinks.

I stare at him, torn. What do I do? Do I ask for help?

"Hey! Martha?" Riley looks past him.

He just stares at us. "Ummm, no."

"Oh my god, I'm sorry!" Riley's voice is concerned. "My coworker's mom wasn't picking up her phone, and he wanted us to check on her since he's out of state."

The man just looks confused. "You have the wrong address."

Riley flashes me a flustered look. "Well, shit." She blows out a breath, then laughs softly. "Damn, I'm sorry. I could have sworn this was the address he gave us."

Riley glances past him again. "Oh my god, you play too?"

The man glances over his shoulder.

"I love that game!" Riley throws the man a shy smile. "I'm not very good at it. Can't find anyone to help me." She starts rattling on about a specific map and layout.

I stand there in utter confusion. Riley is standing there having a normal conversation as if she didn't force me under threat to be here.

I try to plead with the man with my eyes.

"Oh no shit, this is the same map I always get stuck on!" Riley is excited now. "You think you can show me real quick before we have to go?"

The man looks hesitant, but seeing Riley bat her eyes at him, he straightens and steps back.

Anger rushes through me. He's falling for her flirting with him? He's not even that attractive, with his untrimmed hair and greasy face. He ought to know she'd never be interested.

Riley reaches back to grab my hand.

I yank it out of hers. "What are you doing?" I hiss.

For a second, Riley's eyes look dangerous. Then it's gone, and she flashes me a smile. "Grocery shopping. Now come on." And she yanks me inside.

RILEY

18

Dirt Nap - Diggy Graves

I caught the jealousy on Rachel's face, and it shot a thrill through my entire body. Rachel is pissed! I've seen other people get jealous before, but seeing my reserved doe get possessive makes victory run through me.

It's almost as good as winning a fight with Manson, and I can't help but grin.

We move into the house enough for me to shut the door behind us. I just want my woman to have a harder time running from me. I stand behind the couch, staring at the man's TV. His handle is user1995.

I snort. So he keeps the same one across all platforms. Stupid.

"I don't really play the campaign a lot," the man mutters, standing awkwardly.

"I'm sure you're better at it than I am." I laugh, twirling

the end of my braid in my hand. "I really can't stay long, but I've been looking for someone good who can help me."

The man closes out his round and then moves to the campaign. Manson knows I love this game. It's why he dresses like one of the characters.

Beside me, Rachel is stiff as a statue. It's cute. She's way smarter than this dumbass. She, at least, knows something bad is going to happen. This is fun. I like showing off for Rachel. Having her watch me walk inside here without waving a gun around. I also like watching her squirm. How long will she play along before she forgets about my gun and tries to fuck around?

We talk for a bit as the man runs us through a round. Rachel stays silent. Watching. Observing. Taking everything in. Which I've noticed is her default. Rachel won't act until she's sized up her enemies and knows their intentions. She's like Manson that way, and I get a slight twinge of annoyance. I'll show her how fun it can be to be impulsive. Fuck, I didn't plan on coming here today, but I'm so glad we did.

As we chat, I size up user1995's house. It's everything I thought it would be. Sloppy, with dirty clothes on the couches and the sink piled with dishes. He's clearly not used to Mommy and Daddy not doing everything for him. Beer cans are all over the counter, so either he threw a party, or he's a massive drunk. There's trash on the coffee table, along with snacks and a pocket knife.

"Oh my god, you hunt?" I point to the deer's head on the wall.

"Huh?" The man glances up. "Oh, yeah."

I let out a sigh. "I've always thought that was so hot—someone being able to live off the land." I glance at Rachel out of the corner of my eye. She's throwing me an incredulous look, and I wink at her.

"I'm sure you killed that deer yourself," I say.

The man glances up again. "What? Uh, yep." He goes back to his game.

I roll my eyes, then pull the Glock out of my waistband. "You must have used one of these, right?"

Rachel sucks in a breath.

The man glances back, and for a second, his face is blank. Then, he freezes, registering the gun.

I grin at him. "Well, did you?"

"What the fuck?" The man jumps to his feet.

"No." I wave the gun at him. "Sit back down."

"You're fucking crazy!" he shouts but doesn't sit down.

I fire a shot into the TV. "Sit. Down."

Rachel screams. The man trembles, shaking and frozen. I lock my gaze with his until he blinks, then sits down with a thud.

I glance at Rachel. Last time I fired a round, she freaked out and seemed to go into her own little world, and she's doing it again—just standing, frozen.

I don't want her in her own little world. I want her here. I grab Rachel's hand with my unoccupied one and yank her toward me. She has a glazed look on her face, so I smash my lips down on her plump ones. She's so much softer than Manson. So delicate and fucking delicious.

Rachel is still for a second, then struggles to get away, biting at my lips.

I chuckle, licking the sweet taste that's her. Fuck, the blood is rushing to my pussy. Rachel continues to struggle, then reaches up and pinches my nipple. Hard.

I suck in a breath, letting her lips go but keeping her hand locked in mine. I stare down into her pretty eyes, ready to fuck her right here and right now.

"Get out of my house!" the man cries.

I roll my eyes and turn back to the man. "Answer the fucking question."

He's sucking in shallow breaths. "What?"

"Did you use one of these? To kill the deer?" I flick my Glock at him.

"Y-yes?" He gulps.

I smirk. "Really. You used a small-caliber handgun to take down a grown-ass deer?"

The man's eyes dart between mine.

"As an experienced hunter, you ought to know that a 9mm won't take a deer down quickly. Right? You'd probably use a 50 cal, right?"

He nods furiously.

I shake my head. "Do you know what I hate, user1995?"

His eyes widen.

"Liars." I smile at him sweetly, but I don't let the smile reach my eyes.

"Riley." Rachel tugs at my hand. She knows where this is going. She's smarter than he is 'cause he still looks at me with a blank look. What a waste of space. He does nothing to contribute to my world getting better. Instead, he leaches off the success of others. Just like the other people I fuck with. Usually, I do a deep dive into my posers. Flirt with them online. Get them to flirt with me. Then, I send the evidence to their girlfriends, their moms, and their jobs.

But this one had none of that. No girlfriend, no job, and a mom in dementia care. So, I guess I'll have to get a little more creative.

I hear Manson's voice in my ear. *Prove yourself.*

My lips curl in a smile. "Cover your ears, bambi."

I let go of her hand, then fire a round into the man's hip.

For a second after the explosion, there's silence. The man looks down at his hip in shock.

Rachel has her hands over her ears like a good girl. I kiss the top of her head.

"What the fuck?" That seems to snap her out of her trance. She definitely doesn't like loud noises.

I'll get a silencer.

Rachel turns and darts to the front door.

For fuck's sake. The fun has just begun. I lunge at her, snatching her up before she can get outside.

"Don't touch me!" Rachel screams.

"Shhhh." I slam her into the front door, pinning her there.

"No, get off me!" Rachel is fighting for real now. What's wrong with her? Little miss dead-things-collector shouldn't have a problem with me adding to the bones count. I won't even shoot him in the head. His skull will be perfect.

Out of the corner of my eye, I see the man on the couch lean down. He's grabbing his phone.

"Rachel, I'm going to shoot again," I warn her. Instantly, her body locks up, and I hate that. I want her to watch what I'm about to do.

A thought comes to my mind, and I don't think; I just do. I dart over the couch, grab the pocket knife from the coffee table, and pounce. The man is still trying to call 911, the adrenaline making his fingers clumsy.

I slit his throat. The blood sprays everywhere, warm and heavy and alive.

Well, not for long.

I smirk into the man's panicked eyes. His mouth opens and shuts wordlessly. I feel my pussy clench. Fuck, if that isn't the most erotic sight.

Tearing my eyes from the masterpiece under me, I glance up at Rachel. She's still huddled against the door. After a moment of silence with only the man's gurgling, Rachel peeks out at me.

I smile at her and step off of him. "So. About the groceries."

Rachel looks stunned.

I move to the man's kitchen and fling open the fridge door. "Come here and tell me what you want."

I hear no indication that she's obeying.

I glance back. Rachel is looking at me again with a blank look. It's curious. It's like she retreats into some sort of shell involuntarily.

I know exactly how that feels.

I grab a thing of BBQ sauce off the rack and slam it down on the counter, breaking her out of whatever trance she's in.

"What...the fuck?" Rachel gasps.

"Food. Let's go. You don't like venison, and that's about the only thing I have."

"You're fucking insane." Rachel trembles.

I shrug.

"Did you kill him?" Her voice is getting higher.

I give her a blank look. "The human body can't live without blood. So yes. I did."

"What the hell is wrong with you?" Fire lights behind Rachel's eyes.

"Hmmm, nothing?" I motion at the fridge, annoyance flitting through me. She's starting to sound like my mom.

"Nothing?" Rachel's damn near screaming. She stomps over to me, and her body is shaking. She shoves against me. Hard.

"You killed someone!" she screams. Her face is red, but her eyes—her eyes are sparkling and alive. She looks at me with a mixture of hatred and...fear. Not of the noise. Of me.

My pulse pounds in my clit, and I snatch her up. Rachel

fights me, but I don't care. I hold her soft body against me, kissing the ever-loving shit out of her. Reveling in her fight. Soaking in her fear. It's like a drug. She makes me heady.

I shove my hand down Rachel's pants. She screams at me, getting a good scratch down my face. I just push her back into the kitchen island. I flip her over, pinning her solidly with my hand across her back, then put my bloody hand down her pants again.

"Fuck you! Fuck you!" she screams.

The sound shivers down my thighs, and I groan. If she keeps making sounds like that, I'll come in my pants without any touch.

As soon as my fingers hit Rachel's soft pussy, I melt into her body. She tries to squirm away from me, but I don't let her. This body is mine. I own it. And I own her. The sooner Rachel figures that out, the better.

"Let me go! I want to go home. Please, let me go."

I keep a steady pressure on Rachel's clit, rubbing her from behind until she stiffens. Rachel fights the pleasure every damn time. It's like she refuses to let me give it to her.

Which is unacceptable.

I rub until I feel her suck in a breath.

"You gonna come for me?"

"Fuck you," she hisses. "I'm not fucking gay."

"Oh yeah?" I lean down, biting the back of her arm. The movement causes my clothes to shift across my clit. Rachel cries out, and I feel her pulsing on my hand. "This feels pretty gay to me."

Fuck. Her pussy clenching in orgasm makes my own pleasure shoot through me, and I tense, coming. The orgasm locks into me, filling me with overwhelming pleasure.

Under me, Rachel is tense, sucking in deep breaths.

As soon as the waves of pleasure recede, I step back,

blinking. I've never come like that before, with nearly no stimulation. Jesus Christ. My whole body tingles.

Rachel has melted into the kitchen island. She pulls her hands to her face and covers herself. Like all the sensations are too much.

"It's okay, I got you." I pat her back.

She shakes.

I grab some food from the fridge, then turn to the living room. The man's body lays there, lifeless. The blood is everywhere.

The rush that fills my body is unmatched. I feel on top of the world. The best I've ever felt. Why in the hell would Manson try to keep this feeling from me?

I set a light kiss on the back of Rachel's head. "Pick out some food, angel. I won't tell you again."

Now to cover my tracks long enough that Manson can't fuck me over.

MANSON

19

Trick or Cheat - Diggy Graves

As I pull up to the barn, my hands shake. Real, deep rage flows through me. Riley got the drop on me. I was complacent, and she took advantage of that.

I get out of the car and slam the door, marching to the barn. I hope Riley is feeling just reckless enough to be here.

But she isn't. I see the trackers lying on the floor.

I know Riley rarely goes into the house, but I stride there next. The back door is standing wide open, which only makes me more angry. Anyone could come in and hurt her. Riley isn't invincible.

My eyes catch on the mousetraps on the wall, and I arch an eyebrow. Did she think that would keep me away?

Cute.

I don't find her anywhere on the property, but I do find her phone, which she factory reset.

Jesus.

A weird tingling runs through my body. I told Riley to prove herself. I gave her the green light to fuck around and find out. I meant for her to show me what skills she has. But Riley is the most stubborn woman I've ever met in my life, and she's currently pissed off at me. The tingling in my stomach increases. Now we're really playing, and this isn't like when we would mess around as kids. I think Riley's about to fuck shit up.

I try to keep my hands still as I dial my law enforcement connection. He picks up on the third ring. "What's up?"

I rattle off Riley's plate number.

"What?" He sounds confused.

I take a second to suck in a breath. My mask is slipping. I can't be sloppy about this. I put on a friendly voice. "I need you to keep an eye out for that plate."

"Oookay? What they do?"

My blood boils. That's none of his damn business. "I just need to know where it is. Find it for me."

The man mutters on the other end of the line, but I pay him for this shit. The agreement is he's there for me, any time of the day or night. Or I'll find a way for him to disappear. That part wasn't in the agreement, but it was implied.

"It was over in Stark County a few days ago."

"Today." I grind my teeth together.

"Nothing today."

Silence. I consider ripping his head from his body.

"Listen man, you know we don't have shit for shit. There are only a few counties and The City with these cameras. Not much I can do."

I grip the phone so hard that a bolt of pain shoots through my fingers.

I hear the scanner kick on in the background. *Structure fire. 10945 Country Road East.*

"Sorry man. I'll let you know if it pops up again."

One occupant inside.

I cock my head. That address isn't far from here.

Riley has always been obsessed with fire. My stomach clenches, and I launch myself to my car, hanging up the phone.

There are so many things that could go wrong. I haven't taught her everything I know. Mostly because she's not been ready for it. She could get hurt. Worse, she could get killed. And what the hell is Rachel doing? Just going along with it? Did she kill her, too?

Both fear and a thrill run through me. Riley's finally playing the game, and I want nothing more than to stop her. So I will. Ready or not, here I come.

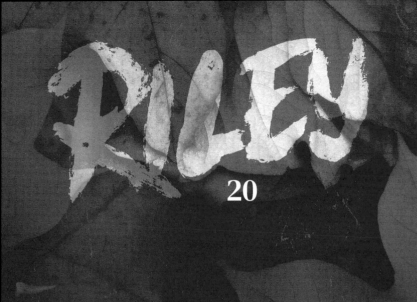

RILEY

20

Evil People - Set It Off

Age 6

"Riley!" My mom screams my name from outside the bathroom. I simply continue to kick my feet in the bath water.

"Unlock this door, or I swear to god I'll beat your ass black and blue."

I uncap the soap and lather some bubbles on. I burned my fingers a little when I was burning Noel's clothes. Noel is my mom's current fling.

My fingers clench. I should have burned *him*. Watched the skin blister off his face from up close. I can't remember why I hate him so much, but I know he's done something.

The door rattles, and I pull in a deep breath. I know what the punishment is. Mom will hurt me for what I did.

On the other side of the door, Mom goes completely silent. I wait patiently, and then I hear her messing with the door handle, and the lock pops open.

Mom rages into the bathroom. She spots me and lunges at me. "You need to learn, Riley." Her hands grip into my hair and around my shoulder. Before I realize what she's doing, she shoves me forward into the bath water.

Warm water surrounds my head, and I scramble. I try to get out, but the tub is slippery, and Mom's grip is iron. My heart pounds. Mom's fingers rip little pieces of my hair out, and my lungs start to burn.

Mom yanks me back up. She's screaming something at me, but I'm just trying to suck in another breath. When I feel like I can breathe again, Mom's voice comes through. "Do you understand?"

I laugh, but I don't mean it. "Yeah."

Wrong answer. Mom shoves me back down. This time, she holds me for longer. I try not to feel anything. Fear, anger, nothing. If I feel nothing, then I'm safe. She can touch me, but she can't touch *me*.

When Mom lets me back up and sees my lack of response, it makes her go crazy. She screams in my face, calling me a psychopath and saying she's going to call the cops on me.

I close my eyes. I'm getting pretty good at blocking out emotions. Noel and the others give me plenty of practice.

Finally, my mom storms out of the room to "call the cops," she said.

I lean back in the tub and pull in a deep breath.

Fire is most definitely better than water. Maybe I'll burn my mom next.

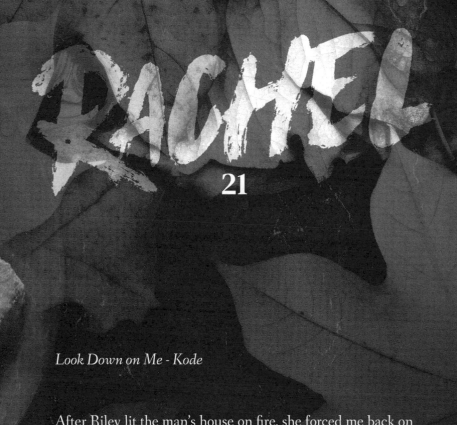

21

Look Down on Me - Kode

After Riley lit the man's house on fire, she forced me back on the bike with her, and we took off. I cling to her back again, barely processing what just happened. I just listen to the sound of my breathing in the helmet and feel her soft body against mine. Pretending she didn't just kill someone in front of me. Pretending she didn't light his body and then his house on fire while I stood there and watched.

Because if I don't pretend it isn't real, I might actually completely check out. I feel it already, the desire to just sign off. Retreat into the corners of my mind to keep from screaming and picking my skin until it's gone. What's more dangerous? Pretending this isn't real or shutting down in the control of a murderer?

We stop at a small hotel. It's an old Motel 6, one story, and breaking down. Riley pats my leg. "Get off. And if you talk to anyone, I'll kill them."

I step off the bike. Riley helps me take the helmet off, then grabs my hand and heads for the front office.

"Wait." I yank back slightly. She's covered in blood. I am too, but less so. We're like a walking crime scene. Scratch that, we *are* a walking crime scene.

"It's Halloween, babe." Riley gives me a cheeky smile.

Oh fuck. Is it Halloween already? My heart clenches, and the reality of the shit I'm in falls over me. It's Halloween, and I didn't find Cali to bring her to the corn maze with me. Instead, I don't think I'll ever survive the corn maze.

Riley pays at the front desk. The employee barely even gives us a double take. "Quiet hours are at ten." Then we have our key, and we're off. The motel is so old that our room opens to the parking lot.

I barely make a fuss when Riley motions me into the room. I'm exhausted and starving, and the reality of this situation feels like it's pressing in from every angle.

I stare at Riley when she rides the bike into the room and shuts it down.

I just shake my head, sitting on the bed. Riley shuts the door, then backs the bike against it, tucking the key into her bra. She disappears into the bathroom, and I hear the bath turn on. I stare at the ceiling. I just want to close my eyes. Close my eyes and keep them closed until this nightmare goes away.

"Come here." Riley pokes her head out of the bathroom.

I don't know if I have the energy to. But Riley marches to my bed and makes me get up. "I drew you a bath."

I blink. She herds me into the bathroom. Sure enough, the bathtub is full.

"Get in," she coaxes. "But keep your leg out of the water. I want to check it."

Staying in these bloody clothes sounds horrible, so I strip

out of them and sink into the water, keeping my injured leg out. Riley checks it and makes a hum of approval. "It's healing nicely. Just keep it out of the water until it's fully scabbed over."

She steps out of the room, and I sink into the tub as far as I can with my leg out. Immediately, I'm surrounded by a warm, comforting feeling. I sink as deep as I can into the shallow tub, soaking in the warmth. I let my brain shut off, bit by bit, and just focus on the feeling of the water on my skin. There's an odd lack of feeling when submerged. It's like feeling everything at once but nothing at all. I want to feel nothing.

I hear Riley messing around in the room. There's the beeping of the microwave, and then she comes back into the bathroom.

"Dinner." She holds out some chicken nuggets microwaved on toilet paper.

Suddenly, they look like the best things I've ever seen. I didn't realize how hungry I was. I sit up, snatching the food from her. My wet hands disintegrate the toilet paper, but I don't even care. I down the chicken nuggets in mere bites, almost groaning at how good it tastes. But I need more.

Riley chuckles. "Let those settle. I'll get you more in a second." She hops on the bathroom counter and sits there, watching me. She's still covered in blood, and the tips of her braids look like they've been dipped in it. I trace the blood over her perfectly proportioned body to her hands. She has long, slender fingers, and as soon as I think that, I frown. Why does everything about her have to be hot? She's a walking red flag.

In that moment, I realize I'm completely naked. My face heats, and I try to cover myself. "Don't look."

Riley arches an eyebrow. "Why?"

I swallow. I'm not sure why. She's seen it all before, but still, I feel vulnerable.

"You killed someone."

"Yep." She pops the p.

"Are you going to let me go?"

There's silence, and I just look at the water pooling around my belly.

"Do you want to go?"

"Yes," I whisper.

"Why?"

"Because!" I trail off. I miss my home. My routine. Nothing here feels right or safe.

"Because why?"

"Because it's my home!"

Riley humphs. "You lived a boring life before me."

Defensiveness fills me. "So?" I pick at the skin around my nails again. It's much softer now, having been in the bath.

"So you don't crave something better? Friends? A boyfriend? A girlfriend?"

My thoughts immediately go to Cali. "Do you know what happened to Cali?"

Riley's voice darkens. "Who's Cali?"

"My friend," I say. "She disappeared a few weeks ago. I thought maybe Manson...did something to her."

Riley snorts. "Doubtful. Manson isn't interested in other girls."

"But he knows her name."

Riley is silent for a while. "Why do you care?"

Defeat fills me. "Because she's my friend."

"Friends, hmmm?" Riley's voice is dark.

"Yeah," I whisper. She was my best friend. She had everything: the looks, the attitude, the spunk. I wanted to be her.

"You know what, I think this is the first time you're not trying to lie to me, but you still are." Riley shakes her head and sounds pissed. "You had a crush on her."

I glance up at Riley, appalled.

Riley shakes her head. "Yep. Fucking hell. Now imma have to kill Cali, too."

Panic flares through me. "No!"

Riley gives me a deadpan look. "Absolutely."

I swallow, then force myself to lean back in the tub. "It doesn't matter. She's probably dead anyway."

"That would save me some time."

"Riley!" I snap my head at her. "You can't just kill anyone you want."

Riley rolls her eyes. "And why not, bambi?"

"Because!" I sputter. "It's...wrong! You'll get caught. They'll throw you in prison for the rest of your life."

Riley scoffs. "In case you haven't picked up on this, they won't. As for the first part, I don't care about what's right and wrong."

"Clearly." I cross my arms over my chest. "'Cause you kidnapped me."

Out of the corner of my eye, I see Riley examining her nails. "Let's save ourselves this tiring conversation again, and I'll tell you right now that I'm a sociopath, Rachel. I don't *care* about what's 'wrong.' Save me your morality speech; it's not gonna work."

I stare at her. Oh fuck. That makes so much sense. I rack my brain for anything I can remember on the term. All I know about it is the stereotypical association with serial killers. I stare at her, wanting to ask all kinds of questions, but I'm not sure what I can ask. Instead, I say, "Manson, too?"

Riley barks a laugh. "He's a psychopath."

"Isn't that what I asked?"

"Sociopath and psychopath. One is made. The other is born."

I pick at my thumb nail again, turning away from her. I have a big piece of loose skin. I know if I pull it away, it'll bleed. I do it anyway. "And which one are you?"

I don't know which one sounds worse. If you're born with it, then you must not ever know what it's like to live life like everyone else. There'd be some comfort in that. But the horrors you'd have to go through to be made one...

Riley is silent for so long that I don't think she'll answer. Then, her rich voice says, "Made."

I wince. I'm not sure what to say. What does one say to that? Sorry?

I glance at Riley. Her face twists into a scowl. "I see that look. Don't try to 'fix me,' Rachel. You wouldn't be the first bitch to try, and you won't be the last."

With that, she storms out of the bathroom and slams the door.

Shit. I fucked up somehow.

I stay in the tub, soaking in the water until it's cold. I think about what this means for me, for my survival, and how I even fit into this puzzle in the first place.

I don't want to get out of the tub, but when I start to shiver, I do. I wrap myself in a scratchy towel and come out.

Riley's on the floor, looking at the ceiling.

"I have no clothes," I say.

"Nothing I haven't seen before, bambi." Riley's voice is monotone.

I stare at her, wondering what made her the way she is. What could have possibly happened to her?

She looks at me, and it's like all previous anger is gone from her face. She's friendly and upbeat and smiles at me.

I wrap the towel tighter. "Can you stop doing that thing with your face?"

"What?"

"That thing." I wave at her. "Where you switch your mood."

There's a small smirk on Riley's face. "And why would I do that?"

"Because." I sit on the edge of the bed. "It's confusing."

"It's meant to be confusing." Riley stares at me. For a second, she looks questioning.

I shift uncomfortably.

"Cali wasn't my girlfriend."

She waves me off. "We have a lot to do tomorrow, so we're gonna get some rest." She opens the drawer beside the bed and grabs a pair of handcuffs.

Immediately, I stiffen and back away.

"Now now. You can't possibly think I'll just let you roam while I sleep."

I jump off the bed, still clutching my towel. "I don't want those on."

"Sorry, bambi. I don't trust you not to run."

"I won't," I plead. "Please."

Riley gets off the bed, a gleam in her eye. "One swing to make you feel better."

"What?" Confusion fills me.

"I'm giving you a pass."

"For what?" I back away as she gets closer.

"To fight me."

"What?" My mouth drops open. "I'm not going to fight you." I back up to the bathroom.

Riley cocks her head. "Wouldn't it make you feel better? Least you fought back instead of taking it like a little bitch."

Rage rushes through me. Who the hell does she think she

is? I make it to the bathroom and try to slam the door on her. Riley just jumps in with me. My heart races and the backs of my knees hit the toilet.

Riley gives me a pitying look. "It's okay. Just roll over and take it. I'll be gentle."

A flash of blinding rage washes over me, and I don't think; I just act. I swing my fist at her face, picturing it going all the way through her skull into the back wall. Instead, it makes contact right below her right eye, and she staggers back.

Shock radiates through my fist, and I suck in a breath.

Riley staggers back. For a moment, she's silent, and pure fear washes through me. She's going to fucking kill me.

Then, Riley starts laughing. She holds a hand up to her face and checks the mirror. "One hell of a swing there, girl!" She laughs again. "But for the love of god, keep your thumb outside of your fist; you'll break it."

I stare at her in horror. Why is she laughing?

"That'll do." She stops looking at herself in the mirror. "Come on. Let's go to bed."

RILEY

22

Bring Me To Life - Evanescence

We sleep with Rachel cuffed to my wrist. I hated sleeping on the bed, but the high from killing that dweeb and burning his house down made me crash. I slept harder than I have in a long time. Even the fact I had a hot, blue-haired number lying practically in my arms couldn't rouse me.

It turns out that killing is good for the sleep cycle. I should do it more.

In the morning, I check Rachel's leg again. It doesn't look irritated or infected. Then I cuff her to the foot of the bed so I can leave. Thank god this is an old hotel, and the bed still has bedposts while being bolted to the floor. Rachel fights me, but I can't take her where I'm going.

"I'm going to have to gag you." I give Rachel a look. She'll definitely scream her pretty little head off while I'm gone. And oddly enough, I don't want to lose her. Despite the fact she pissed me off last night, I'm growing fond of the little horrified looks she gives me. It's like having my own personal cheerleader.

I do throw blankets on the floor so she's more comfortable. I use her leggings to gag her, which means she's pantless, and then once I'm sure she's secure, I leave her. My first stop is the sheriff's department. I hate even going in there, but it can't be avoided for what I want to do.

When I'm done, I go to Walmart to get a cheap burner phone and a few other things, like new clothes.

Manson wants me to prove myself? Fine. Let's play.

MANSON

23

Therapy - VOILA

After checking out the structure fire, I drove around all night looking for Riley. The fire had her style all over it. They said it was more than likely arson since the living room, in particular, was so severely burned. The fire burned so hot there that it melted the vinyl siding on the front edge of the house. So, the person—Riley—used an accelerator.

There was also a body found, charred to a crisp. They're going to conduct an autopsy on him, but I already know the answer. Riley killed him.

But why? I couldn't find much on him. He graduated high school in the area and didn't do much afterward. His parents are rich farmers, and it looks like he had his whole life set up for him.

Which, I'm sure, pissed Riley off.

I grip my hands harder on my bike. I don't like playing catch-up.

My phone rings through my headset, and I answer it. "Yeah?"

"Hey, you told me to call you if that plate shows up."

"Where," I grind.

"Uhhh, the sheriff's office. Like thirty minutes ago."

"Jesus." I pull a U-turn. That's not too far from here. Why in the hell was she going there?

"Why didn't you call me earlier?" I'm already planning his death. This man is useless.

"I was on another call, Jesus. I didn't see it till just now."

I grit my teeth.

"There's something else you should know. She uh...she filed a report on you."

"What?" I can't keep the bite out of my tone.

"Yeah. Said you hit her. I'll send you a pic."

I yank my bike to the side of the road and dig my phone out of my pocket. He texted me a picture of Riley, her face red like she's been crying. And she has a black eye.

What in the ever loving...

"So like...I can squash it, but just know any more, and we'll get people breathing down our necks. The state is serious about that stuff when you're married."

My phone buzzes, and I glance down. It's a blocked number. I end the call I'm on, then hit the accept button.

There's silence on the other line.

"Riley," I growl.

"Oh hey!" She sounds cheerful. "If it isn't the wife beater himself."

I try to hold the anger back, but it seeps into my words. "What are you doing?"

"Talking to you," she says, flippantly.

This little...

"I didn't realize that we were married, *husband*."

I grit my teeth. I had us married legally as soon as she turned 18, although I didn't change her last name, so I didn't tip her off. I wanted to keep her safe, and an owned woman is a safe woman in my world. This isn't the way I wanted her to find out, though.

That bruise looked pretty real. "Who are you with? Who touched you?"

"You did," she chirps. "Or didn't you read the police report?"

"Riley, enough."

"No, Manson." Her voice gets angry. "You told me to prove myself. So I'm doing it."

"Offer is off the table." I keep Bluetooth on, throw my phone in my pocket, and fly down the road, doing a hundred to get to the last place she was seen. "I'm going to make your life a living hell."

"Already have. That threat won't work anymore, Manson. I'm going to find a new target, and you're gonna stay out of my way. Got it?"

"No, don't you—" the line goes dead.

"Fuck." She could be anywhere by now. There's no way she's still at the station.

I check anyway.

Nothing.

Despite my rage, there's a flicker of amusement. I'm done running around the town. I have to strategize. Research. Find out everything I can about Rachel and everything I don't know about my wife so I can take her down once and for all. And by down, I mean under my thumb and out of trouble. When I find her, I'm never letting her out of my sight.

RACHEL

24

Grave Half Empty - Diggy Graves

The time Riley's gone is some of the longest of my life. She's gagged and cuffed me, and the only comfortable spot I can find is lying on my side on the floor with my hands twisted behind me.

As I lay on the ground, smelling the old carpet, I realize that Riley is starting to make a whole lot more sense. She feels nothing, and anything she does seem like she's feeling is fake.

I try to shift to a more comfortable position, and the smell of feet hits me so hard that I almost gag. As much as it terrifies me to be with a sociopath, there's no more guessing here. Everything Riley does is driven by intellect or impulse, not emotion. Which means things have just become a million times simpler. It takes the guesswork out for me.

Riley wants to get back at Manson and win whatever competition they have going on. Somehow, I became a part of that, so I just have to figure out how *not* to become a part of it.

Time drags by painfully slowly. When I hear the rumble of the bike, I shudder in relief, and it's quickly followed by a hollow feeling in my stomach. Was I actually excited to see her again? Do I have a self-preserving bone in my body?

When Riley breezes through the door, she releases me from my spot and then tells me to get ready and that we're going out. She brings out a change of clothes for me and herself, and relief rushes through me. Honestly, anything other than being trapped in that tiny room.

We mount up on Riley's bike, and she takes off again. I wrap my arms around her, ignoring the electricity I feel at our touch and reveling in the speed. The freedom.

I expect Riley to stop at another house, but we don't. We pull into a small cemetery off the side of a country road. The lead-up is dirt, and Riley slowly rolls to a stop.

Getting off the bike, I pull my helmet off before she can help. "Where are we?"

Riley just grabs a bag out of the saddlebags and walks up to the cemetery. It's fenced with pretty white wood, not dilapidated and falling apart like most of them. Which means that whoever owns this has money.

Riley walks to a fancy marble headstone and then stares down at it.

I follow slowly.

Pam Kennedy. The date of death reads a few years ago. We stand there, with the fall sun beating down on us and the long grass swishing around the outside of the cemetery.

"Who is this?" I ask.

"My mom." Riley starts unbuttoning her pants.

"What are you–" I step back as Riley drops the bag, yanks her pants down, squats over the grave, and starts pissing on it.

I stare in shock. It's silent, except for the sound of pee on the hard ground. When Riley is done, she yanks her pants up and grabs the bag. She pulls a can of spray paint out, starts shaking it up, then pops the lid off and starts spraying the headstone. I stand back until she's done. She painted the word "whore" in red over the white marble.

I swallow.

"Rot in hell, Mom."

I wait, unsure of what to do. Riley stands there in the hot sun, just staring at the headstone. Sweat rolls down my back.

As I'm about to say something, Riley snatches up the Walmart bag again and grabs a pack of cigarettes. She offers me one, and I shake my head.

"Suit yourself." She hops up on the gravestone next to the one she painted and lights one up.

The smell of spray paint and cigarettes fills the air. Riley is silent. I wait while she smokes two cigarettes, then scoot away, looking at the other headstones in the area. I look at the names, curious if they'll be useful for getting to know Riley or any of this mess. I'm careful not to step on any of them. Some of them are old—too old to read—but the grass here has been trimmed pretty well.

Again, rich.

I almost trip over a snake curled up in the shadow of one of the headstones. It's gray, with a little bit of its orange belly peeking up at me.

"Oh shit!" I squat down.

The snake curls up, hissing at me. It's gorgeous in person. I've seen them before, but never one with such a bright orange belly.

I reach out to grab it, snatching it behind the head. The snake hisses, whipping its body back and forth, the bright color of its belly flashing in the sunlight.

"You're okay." I carry the snake back to Riley. "Look!"

She gives me a bored look.

"It's a ring-neck!" I admire the yellows and oranges on its belly. I love the smooth motion as it curls and tries to get away from me.

Riley raises an eyebrow.

"I have a skeleton of one of these at home." It's one of my favorites too. I found it by a creek bed, perfectly preserved. I must have found it right after it died because it hadn't been eaten or crushed by anything yet.

I let the snake go. It slithers into the tall grass around the fencing.

Riley just pulls out another cigarette.

"So..." I rub the back of my neck. "Now what?"

"We wait until I can take a shit. Then we'll go."

I blink. Jesus. I almost ask what her mom did, but I catch myself at the last second. "She was young," I note. Immediately after saying that, I freeze. I realize that it's likely Riley killed her, and that's why she was so young.

"Heart attack, few years ago." Riley takes a long drag.

I'm silent. I don't think 'I'm sorry' is the right response in this situation.

"I don't regret much," Riley puffs out smoke. "Anything, really. But if there was a regret in my life, it'd be that I wasn't the one to kill her."

"Oh." Once again, I don't know how to respond to that. Oddly, I feel a rush of familiarity. Papa died a few years ago, too, and it always gave me a mix of relief and anger.

Riley shakes her head. "Relax, Rachel. I don't need your sympathy."

"Whatever." I glare at her. I wasn't trying to give her sympathy.

We're silent again for a while. I'd prefer it to be that way since this whole exchange is making me feel awkward.

"You talked in your sleep last night."

I glance at Riley and feel my face flush. My ex told me I used to do that. I still have vivid dreams, and I guess it's still happening.

"Yeah." Riley blows out another breath. "You were crying. Said something about Papa."

A horrible feeling hits my stomach, and I stiffen. I do everything I can to avoid that memory. I never told anyone about him. Well, I told my mom when I was seven. But she said I was lying and he'd never do that. When Papa found out I told her, he yelled at me and asked me why I talked about our love and if I told her my secret—that I liked it. So, I never said anything else from then on. Shame fills my body. The deep shame I feel anytime I think about *that*.

Blessedly, Riley doesn't grill me. The only sound is the wind whipping around us and through the grass.

She lets out a breath, grabbing another cigarette. "He still alive?"

I swallow. "No."

"What happened?"

"Renal failure." I pick at the skin around my nails. I feel my pits start sweating.

Riley offers me a cigarette. I'm not sure why, but I take it. I don't smoke, but I need something to do with my hands.

"We can stop at his grave next if you want."

I glance up at her.

She shrugs. "I'll schedule pissing on another grave into my day."

I stare at the violent woman in front of me. She's been nothing but aggressive and mean, but...in this second, she looks...kind. As I watch Riley take a draw and stare out into the desert, I get the feeling that Riley would believe me, even though I haven't said the first two words about it.

Some odd part deep in my chest warms.

Riley glances at me, and I rub the back of my neck, suddenly self-conscious that I had left her offer hanging. I ask, "Is it a requirement to piss on it?"

Riley laughs, looking me up and down. For once, I feel her look isn't calculated. There's just enough of her dead eyes in it that she looks natural.

I crack a tiny smile.

She stands, brushing herself off. "Yep. We'll rain-check it. C'mon, I'm not done raising hell."

MANSON

25

Who's a good girl? - Manic Kazzy

19 years old

I grip the edge of Riley's porch, fingers digging into the wood, as I do a pull-up to get to her second-story apartment. I lift the rest of my body up easily. Quietly.

This is unacceptable. *This* is what she picked? Instead of our house, with the security system, the fence, and myself inside?

I stride up to the sliding glass door, and it pushes open easily.

Jesus. Adjusting the ski mask, I step into the dark room.

It's late. I wanted to make sure Riley would be asleep. I checked out the floor plans before breaking in, so I know the exact layout. I turn left to head to the bedroom, but when I get there, Riley isn't in bed.

For a second, my chest tightens. Where is she?

I stride back out to the living room, whipping my head back and forth. There. She's on the couch, passed out. There's an empty bottle of wine on the coffee table.

My dick hardens at the sight of her splayed on the couch, pretty lips parted. Riley has always been pretty, but now that she's a grown woman, she's absolutely stunning. Her breasts have filled out, and her hips are full and have perfect handles to grab.

I drop down on top of her, holding my gloved hand over her mouth.

Riley's eyes flutter, and then they open. They widen when she sees me on top of her, and her whole body stiffens. My dick hardens further. Painfully. I never get to see her so helpless. So fragile.

Riley doesn't buck like I expect. She just lays there, looking at me, which pisses me off. *Fight, woman!*

Something changes in Riley's gaze, and she looks...distant —gone. I raise my hand off her mouth.

"Noel." She breathes the word so quietly that I'm not sure I heard it right. Did she say no? I lean my head down, but she doesn't say it again—and doesn't fight me either.

Which makes me mad. Would she do this if someone other than me broke in? Just give up? For all she knows, I'm a stranger. So, yes.

I pull my hand back and slap her hard enough to wake her up. *Get up, Riley. Fucking fight.*

That pisses her off. An angry light fills Riley's eyes, and she bucks up into me. She tries to throw me off by twisting her upper body, but I'm big. I've filled out over the past few years, and Riley isn't small, but she isn't a match for me.

I pin both her shoulders down. Watching her fight gives

me life. I expect fear when I look down at her, but instead, her eyes are flashing. She looks feral and...excited.

What the hell? This shouldn't excite her.

I reach down, grabbing the panties she slept in and ripping them off her.

"Fuck you." Riley lifts a knee and kicks me in the chest. It makes a puff of air escape me, and then I laugh. I pin my body on top of hers so she can't get another blow in, panting until I can catch my breath again. Meanwhile, Riley is clawing at my mask.

I pull up and try to flip her over, but it's like fighting a wildcat. I can't help when another small chuckle escapes me. But I get my hand between her legs and leverage her over.

Riley screeches. She feels so good struggling under me. I grind my hips into her.

"Get off me, fucker," she says with a groan.

Fuck. My dick throbs, and I pause. I smack her ass. Hard. I see her cheeks bounce back and forth.

Riley just groans, pushing back into me. She likes this, and she doesn't even know who's fucking her. I could be anyone.

Rage flashes across my vision, and I yank my pants down. I shove inside her in one push. I want it to hurt. I want Riley to know why she has to fight.

Immediately, her tight pussy squeezes my dick, and I groan as a bolt of pleasure shoots through me. Fucking hell. I haven't fucked Riley until now. She was just a kid before. Acted and looked like one. She always acted so much better than me. Always rejected me. And no way in hell was I going to follow her around like a puppy.

That doesn't mean she wasn't still mine.

But now? Now she's grown. Now she moved out on her

own, got her own job, and otherwise ignored me. Now, I get to teach her a lesson—that she never gets to ignore me.

Now she's my wife.

Riley clenches down around me. "Fuck you!" She arches to get away, but I just press deeper. I have her now. There is no escaping me.

Pleasure fills me, and I pause to keep from coming right away. The sensation of being inside her tight, perfect pussy is too much. Too fucking much.

Riley is wet. Wet and warm and so fucking good. I pull back and slam into her. Making a burst of air come out of her. I get off on reminding her who she belongs to.

"Get off me." She tries to claw away, and I jackhammer in and out of her. I want to say something. Want to teach her just how at risk she puts herself. Tell her that she's mine. *Mine, mine, mine.*

Riley groans, her pussy clenching around me. She loves this. But she doesn't know it's me. Both elation and anger mix, and I pound into her harder. No part of me is gentle with her. That's not how the world will be with her. But instead of it scaring her, she just bucks into it harder.

It drives me wild. I have to actively hold myself back from coming. But when I see Riley's hand inch down so she can play with herself, I explode. I come inside her, pumping her full of my cum as deep as I can. The last thing I want is kids, but I refused to fuck with rubbers. Not with Riley. I need her to feel me. All of me. So I got fixed, knowing the day would come when I taught her just who she belongs to.

When Riley's pussy clenches around me, and she comes, I come to my senses and yank out of her. She's not supposed to enjoy this. Not with a stranger. For a second, I see my hands around her neck, strangling her. Cutting off the blood until her lips turn blue.

I force myself to take a step back. I will not be impulsive. I'm not done tormenting my little pain. She hasn't suffered enough.

I'll make her suffer for ever ignoring me.

MANSON

26

Something To Hide - Grandson

I'm so fucking pissed off right now, and when I'm pissed off, I usually fuck Riley so hard she can barely walk.

But Riley isn't here.

I grip my hair and rip, enjoying the little shock of pain. I've always fucked Riley to let off steam. Even the first time. The moment I got addicted to her pussy and haven't gotten enough since.

I pace our childhood home, eventually ending up in Riley's room.

I can't get the first time I fucked Riley out of my head. I can't stop thinking about that thing she said when she saw me. I thought it was no, but it sounded odd. Was she saying a name? I curse myself for brushing it off.

I sit in the house we grew up in together, thumbing through our old yearbooks. I find one Noel, but I don't remember him, and he never interacted with Riley. I kept close tabs on everyone who did. Obsessively. Anyone she fucked in high school ended up dead, so pretty quickly, they stopped coming around her.

So who the hell was it?

I've known everything about Riley since she came into my life. I know her favorite music, her strange obsession with the Holocaust, and her hatred for animal farms.

But what about before?

I clench my jaw. Riley was always quiet about what happened before. I wasn't worried about it when I met her. She was only twelve—she wouldn't have had any other serious boyfriends or competition.

A horrible thought fills my head, and I swallow. *No.* She would have said something.

I snatch up my phone and hop on social media. I find her mom's page and start scrolling through it. I go back years, shifting through endless data. I find nothing for hours. It makes me want to throw my phone against the wall. Then I scroll past a name, and my stomach drops.

Noel Callum. He's around the same age as her mom and hasn't updated his profile in at least ten years.

I google him. I find a Noel Callum, sent to prison ten years ago for child porn and rape, the victim being under 12.

My entire gut feels like it ignites on fire. I can't do anything but stare at the screen.

Ten years ago, Riley was 16. Was this about her or someone else? I've never known Riley to work with the cops.

I scroll through his social media page, and the uncomfortable feeling starts to turn to rage. Noel posted several pictures with Pam, kissing her with his arm around her. As I scroll back, I see they were dating, so he would have had unfiltered access to Riley.

Rage boils up in me, and I see red. Why didn't Riley tell me?

I rip my room apart. When it's completely shredded and the walls have holes, I force myself to get back on my phone. I will find the answers, and I will make things right.

No one touches my fucking wife.

No one.

RILEY

27

Side Effect - FKA Rayne

Rachel hops on the bike behind me. It's still mid-afternoon, but we have a long trip to my next spot. It's a spot I haven't wanted to ever think about again.

Manson yells at me for being impulsive, but there's a reason I don't dwell on things. Especially *this* thing.

Rachel has started to relax on the bike. She leans back a little more now, not gripping me like I'm gonna kill us both. It's kind of nice to have a backpack. It's nice that she knows I hold her life in my hands, and she still gets on the bike anyway. It makes me smile.

Sure, I kinda forced her to. Po-tay-toe, Po-tah-toe.

A small animal darts into the road, and I swerve sharply to avoid hitting it. Rachel scrambles to grab me and grips me around the tits, which shoots a sick feeling through me.

As soon as I right us, she lets go and wraps her hands around my waist.

I freeze up. Fuck. The pressure on my chest brings up all kinds of old memories I want nothing to do with. Suddenly, I feel like I'm going to get sick.

I spot a picnic spot ahead and whip my bike off to the side of the road.

"Get off," I bark.

"What?"

"Get the fuck off!" Heat rushes through me, and I jump off the bike, barely getting the kickstand down and my sunglasses off before I hunch over the grass. I puke up everything in my stomach.

Still, I can feel the touch. It's pawing at me, moving up and down my whole body. I want it off. I want it fucking off!

Rachel stands silently, watching. The bike rumbles beside us.

My body shakes, and I try to suck in a breath. I hate this. I hate every second that Rachel's watching me. Watching me be weak.

"Turn it off," I snap.

"What?"

"Turn it off!" I motion at the bike.

Rachel jumps to obey. I suck in deep breath after deep breath. Rage at how defenseless I'm being rushes through me. Immediately, I hate the hot sun beating down on us, hate the way my jeans are touching me, and hate the way Rachel looks at me like I'm crazy.

I snarl at her, "Don't you ever, ever feel me up again. Got it?"

Rachel pales. "I didn't...I'm sorry, I..."

I straighten, staring her down, letting all the anger rush through me. "I'm not your plaything, you got that? You don't get to touch me whenever and however you please."

Rachel's pretty eyes widen. I can practically smell the

fear. I know this reaction has nothing to do with her, but I can't stop. I need her to know. To never fucking touch me there. I smile through my rage. "Don't mistake my familiarity with kindness. I kill people for less."

I see the subtle flick of emotion. Rachel doesn't show much, but it's there. You just have to pay attention.

I step back. "Now. Stop looking at me like I'm crazy."

Immediately, Rachel looks away.

I run my hand over my hair. My braids are sweaty and messed up from the wind. I pace back and forth. I want to clench my fists until my fingers dig into my palms. I want to feel the blood. I want to dig around in someone's brain with my bare fingers.

Fuck! Why couldn't we be at our next stop already? I need it *now*. I need it more than my next breath.

It's hard to breathe. Everything that I keep locked up so carefully wants to come out. It wants to fucking come *out*. As soon as Rachel closed in on herself after I mentioned her Papa, I knew what happened to her. And now my memories are screaming to be let out.

So I scream, letting the pent-up energy out. I knew I shouldn't have started this journey. I never should have visited my mother's grave. As soon as I did, I knew it would all come back in a rush, and I'd never be able to stuff it back in.

Maybe that's why I did it.

I kick at a clump of grass. It goes flying. I need much, much more than that. I need release. Acid, beer, sex. Dirty, rough sex that hurts.

I scream again. Manson is the only one who can fuck me when I feel like this. It's like he has a sixth sense when he knows things are hard. He'll break in through my window and fuck the shit out of me, whether I let him or not. He wears a mask and never says it's him, but I know it's him. It's fucked up and wrong, but I always feel better after.

My chest aches with how much I wish he were here. But Manson isn't here. In fact, he's actively tracking me down. Trying to prevent me from hunting down my nightmares. After telling me he buried Pup.

I whirl.

Rachel's still standing there, quietly. She's gripping her arms and biting her lip.

Fuck. She thinks I'm crazy.

"Don't look at me."

Again, she looks away. "I'm sorry, Riley."

Sorry? She's sorry? I scoff. "Fuck off." I don't need her pity. I want to rip my hair out. To scream and go crazy and kill everything that ever hurt me.

Softly, Rachel says, "I would have helped you kill her if that means anything."

I freeze. My entire body locks up.

She's mocking me.

I whirl on Rachel, about to lay into her, but her face is angry. She isn't looking at me, just kicking a clump of grass. She doesn't usually show emotions, but right now, there's pure, venomous rage all over her face.

I falter.

Rachel is a terrible liar, but she looks serious. For a moment, she looks like me—a little wild. And that makes me pause.

No one has ever offered to kill for me. *No one.* They all told me how crazy I was. How I needed therapy. How I couldn't kill her, as Manson said.

I force a swallow, then immediately straighten. Rachel was mocking me. She had to be.

"Get on." I motion at the bike. I have people to kill.

Ready or Not

I get us going again, but the whole ride, I can't get my quiet doe's offer out of my head.

28

Dark Room - Foreign Figures, Jonny T

Age 6

"Riley bear," Noel's voice comes from the house. A cockroach skitters past me, but I barely notice. This place isn't as bad as some of the other ones before.

"Riley! Where are you? Let's play." The sounds of his friend's voices filter into the shed. It's hot in the shed, but I knew he'd look for me in my room. Mom's at work. She always is when he has his friends over. They look at me in a way that makes me uncomfortable. When I told her that, she shrugged me off. Said I was being dramatic.

A shiver runs through me despite the heat.

"Looks like she's already playing." There are deep chuckles.

I squeeze my eyes shut. I should have run farther. Surely, they'll leave me alone.

"Ready or not, here we come."

I shrink further behind the lawn mower, breathing in the hot air and smell of stale grass. I crouch there for what feels like hours. Then, I hear deep voices outside.

"You're just making this more fun, Riley."

The shed door opens, and heavy footsteps pound in. There's silence for a second, and I hold my breath.

"There you are." A heavy hand lands on my shoulder.

I dart to my feet. It's one of Noel's friends. One who watches me heavily. His eyes are dark and full of something mean. I smile, trying to lighten the mood. "Sorry, I fell asleep."

"Yeah?" His mouth kicks up in a smile.

"Yeah." I glance out the door.

"In here!"

I see Noel and two more of his friends come up. Despite the heat, they step into the shed. All of them are smiling at me. One rubs his pants where the zipper is.

"You're pretty good at hide and seek." Noel smiles at me. "Want to play another game?"

No. I don't. I try to back away, but there's nowhere to go. "I'm kinda hot," I laugh nervously.

The men just grunt, looking at me.

"Come on, it'll be fun." Noel pats his knee.

When I don't move, he waves me over. "C'mon, you can have a popsicle after."

Despite the tingles moving over my skin, I move to him. I have no other choice. I'm trapped, and closer to him is closer to the way out.

The rest of that afternoon feels like a blur. A blur of pain and fear and confusion. I don't remember why. All I know after is it hurts to sit, it hurts to pee, and there are marks all over my chest. I'm bleeding, but Noel says I got my period, and that's what happens when you become a woman.

It's not the first time it has happened. But I can't remember. Little snippets come back to me, and I force them way back down.

But I remember that I get my popsicle every time they leave.

29

*Take What You Want (feat. Ozzy Osbourne & Travis Scott) -
Post Malone*

Riley and I ride for what feels like hours. My back aches, my
mouth is dry, and my whole body hurts from trying not to
touch Riley so I don't set her off again. I know whatever
happened to her was so bad she doesn't want to talk about it,
and she doesn't want to be touched. And I get that. On a
deep level, I get that.

So I just ride behind her. Stiff, uncomfortable, and
fucking starving.

When we finally slow, it's to a small town. Riley takes the
neighborhood streets slowly, and I barely notice the houses
we're passing. Not many people are out.

We roll into a lot of land covered in tall grasses. At first, I
thought it was an empty lot surrounded by trees and scrub at
the edge of town. But then I notice the tiny house tucked into

191

the back. The windows are broken in, and the door is off its hinges.

Riley stops the bike. I struggle to get off. My legs are stiff, my back is stiff, everything is stiff. Riley gets off first and offers me her hand.

I'm so exhausted, I take it.

Riley motions at the saddlebags. "Water and snacks." She barely looks at me.

I open the bags. There's a Walmart bag of snacks and a big thing of water. I rip into them, picking out the pretzels. I love pretzels, and I down as many as I can, then follow them with water. The water is warm, but it feels heavenly. I root through the rest of the snacks. She got fruit snacks too, and I rip those open.

When I finally feel satisfied, I stretch and look around. It's right before sunset, and the world is brilliant and bright. For a second, I don't see Riley. Then she comes out of the house. She gives me a dark look and motions me over.

Whose house is this? It looks like it's been abandoned for a long time, and Riley's face is angry. Cautiously, I walk up to where she's walking. Riley stops suddenly, and I stop abruptly so I don't run into her. I glance up to where she's looking, but I don't see anything. It's just an old shed.

"Riley..."

She says nothing. When I glance over at her, she's as still as a statue. There's no expression on her face. It's like she's somewhere else.

I glance at the shed again. The doors are open, and I can see inside. No one's in there. There's junk and old pots and old wood.

She's still frozen. Unmoving. It makes an eerie feeling wash over me.

"Riley?"

Nothing.

I glance around. Is she okay? I don't touch her. I know it won't help her.

I look around, looking for help, when I freeze.

Riley isn't watching me. And I realize that for the first time, she isn't paying me any attention, and I'm not chained up. This is my chance. My chance to get away.

I look at Riley and take a small step back.

Riley doesn't move.

I take another step.

Still, Riley doesn't react.

My heart races. If I go to the cops, surely they can protect me against Manson. If he's as bad as Riley says, they're probably looking for him anyway. I can tell them where he lives, and they'll arrest him, and then I'll be safe. But that means they'll probably arrest Riley, too.

For some reason, my heart twists. I hate that idea. Even though this is the woman who helped kidnap and drug me. The woman who killed someone in front of me.

So why the hell am I hesitating?

Something isn't right with Riley. She tried to hide the pain earlier, but now it's all over her face. And for some unknown reason, I hate that.

I back away from her, but it physically hurts. Riley doesn't notice. Adrenaline washes through my body. As I back up, my foot crunches on something. I glance down and lift my foot. I see a tiny skull, probably belonging to a squirrel, crushed to pieces under my boot.

Fuck. I broke it. Sadness fills me. As I stare at the fractured skull, I realize that staying means the end of all the things I know. To ever being able to go home. To collecting my skulls and minding my own business. To maybe even live my life.

So I do the only thing I can do. I run.

I dart toward the road, blindly running toward the rest of the town. My body feels sluggish, like it doesn't want me to run, and my leg twinges in pain. But I have to. *I have to.*

Suddenly, my foot catches on something, and I crash to the ground, hands skidding on the dry dirt. I grind to a halt, suddenly hyper-aware of all the sounds around me.

"Rachel?" Riley asks.

I dart up, sprinting toward the road. My feet hit the pavement, and I turn left, running faster than I have in my life. Things blur past me as I go.

"Rachel!" The shout is a warning.

Fuck! I dart to the left. Maybe I can lose her in the brush. I jump into the bushes, only to get held back momentarily by the sticks. I push forward, pressing into the tree line.

I hear Riley chasing me. She's close. So fucking close.

I heave for breath. This is it. She's going to kill me if she catches me. I fucked up.

A body slams into mine, and I stumble forward. I rush toward the ground, and at the last second, I'm flipped around, so I land on a soft body as we go crashing into the dirt. In a second, Riley is hovering over top of me. Her eyes are bright and manic.

I scream, thrashing, trying to get away. Riley pins me down, laughing meanly. "Were you trying to run, Rachel?"

"Help!" I scream. "Somebody help!" I kick and buck.

"Don't worry." Riley struggles to get my hands pinned in her one. "I'll kill you quickly." She looks down at me with a mocking smile.

I fight to get away, but I'm stuck. Again. I'm trapped under someone who pities me and my weakness.

Just like with Papa.

Blind rage rushes through me. This may have been how it

went as a child, but I will not die without a fight. I will not hide any longer.

"Fuck you," I hiss. Fighting her fills me with adrenaline and fear, but I keep going. "I'll take you down with me." I struggle and glare up at Riley with all the hatred I can muster. Suddenly, all of the adrenaline that races through me feels good. I'm tired of taking everything quietly and never causing a scene. This will not be how I go down.

I butt my head up into Riley's, and they crack together so hard I feel it in my teeth. She lets off my hands for a second, and I rip them out from under her.

Adrenaline rushes through me. If I'm going to die, I'll die fighting.

30

TRIALS - STARSET

Pain lances through my nose and fills me with vigor. I jump off Rachel just enough so she rolls to her stomach to get up, then I drop back down on her. I snake my arm around her neck, sinking her deep into my elbow. Elation fills me as I grip my bicep and feel her arteries compressed by my arms.

Rachel struggles, but there's no escape once I've sunk in. I have her completely under my control. And that makes my pussy pound. Her pretty little body is totally and completely mine. And for a second, it feels like what I imagined I'd do to Noel.

It feels good.

Rachel doesn't stop fighting. Something shifted in her eyes right before she headbutted me. Something...dark. And it turned me on.

I squeeze harder. Rachel's movements are slow. It only

takes seconds to make someone pass out. Just a little longer to kill them.

Kill her, the impulsive thoughts in my head scream. *Kill her and be done with it.* But something odd scratches at my chest. Manson's annoying fucking lectures about impulsiveness are there as usual, but there's also something else. Some odd...sense of loyalty.

Rachel slumps, and I hesitate a half second longer, then release my pressure.

The odd feeling swells, and I jerk back, pressing my hand to my chest.

Rachel twitches, then moans. She brings her hands up to her head, groaning.

I stare at her, not quite sure what to do with myself. Rachel ran away. She ran from me. So why do I feel this weird desire to keep her alive? Which, I may add, I've never felt for anyone before. Well, anyone except Pup.

And possibly Manson.

No, cut that. Not him.

Rachel coughs, then looks up at me. She squints in the twilight, then backs away. She doesn't make it far before wincing and holding her head.

"That's what happens when you headbut someone," I say monotonously.

"You didn't...I thought you were going to..."

"Kill you?" I cock my head. "Don't tempt me. I'm still not sure why you're still alive." I stare at her. She looks the appropriate level of afraid, and it makes me horny. I lift an eyebrow. "You don't think things through, do you?"

"What?" She coughs again. Her cheeks are pink, and it makes me want to bite them. They won't be scratchy like Manson's. They'll be soft and pillowy and—I blink back into focus. This is the girl that just fucking betrayed me. I ask,

"Where did you think you were going to go that Manson wasn't going to find you?"

Rachel turns her dark gaze on me, and even in the darkness, I see the flash of fire. She's fucking angry. At *me*.

"Don't be mad, I just saved your life." Or do. It's kinda doing something for me.

Rachel sputters.

I laugh.

"Well, even if Manson found me, it would still be better than you!" Rachel scrambles to her feet. "He'd just kill me and get it over with instead of playing with me like a cat with a mouse!" She scrambles to her feet.

"I prefer hunter with a doe, but okay."

That really pisses her off. Rachel launches herself at me, and I duck her swing.

"You're no better than him," she cries. "You try to sound all high and mighty, but the only reason Manson wants me is because I'm with you. So let me go, and you can keep playing your fucked up little game of murder hide and seek without me."

Anger fills me. She has no idea what she's talking about. Who she's siding with. My voice gets low. "No." Rachel is *mine*. I'll be damned if I let Manson get her.

She curls her lip at me. "If I'm such a burden, let me go. Let me go or kill me, but stop with this halfway fucking bullshit."

Her attitude fills me with lust. I want to slam her against a tree and fuck the fire out of her. I want her to squirm on my fingers as I jam them inside of her.

I cock an eyebrow at her. "I can't let you go. My business has always been Manson's business. You were fucked the moment I saw you at the corn maze."

Rachel has partially turned away, but she whips around.

She looks deep into my eyes and snarls, "Why? Because he's in love with you?"

I freeze. My entire body goes completely still. Love? Manson doesn't love me. My mom loved me. Noel said he loved me. I've seen what love does to people.

For some reason, I don't want Manson to be on the same level as them.

My chest feels like all the air has been vacuumed out of it. It's quiet out, just the sounds of a dog barking far off.

I try to suck in a breath. "No, he isn't."

"Really?" Rachel's voice is just a whisper now. "Because I've never seen anyone who doesn't care just a little act like this."

I tremble slightly, and it makes more anger rush through me. Hot, saving anger that jerks me from my frozen state. The words come out of the depths of my chest. "If he loves me, I'll kill him."

We stand in the dark woods, and I feel murderous. Why does Rachel always bring out the weakness in me? It's like she has a knack for it. She's hit me in all the spots Manson has been aiming at for years, and she hardly even knows me.

I narrow my gaze at her. Is she working with him? Did he send her with me just to spy and report back to him?

My vision darkens around the edges. "Were you *trying* to run to Manson?"

Rachel sputters. "What?"

I take a step toward her. "That's the only reason you'd run. Surely, you knew you couldn't escape him. So maybe you were running to him."

Rachel sputters. "Fuck no."

I shake my head. "Do you need a better idea of what he's like? You said I'm worse than he is." I grab the phone out of my back pocket. "So call him."

"What?" Rachel takes a step back. "No. I just want to go home."

I'm shaking with anger. This is a bad idea, but she needs to learn. I dial him, then hover over the call button.

"Riley..." her voice has lost the bravado.

I raise an eyebrow. "Your move." Then, I press call.

31

When The Darkness Comes - Jeris Johnson

I've just pulled into the lot when my Bluetooth kicks in with a call. I park and check my phone. It's the blocked number again, and I immediately answer.

"Riley." I grin. If she's where I think she is, this call is coming right on time.

Silence.

"Riley."

There's a sound, and then Rachel's voice comes across the line.

"Manson."

Immediately, I still. I didn't expect Rachel. I'm not sure what their dynamic is at this point, but if Riley is good at her job, which she is, Rachel is deep in the grips of Stockholm right now. Probably thinks she knows Riley and that Riley likes her.

Part of me wonders if Riley does like her, and that thought makes me mad. What does Rachel have that I don't?

Nothing. The answer is nothing, and Riley is just doing this to piss me off.

Riley's voice comes across the line. "Rachel wanted to tell you where she was. Says you can come pick her up since you're less dangerous than I am." Her tone is mocking.

"Oh yeah?" I watch the traffic move across the street in front of me. "It's a bit of a drive out to Noel's place. Not sure I want to come get her."

Silence.

That silence confirms exactly where they are. I keep talking, "Noel doesn't live there anymore. But you could have just called me, and I would have told you that."

In the following silence, I know Riley is seething.

"Let's stop playing games, wife. Come back to the house." I say it gently, but I want nothing more than to punish her. I hate that she never told me. I hate that she just confirmed my deepest fear.

Riley's voice comes on, just as melodic and pretty as it's always been. "Manson, get this through your head. We aren't a thing. I'm not your wife. I don't want you. Never have, never will."

Something odd rushes through my chest, and immediately, a flash of anger follows it. "Rachel." I grit my teeth. "I'm gonna need you to bring your girlfriend back here. Meet me at The Landings. By the way, your mother is such a nice person. Though, too sweet for me." I let out a short breath. "Riley, we can discuss Noel when you get here."

Silence, there's a scuffle noise, and then the line goes dead.

I throw my bike in gear. Your move, Riley. It's time to see how far she's willing to go to play this game.

32

Harder To Breathe - Letdown

That fucking prick bastard. I will get great pleasure stuffing my gun in his smug mouth.

For a second, I forget Rachel is beside me, but then she breathes, "My mom."

I toss a look at her. It's almost dark now, so she probably doesn't notice it. It's a shame 'cause it's a scorcher. "No."

"Riley!" Rachel grabs my arm, and immediately, I shake her off. "No. He's throwing a fit because, for once in his life, he isn't getting what he wants."

"He knows where my mom lives."

I start walking back to my bike. "Of course he does. Did you think I was kidding when I told you he's not a good person?"

Rachel scrambles to follow. "He's going to hurt her."

"Yes," I drone. "He is."

Rachel will be miserable thinking about it too. Once

again, I'm grateful I don't feel such things. They're counter-productive.

"We have to go," Rachel says.

"By all means, keep begging. I might come."

Immediately, Rachel clams up. She just follows me to the bike. When we get there, I expect panic. Useless tears and emotions. But I get nothing. Despite myself, I turn to look at her.

Rachel just stands there, watching me. I can see the calculation on her face.

I stare at her. I make it a general rule not to be friendly with women. With anyone, actually. Usually, they end up acting like my mom or the men in my past—emotional and abusive.

But not Rachel. She's calculating. Cold. A planner. It makes me smirk. She's capable of playing the game. Good. If she's playing, then maybe I should focus. Be a little less impulsive. A little more strategic.

I stick the key into the bike. "Let's go, little deer. We'll see if you're just as brave when Manson realizes we're not playing his game."

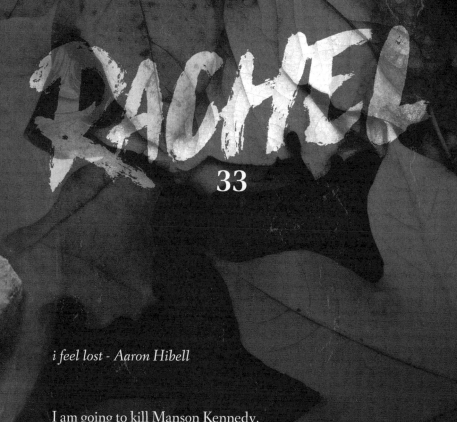

RACHEL

33

i feel lost - Aaron Hibell

I am going to kill Manson Kennedy.

I stare into my French fries, plotting. Riley dragged us to a fast food place and hasn't gotten off her phone since we got here. She clearly has no fear of bringing me out in public now because she knows she has me trapped. If I say anything, both myself and my mom will die.

The thought makes a shiver run through me, but I quickly shut it down. Emotions have never helped me in the past, and they won't now, especially with Riley eating up all my reactions with her dead gaze.

I don't know who Noel is, but I'm guessing he's the guy we were supposed to kill next. And that he's part of the reason for the pain on Riley's face.

I pick at my fries. I forced myself to eat the nuggets, but these feel cold and soggy, and the texture makes me want to gag.

Manson is the head of all my problems. I just need Riley to let me get close enough so I can kill him.

I grit my teeth. "I know you don't want to go to Manson 'cause you don't want to lose the game."

Riley barely glances up at me. "Yep."

I pull in a breath. "So drop me off with him. Drop me off and leave."

"He'll have you, which means he'll win this round."

I shrug. "He'll get me eventually."

Riley gives me a blank look that I've come to interpret as dangerous. "Are you saying he's better than me?"

I feel the tension from across the table. "No, Jesus." I run my hands down my face. "Manson's obsessed with you. You're obsessed with him. The reunion is inevitable."

"I am not," she snaps. "He's the worst person on the planet."

"Then why isn't he dead?" I arch my eyebrow at her.

Riley puts her phone down on the table and stares at me. She keeps her voice low. "Manson is a part of something much bigger than himself, Rachel. I'd be dead in twenty-four hours."

"But you'd win the game." I cock my head at her.

She snorts. "I'm not suicidal."

I eye her. Do I risk telling her that I want to kill him? She says she's not loyal to him, but she seems to be in denial about a lot. Saying what I'm thinking could get me killed where I sit. But my mom and I are dead men walking anyway, and I've spent too long hiding. I take a deep breath. "Then let me do it."

Riley snorts, picking up her phone.

I lean in. "Let me do it. Let me kill Manson Kennedy."

My heart is racing. I can feel it in my chest, and my fingertips are tingling. But I mean it. I've never thought about killing people more than I have in the last few days, but it seems inevitable around Riley.

Finally, Riley lifts her gaze to mine. "Did you just threaten to kill my brother?"

I stare into her dead eyes. I can't tell what she's thinking. He's her brother? I completely read the room wrong.

A tiny smirk settles over Riley's face. Then she starts laughing. "You really meant that too."

I stare at her. She doesn't lunge over the table or threaten me; she just laughs.

I feel the heat rush over my cheeks. "He's your brother?"

"Stepbrother." She shakes her head, and then her face grows serious. "You sure threaten to kill people a lot, bambi." Her eyes spark with something. "In order to do that, you're gonna have to stop being so helpless."

I glare at her. "I'm not helpless."

"Sure," she smirks.

I cross my arms. "If you can't win, why not team up with him? He has all these resources you keep talking about, so why not use them?"

"Now you're just talking stupid."

"Am I, though?" I stare at her.

"Yes." Riley lifts a thin, dark eyebrow.

"What is that saying, keep your friends close but your enemies closer?" I motion at her. "You're good at getting what you want. Why don't you pretend to work with Manson to get what you want?"

Her dark eyes take me in. "You can't manipulate me into saving your mom. You're shit at it."

I narrow my eyes at her. "I'm just saying. Manson seems like the kind of guy who can get you what you want. So why not at least pretend to like him?"

Riley watches me, taking everything in. I feel like she's looking into my soul, and I hate it. But I don't back down.

Finally, Riley smirks and motions at my French fries. "A potato died for you to eat that, so stop wasting food."

I do, in fact, waste my food. I drop the rest of the soggy, gelatinous mess in the trash while staring at Riley, saying fuck you in the only way I can. Something about always being under the threat of death makes me reckless. And oddly, it feels freeing.

Riley's eyes flash at my disobedience, and I think I see the tiniest hint of a smirk before she motions me outside. We get back on the bike and drive into the night. I'm not quite sure where we are, but we're headed east. Which is the general direction of my mom's nursing home.

But I don't think Riley is headed there. She has no reason to. She doesn't care that it's my mom because she doesn't really care about anything, and I have nothing to bargain with. I have nothing that Riley or Manson needs.

The bike rumbles underneath me, and I'm both exhausted and wired at the same time. My gut twists. There's a huge chance my mom will die, and that reality sinks into me. I'm filled with mixed emotions. I flashback to my mom's disinterested face when I told her about Papa. She shrugged me off and looked at me like I disappointed her. For the longest time, I felt bad and tried to make it up to her. Then, during my teen years, I hated her. That old anger fills me and rushes through my body.

Could I let my own mom die? I remember the times she bought me smooth peanut butter instead of crunchy after I almost puked from the texture. She never belittled me, just asked me what I wanted instead. When I told her I wanted to stop picking my fingers and face, she took me to get acrylics so it would be easier. She didn't have a lot of money, but she always saved to make sure I could have a fresh set every few weeks.

I feel sick. How could I even consider letting this happen?

I stare at the land around us. We're flying down a deserted highway. Most highways in this state are empty, especially at night. We've been driving for a while, still heading east. I start to recognize the area, and as I do, nerves fill me.

Is Riley going to stop? Maybe she will. Maybe she wants to work with Manson like I suggested. My hands are slick with sweat, and I want to pick my nails.

We get close to the exit, and I hold my breath.

Riley flies past it.

No, no, no. My gut is in knots, and I need to throw up.

"Where are we going?" I try to shout the words, but they're eaten by my helmet and the rumble of the bike.

Riley passes the next exit. One more, and we won't have a place to turn around for miles.

Once again, someone is making decisions for my life, and I'm stuck and forced to be silent.

I shift, and as I do, my hand bumps the gun. I freeze.

Shoot her. The thought pops into my head. *Bang, bang, bang, done.*

I suck in a breath. I've never shot a gun before. It will most definitely be suicide.

Unreasonable anger bubbles in my gut as the last exit approaches. I will not be silent anymore.

I dart my hands to Riley's waistband, using one to yank her shirt up and the other to grip the gun. It's warm and rough against my hands. Riley slows, and I have to yank twice before I get it out.

"Turn around!" I scream, pressing the gun into her side.

Riley slows the bike even more.

"Go back!" I shove it into her more.

"Rachel," she growls. We're going slow now, and I can hear her over the bike. "You really want to do this?"

My body shakes. Yes. Yes, I want to do this. "The Landings," I growl. I don't know where to put my finger. I don't want it on the trigger because I'm shaking so bad I'll accidentally pull the trigger.

Riley takes the exit. We rumble to a stop sign, where Riley stops.

"Keep going," I hiss, jabbing her. I know I'm ruining any progress we've made.

"You have a gun. I get it." Riley sounds bored. "Keep my ribs out of it." She picks up her feet again, and we keep rolling slowly.

"Where am I going, bambi?"

"The Landings."

"Well, I know that. Where is it?"

I give her directions.

As we roll up, panic fills me. What if he isn't there? What if my mom is already dead? But when we roll slowly into the lot, there's one bike in the lot and a huge man standing there waiting.

I have one shot.

MANSON

34

Hole In Your Head - Ekoh

I hear Riley's bike coming down the dark road, and the rumble fills me with a sense of satisfaction. She's here. The last few days of not knowing where she was has been torture.

But as I watch her headlight pull in, I feel my muscles tighten. Riley is here because she has a weakness. She has someone close to her, which makes her vulnerable. Anger, my only true friend, fills me. How dare she make herself weak. And for what? A girl?

I crack my neck as the bike rolls up. As it stops, I meet Riley's gaze. Even in the dark, her eyes flash with something... amusement, maybe?

She's not wearing a helmet. "Riley." I growl out her name. Rachel scrambles off the back of the bike.

"Manson, don't," Riley demands with a slight panic in her voice. I look for what's scaring her as I watch Rachel lift a gun and point it at me.

I duck, jumping back and yanking my own gun out as I do. I aim down the sights, but Riley jumps in the crosshairs.

"It's empty, Manson!"

I try to get a sight picture of Rachel without Riley in it, but Riley is fully in front of her.

"Move," I demand. This is the second time Riley has gotten in the way of a bullet for her toy, and it's really pissing me off.

Rachel's gasping. Riley yanks the gun from her, turning to yell at her, "Are you suicidal? You really think I'd put a loaded gun near you after all this?"

"Fuck you!" Rachel scrambles back, but Riley just presses her into her bike. She's all over her, glued to her body. For a second, I see her grab Rachel's tit. Then she glances back at me. "Oh, you're welcome for saving your life." She winks.

In four strides, I'm beside her. I grip Riley's hair and yank her head back. "What in the actual fuck?"

"Shoot her, and I'll never speak to you again." Riley glares up at me, but her pupils are huge. I think about shooting Rachel. Putting a bullet in her head, then locking Riley up for the rest of her life. But shooting Rachel would be impulsive.

And I'm not impulsive.

"Do you get off on defying me?" I grit.

"Yes." Riley smiles at me sweetly. Then, she grabs Rachel's face, yanks her to where I have her held, and kisses her. She leans into it, even as Rachel pushes back against her. Riley's damn near humping Rachel right in front of me.

I yank Riley back, and as she comes up for air, she laughs, "Now, dear brother, since we did as you asked, kindly leave that old fuck alone so I don't have to listen to my girlfriend whine about it."

I tuck the gun into the back of my pants as I rip the two girls apart. I swear it almost sounds like velcro, and I yank

Rachel back into my body. I have the impulse to kill her again. But no. I can't shoot someone in front of a building of people who have nothing better to do than get in other people's business.

"My house," I growl.

Riley just tosses me a flippant look. "Is your bed still bloody? If I'm going to fuck in blood, I prefer it to be fresh."

"That can be arranged." I toss Riley a look that's meant to be threatening, but she just licks her lips.

"Let me go." Rachel struggles.

"Not a scratch, Manson, or your wife will file for divorce in the morning."

I snort. As if I'd let anyone dissolve our marriage. Once I have Riley back at my place, I can keep her safe...and if that means keeping her there for the rest of her life, so be it.

"Put the goddamned helmet on," I snap at Riley and yank Rachel to my bike.

35

IF IT DOESN'T HURT - NOTHING MORE

I race Manson back to his place. The ease of riding without another person sends a thrill through me, and I lean into my bike, feeling one with it and the wind. I drive recklessly, loving the power that hums between my legs.

I beat Manson and Rachel to his house, which makes me smirk. I drive right up Manson's front yard, bumping along the grass, and park in front of his front door.

Manson arrives shortly after with Rachel, glaring at my bike haphazardly in front of his door. I grin now, moving into his kitchen and flipping on the lights. As much as I love giving him shit, I'm shocked he's still here. I've pushed him to the edge over and over again. Why won't he just give up?

I ignore the teeniest, tiniest part of me that says I don't want him to give up. Because that tiny part of me also gets all panty when he's around. And that is an absolutely dangerous response around Manson.

I shove around in his kitchen. I'm exhausted, and yet, I don't think I'll sleep for another three days. As I open his fridge, Manson shoves Rachel past me.

"Where you going?" I glance at him.

He ignores me and just shoves her to the basement door.

I straighten. "Don't—"

"I heard you the first time." Manson shoots me a glare and puts on a pitiful voice. "Don't hurt her."

I snort. "Remember. I'll never speak to you again."

The look he gives me is worth every bit of annoyance keeping her around. I grin, yanking food out of the fridge. Everything is meticulously organized. Hell, Manson has prepared meals stacked up for the next week. I glance in the freezer. Yep, even more.

Jesus. This guy couldn't live by the seat of his pants if he tried. It's boring.

I grab a meal and stick it in the microwave. Except for the hum of that, the house is silent. I find my fingers tapping against my arm. Manson being down there with Rachel alone makes this odd feeling run through my body. It's like there's vibrating in my legs, and I can't keep my hands still.

I blink. Oh fuck. Am I feeling something? I haven't felt something since Pup died. Well, since Manson killed him. Swallowing, I stalk to the top of the stairs and glance down.

Rachel and Manson are at the bottom of the steps, and he's chaining her there. There's a blanket, a bucket, and water.

I turn and stalk back to the microwave. I really shouldn't care. I *never* care. Rachel is loyal. I know it. She's scared and impulsive right now, but the way she looks at me when she thinks I'm not paying attention is...everything. Also, Rachel needed this. She needs a push into the big wild world where she can live a little.

That's it. That's all I'm doing. Pushing her to live. Plus, I won't let Manson kill another one of my pets.

That's it.

I pull my food from the microwave and open the lid. It's a steamy mess of beef, mashed potatoes, and veggies. I take a sniff. Okay, maybe that's not beef. Is that...I frown. Is he stealing my venison?

Manson appears at the top of the stairs, and I wipe all traces of anything off my face.

"Did my girlfriend behave for you?"

He snaps a glare at me.

I grin. Egging him on is so easy. I love when he's mad at me. It sends a thrill straight through me.

"She's not your girlfriend."

"Yeah, she definitely is." I take a bite of the food, and it's fucking delicious. The meat has some sort of gravy on it, and it's tender. Fucking hell, Manson's a good cook. Just one more thing I'm gonna have to add to the 'don't-think-about-this-you'll-get-wet-it's-Manson-you-idiot' list.

When I glance up, Manson's gaze is fixed on mine, and I realize I must have moaned a little. The look in his eyes is feral, and I almost lose my resolve.

I motion at him. "Well, you're gonna have to feed her. You have any chicken nuggets?"

A scowl starts to form. "I don't *have* to do anything."

I take another bite. Fuck, it's so good. I wonder if Rachel will eat this. I turn to see what other meals are available, and Manson slams his hand on the fridge and closes it. "Stop messing with me, Riley. Rachel makes you weak. Anything connected to her is now a liability. I found her mom without even trying."

"I didn't come back because you threatened her mom." I shoot him a glare.

"But you're here."

"If you must know, she threatened me with a gun."

"An empty gun," Manson growls.

I smirk. "My ribs were in danger." Fuck, I love her fire. She's sexy on a normal day, but when she's threatening my life? Makes me want to shove my face into her pussy and make her scream.

"Riley!" Manson slams his hand against the fridge again. I'm reminded again of how big he is as he looms over me. Despite myself, the blood shoots to my pussy.

"What?" I toss my meal down on the counter. "*What*, Manson? What is possibly so important you brought us back here for, hmm?" I want to push Manson. I can't help but push him. It's the toxic push and pull we've had ever since we met. "You jealous? You mad you're slipping, and I can do whatever I want?"

Manson's green eyes watch me, and his mouth is tight. Quicker than I can track, his hand snaps out, and he grabs my upper arm with a vice grip. Yanking me to him, Manson doesn't break eye contact. "Who's Noel?"

A horrible rush of tingles pushes through me. I never wanted Manson to know about that. I didn't care about anyone else, but him? He couldn't know. Could never know how weak I was. Could never look at me with pity.

Blinding rage fills me, and I yank back against his grip. "Let go of me."

Manson just tightens his hold, pressing me back into the counter. "I want answers, Riley."

"Fuck off." I scramble for my fork with my free hand, grab it, and use every ounce of power I have to stab it at him.

Manson dodges back, then cusses, ripping the fork from my hand and dropping his shoulder into my stomach. He picks me up, and I scream, pounding into his back and kicking my legs. That doesn't keep him from marching me upstairs. We don't go to the room we fucked Rachel in before. Instead, he carries me as I scream down the hall to a door that's always shut. He walks us into a softly lit bedroom.

"Let go!" I claw at him as he throws me over his shoulder onto the bed. I scramble up as Manson takes a step back. The room is actually nice, with a king-size bed, cozy furniture, gabled ceilings, and what looks like a pink-themed bathroom. There's also a wide couch under the windows.

Manson glares down at me. "You're not leaving this room until I get answers."

I step up into his face, which is really just his chest because of how tall he is. "You can fuck all the way off."

Manson's eyes are filtered. "You're mine, and you'll do as I say."

All the years of his bullying and domineering fill my mind, and I can't help the real snarl that curls my lip. I look into his eyes, making sure he sees every ounce of hate there. I want to watch it push him over the edge. For that delicious control to snap. "I'll never be yours, Manson Kennedy."

The words fill the room. Manson stares back at me, giving me no reaction. The silence kills me. I want him to fuck me. Force me down on the bed and take from me. Replace the horrible grip on my body that's had me since he mentioned Noel.

Treat me like he always would.

Manson's eyes flash with something, and then he stamps it back down.

And there's the pity.

"You'll always be mine, wife."

Then, he steps out of the room and closes the door.

MANSON

36

Love is Madness (feat. Halsey) - Thirty Seconds to Mars

I leave Riley for two days. And by leave, I mean I watch her obsessively on the cameras, and sometimes—often—I sit outside the door as she rages inside. Everything in the room is bolted down. The mirror isn't breakable—she tried—and the windows are bulletproof glass. I took away anything that could be used as a weapon, and I just watch her. She's beautiful, even when she's angry. Especially when she's angry.

She refuses to speak to me.

Which will simply not do.

I stand in the bedroom across from hers, staring at my phone screen. Like I have twenty times already today, I stare at the prison's number on my screen. I should just call and have Noel dealt with. I have the people, and I have the money.

But I don't call. Because what I need is details. I need to know how exactly I'm going to ruin Noel's life, minute by minute, hour by hour, year by year. I could do anything, but I want this to be personal. I want to know every single thing he did to her so I can pay it back tenfold.

The thought crossed my mind to pay my people to beat the truth out of him. But I immediately shut that down. I refuse to let anyone else hear my wife's intimate trauma. That's for me, and me alone, so I can protect her from it.

But Riley won't talk to me. So, I tried other methods to find exactly what Noel did. I searched police records, I called my contacts, and I cussed Riley's mom out for dying and taking what she knew to the grave. My contact knew about Noel—he was a low-down member of our organization at one point—but all he knew about was the arrest, and he confirmed it wasn't because of Riley.

I clench my jaw and slowly put my phone back in my pocket. She just needs to talk to me. I want to shake the truth out of her. My vision has been blurry since I found out, and my body practically vibrates.

I stalk to Riley's room, unlock it, and push in.

She's lying on the couch, as she usually is. She hasn't touched the bed.

"How long?" I can't look at her. I'm already breaking my rules: don't do something without thinking.

"Have you been feeding Rachel?" she asks, sounding bored.

My skin gets hot. "Answer the question, Riley. How long did Noel do what he did?"

Out of the corner of my eye, I see her sit up. She raged and screamed the whole first day, but she's gone oddly quiet. Now, her voice is calm. "I want to talk to him."

Immediately, I snap my gaze at her. "No."

She shrugs. "Don't worry, Manson, I won't fuck him. Not that you have a say over who I do and don't fuck."

She says it so flippantly that I want to wrap my hand around her throat and squeeze. I want to watch the oxygen drain from her blood until she acknowledges that I'm the only one who gets to touch her. That I'm the one who will punish anyone for daring to do otherwise.

"No?" Riley shrugs. "Then enjoy your silence. Oh, and I want a pack of cigarettes." She rolls over on the couch and gives me her back. Her pretty, curvy shoulders, waist, and ass.

I stalk out of the room before I actually choke her. It takes a full twenty minutes of pacing the house before I calm down enough for my hands to stop shaking.

It's nearly five, so it's time for me to feed Rachel. Not that I want to, but Riley asks about it every time I go into her room. I know she's doing it to piss me off, but still, I feed her.

Today, I bring down a sandwich on a paper plate. I take a deep breath at the top of the stairs, then head down. As usual, Rachel doesn't try to plead. She hasn't cried, not once, but I know she knows she's screwed.

This time, when she takes the plate, she frowns at me. "Are you both done being idiots?"

I blink.

She just glares at me. Rachel has pretty eyes. They're softer than Riley's and quieter. More observant with a lighter, golden brown hue.

"Excuse you?" I look her up and down.

She just starts picking the crust off the sandwich. "I can hear her screaming, you know."

She can hear it all the way from down here. I hate that. I cock an eyebrow. "You think just because Riley defends you that you're safe?"

"No, I know I'm not safe at all." Rachel takes a bite, and despite myself, I sit there and watch her. She's mouthy. Riley definitely likes mouthy. She picks fights with me any chance she gets. Is that what Rachel has that I don't?

I watch Rachel eat, noticing the skin around her nails is bloody and ripped up.

Rachel sighs. "So, like, are you gonna kill me now or later? The suspense is killing me."

"Later. Once I can convince Riley she's making a huge mistake." Again, I expect some big emotion out of Rachel, but she's just still for another moment, then takes a bite. Slowly, she starts picking at her bloody fingers absently.

"What did Riley say?" I ask. "When you were at Noel's?"

Rachel blinks, then focuses on me. "What?"

"What did she say? About him?"

She looks up and away, which I know means she's remembering. "Nothing, really."

"Right." I draw the word out.

Rachel glares at me. "I told you the first time I met you that I'm an honest person. I don't lie. Riley said nothing. There was no one there. Nothing there."

"Then why did she take you there?" I narrow my eyes.

Rachel snorts like I asked something amusing. When I just look at her, she stares at me. Then she shakes her head. "You're just as clueless as she is, aren't you?"

I clench my jaw.

"How? How is this my life?" Rachel's voice is pitched high. "My whole life, I've struggled to understand people. I'm always thinking about how I read a situation wrong, but there are people out there who are worse than me, and now I have to explain it to them in a way that won't get me killed?" She gives an incredulous laugh. "Man, fuck my life."

I just eye her.

"Look." Rachel runs a hand through her blue-streaked

hair. "You guys need to figure out a way to flirt with each other that isn't fighting. And killing."

I stare blankly at her.

"You've really fucked up. I've never seen a woman more pissed off at someone in my life. Whatever you did, you royally fucked it up."

I'm up and at Rachel's throat in a flash. I pin her against the stairway railing. "What did you just say?"

She laughs, and I can feel her throat bobbing in my hand. How easy it would be to crush it.

She puts her small hands over mine. Her touch is so delicate, I hardly feel it. I apply pressure, watching her arch her back.

"I could help you." She gasps. "But you'd have to keep me alive. Give me a bed. And a real toilet."

I stare down at the tiny woman who's become almost as big a pain as Riley. Is she actually...bargaining with me? "And why would I do that?"

"Because," she coughs and laughs. "I have something you don't."

"And what's that?" I narrow my eyes.

"Love." She meets my gaze. "I know how to love. And you need that if you're ever going to get your wife to love you back."

MANSON

37

Antisocialist - Asking Alexandria

Age 10

Smack! The sound of my dad's hand hitting skin is loud in our living room. My mom cries out, clutching her face. Dad looms over her, stomping his foot down on her ribs. I hear a crunch, and my mom screams.

"So you chose being a whore over being loyal?"

I watch from the other side of the couch. Dad came home in a fit of rage, with his face all red and his body jerky. He spotted my mom and laid into her. I've seen what my dad does to those who defy him. He makes me watch as he kills them slowly. Why did my mom not know not to cross him?

My mom screams loudly as my dad stomps her in the crotch. I swallow. My body feels like it's being ripped in half. I want to stand by my mom and my dad at the same time.

I've never seen my dad so out of control. His movements are explosive and blind. Usually, everything is planned down to the smallest detail. He's made me study anatomical charts to read off to him the most sensitive parts of the body, and we take days to test those parts on real people.

Dad stumbles partially, righting himself. "You betrayed me, Olivia."

"No, please," she sobs.

"Couldn't keep Rob out of your inbox, hmmm?" Dad's voice wobbles, and it makes a cold feeling run through me. Dad is never weak.

My mom cries harder. Dad snaps his gaze to her face. Snot is running down her nose. I want to scream at her to stop. Stop being weak! Dad has never acted like this. Why is she making it worse?

Everything feels wrong. My whole body feels wrong. I feel weak.

Dad raises his boot and crushes it down on Mom's face.

I watch, blinking slowly. I want to sink back down inside myself and never come back out. Goosebumps run across my skin, and I feel prickles on the back of my neck. Not safe. *Not safe!*

It's a while before I realize the room has gone silent. There's no more sound, and I peek out from behind my hands. Dad is bloody. The floor is bloody. My mom is bloody. My dad's chest heaves. He turns to me, and the look in his eyes is unsettling. He looks wild. He doesn't look like my dad.

Not safe. *Not safe.*

"Where's her phone?" His voice is pitched high.

Slowly, I glance around. I don't know.

Dad rustles through her pockets and yanks it out. He waves it in the air. "This is what you get when you're not loyal, son."

I swallow.

Dad drops to the couch and starts going through her phone.

I've been around enough dead people to know my mom is dead. There's too much blood. Too much...stuff that should be inside on the outside. I don't want to look at her face because I don't think it's there.

I don't move. I don't want to draw his attention.

Dad is quiet for the next week. I move carefully around him, trying to figure him out. Finally, after a week, his behavior changes. His shoulders loosen a fraction, but he never explains anything to me. It's only years and years later that I learn that after hiring a hacker, Dad found out Mom wasn't talking to Rob at all. Rob had created fake conversations between the two of them to make my dad mad. To make him weak.

Now, every time I think of impulsiveness, I remember scraping my mom's body off the carpet. Impulsiveness is never safe, and I decided I was never going to be like that.

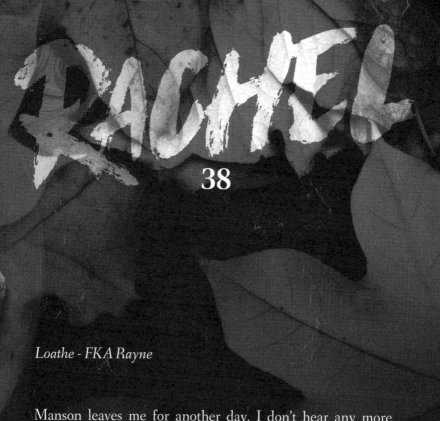

RACHEL

38

Loathe - FKA Rayne

Manson leaves me for another day. I don't hear any more screaming from upstairs. Which either means he's killed Riley or she's icing him out.

I hope she's icing him out. She has to be. Otherwise, he'd have no more use for me, and I'd be dead.

I shift on my blanket, moving to a new position to get some feeling back in my ass. Manson has chained me to the steps with a handcuff around my ankle and a chain. I have enough room to move around, use the bucket he's left as a toilet, stretch, and sleep. The basement is old and empty, smaller than the rest of the house. There's a small part of the wall that's crumbled down, leading to the crawlspace under the other part of the house.

I've picked every last bit of my scalp and the skin around my nails. It's taken everything I can not to pick the scabs on my leg off. The only thing keeping me from doing that is the fear of infection. If it gets infected, I can't run. But that doesn't stop me from picking just the edges. Not enough to bleed, but enough to occupy me. There's nothing else to do down here. Well, that and think about how royally fucked I am. I hoped Manson would take my offer. I've been running their situation around and around in my head, and this is the best thing I can come up with to save my own ass.

At first, being down here in the quiet calmed my nerves. Being alone after days of being scared for my life helped regulate me. But now, I want a shower. And something comfortable to sit on. I just want to get out of here.

The door at the top of the stairs bursts open, and after so much silence, I jump. I cross my arms and stand, watching Manson watch me. His gaze is dead. "You have a lot of nerve."

I stiffen. Manson seems to catch the movement and cocks his head. He takes a slow step down. "Demanding things of me."

I swallow.

"You're counting on Riley to keep you alive."

Another step.

"But you know, there are things worse than death." Another step.

I don't move, but I want to. I feel his slow approach with every piece of my body. I want to run. But there's nowhere to go.

The closer he gets, the more I realize how much stronger he is than I am. Panic kicks in, and my whole body trembles.

Manson's hand snaps out, and he grabs my neck again. He pins me to the stair supports so hard my breath bursts out of me. In a second, he ducks down and unlocks my ankle, then throws me away from the steps.

"Run." His voice is soft.

I scramble away. There's nowhere to go, but I still run. The movement pushes power into my limbs, and everything buzzes. The basement isn't that big, but I try to get him to chase me far enough that I can double back and get to the stairs.

Manson follows slowly, his face in shadow. "Run faster, little deer."

The words crawl up my skin. It feels wrong when he calls me that.

I dart around the room to the stairs, but Manson darts after me. He's fast, and he grabs my arm. I scream, trying to rip it away from him. He shoves me backward, slamming me into the wall. I grit my teeth, expecting my head to slam into the concrete, but it doesn't. I see him pull his hand away from my head and the wall.

"She wouldn't want you to hurt me." The words come out laced with venom.

Manson looks down at me. His eyes are so expressionless they shoot fear through me. "I don't have to hurt you to make you miserable."

I scream, clawing my hands out at Manson. He catches my hands, pinning them above my head and pressing his body into mine.

"Atta girl, fight me. Show me how much you hate me."

"Fuck you!" I try to headbutt him, but I can't get enough space between the wall and his body to make any impact. I jerk my foot up and try to slam it down on his feet.

Manson chuckles, running his hand up and down my side. It's gentle and sends a shiver up my body. I hate that I like it.

"No!" I scream, kicking out at him. He just laughs, continuing to touch me. He lightly runs his large, tattooed hands over my breasts. It makes me shiver, and against my will, I feel myself get wet.

Fuck, fuck, fuck.

"Who's in control here?"

I squeeze my eyes shut. Manson's voice rumbles over me in a delicious growl. I hate that I like it. I hate that it feels good when he's gentle. It reminds me of Papa. I want to run from it like I have my whole life.

"Rachel," his tone is warning.

I grit my teeth. I know Manson wants me to cower—to submit to him despite all the things they've done to me. But I am not just a toy. This isn't right. An angry curl of emotion fills me. I look up and meet his gaze. "Fuck off, Manson."

His eyes bounce between mine, then his chest shakes as he chuckles, running his hand up to trace my neck. It makes goosebumps skitter across my skin. "You're just like her."

I hold his gaze until it makes me uncomfortable. An evil grin crawls across his face, then he grips my shorts and rips them down. In a flash, I'm bare, and his own pants are down. I feel his dick pressing against me. He leans into my body, his breath hot on my ear. "I told her I wouldn't hurt you, little intrigue." He rocks against me, all muscle and power. Despite myself, I feel the electric shock of his friction in my clit. "So I'm going to make you come, over and over, all over the person you claim to hate."

He adjusts, and I feel the tip nudging at my entrance. I try to get away, but there's nowhere for me to go.

"Good girl. Fight me." He pushes slowly into me. The stretch immediately fills me, and I scramble up on my toes.

Manson groans, pushing farther in. The fullness and pressure don't let up, and I'm on my toes as far as I can go.

"Yes, Rachel. Let me hear how much you don't want it."

"Fuck you," I hiss.

"You are." Finally, he seats himself fully and just stops, his heavy breathing in my ear. He sounds like he's holding himself back, and a shiver runs across his body. It makes my clit tingle.

I squeeze my eyes shut and wait for him to pound into me, but he just waits there. He traces his free hand down my body and wedges it between us, moving down to my clit. His fingers brush it, and I jump.

Manson chuckles. He brushes his fingers across it again, and it's everything I can do not to react.

"Mmm," he says into my ear. "You like that?"

"No." I grit my teeth. The gentle touches remind me of something else, and it brings back a wash of shameful memories.

"Really? Cause you're soaking my dick."

I squirm. "Get off me!"

"No, no." He continues playing with my clit, pressing down in circles. My muscles tighten as a pleasurable sensation washes through me. His voice is warm in my ear. "You feel so good."

"No." I shudder, trying to put myself anywhere else but here as shame washes over me. I think about home, about my collection, and the little mouse head I found the night of the corn maze that's sitting on my nightstand.

A bolt of pain shoots through my clit, and I gasp, stiffening.

"No, Rachel. You stay here with me. Don't you dare think about anything else while it's *my* hand getting you off and *my* dick you're going to coat in your cum." He starts in on my clit harder, and involuntarily, I clench.

"Fuck, you," I pant.

"As I said." Manson leans in to nibble up my neck. "You already are."

I buck against him. I want him to fuck me. To pump into me until he gets himself off. To do anything other than focus on me.

He bites my earlobe, continuing to work me. His fingers are skilled. He circles my clit over and over with steady pressure, and I hate how good it feels. I hate it, I hate him, and I hate myself. I feel an orgasm coming, and still, he's just seated in me.

"Hmm," he groans. "You're so wet. How embarrassing to come all over the man who wants to kill you."

"No." I grit my teeth, my body tense.

"Well, that's funny 'cause you have no choice." He presses his body harder into me, overwhelming me with his scent. I can feel the muscles rippling up his body. "Come for me, sweet little intrigue."

I try to escape his fingers, but they follow the little shifts I make with my body. Moving doesn't help; in fact, it shoots more pleasure through my muscles. I feel my pussy clench, and his dick pulses once. The sound he makes in my ear is a low grunt, and that's all it takes. Pleasure shoots through my body, and everything tightens. My orgasm explodes over me, ripping through me against my will. I clench down hard on his dick, my pussy gripping him in waves of pleasure.

Manson shudders. "Good girl. Good girl, come on my dick like a sweet little thing."

I groan, trying to stop, but I can't. My body reacts with or without my consent. When the pulses slow, Manson chuckles in my ear. "That was a good start."

He starts in on me again, relentlessly chasing my pleasure. My clit is sensitive from the first orgasm, and quickly, another one chases it. Faster than before, I come again, clenching on him. This time, Manson lets out a soft grunt and shoves into me once, then again stills.

As soon as I come off that high, he starts again.

"Manson, please." I shift to get away, but he keeps me pinned solidly against the wall.

"Hmm?" He continues rubbing me. I'm sensitive and swollen, and the touch is overstimulating. His body all over me is overstimulating, and I just want a chance to breathe.

"Stop." I try to yank my hands down.

His dick pulses. "Say it again."

"Fuck you." I try to catch my breath.

"Yes," he moans, relentlessly rolling my clit in his fingers. It hurts while feeling good, and I don't think I can come again.

But I do. And again, and again, and again with each gentle touch. With each time, my breathing becomes more jagged. My body is filled with both pain and shame. I don't know which one to focus on, and it makes my head foggy.

At some point, Manson lets go of my hands. They fall to his chest, numb. I drop my head into them. The overwhelming sensation makes me want to cry, and I don't know why.

"Are you crying, sweet little thing?" Manson's voice is soothing.

I clench my eyes shut, my cheeks burning. I don't want him to see that.

I feel Manson pulse inside me. He pulls his dick back, then pushes it deeper. "That's it. Cry for me."

The humiliation rushes through me, making my skin hot. Manson starts pumping into me, and I can feel every stroke in my sensitive pussy. He drags against my G-spot, making me shudder. Manson must mistake it for crying 'cause he shushes me, increasing his pace.

"I'm going to pump you full of my come, Rachel."

"Wait," he doesn't have a condom on.

"And you're going to remember just who owns this pretty little body and just who made you cry." Manson's pace is brutal, but his dick drags against that spot in me with every thrust. Against what I thought possible, I clench up again, pleasure shooting through me.

Manson groans and slams his dick into me, pinning me against the wall. His dick twitches, and I feel his hot cum filling me.

"No," I whisper.

"Yes," he grits, still locked in pleasure.

We stand there for a minute, both panting. Manson just fucked me. He just fucked me and made me come over and over, just like he said he would. Sweetly, without hurting me.

I hate him more than I ever did.

In the silence, Manson's voice asks softly, "How do I get Riley to love me?"

I catch my breath. He's going to give me a chance.

Manson drops his head against the basement wall. "Do I have to buy her flowers? Sing to her a few times?"

"I...it's not that simple. Love isn't a formula."

Manson pulls out of me.

I stiffen.

He glares at me. "Tell me what it is then."

"It's...I don't know. It means different things to different people. I need to know Riley so I can tell you what she wants. I need to find out what she's mad about too."

Manson shakes his head, pulling up his pants. I scramble to get mine up. He isn't going to believe me. He'll have no use for me. Manson turns and stalks to the stairs.

I stand there, dripping his cum, and never feeling more alone.

At the bottom, Manson turns. "Let's go, lovebird." He looks me up and down. "If you tell Riley about this, I'll kill you. Fuck what she thinks." Then he turns and walks up the stairs.

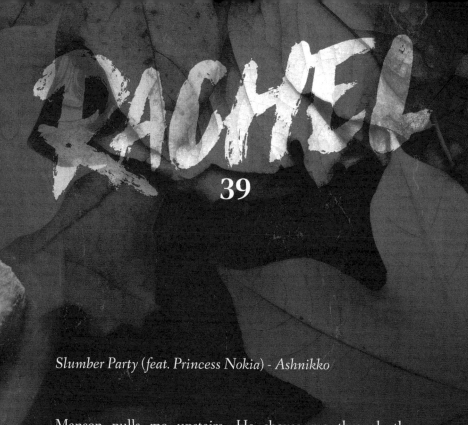

RACHEL

39

Slumber Party (feat. Princess Nokia) - Ashnikko

Manson pulls me upstairs. He shoves me through the kitchen, then around to the stairs. He marches us both upstairs, past the room where they fucked me when I was tripping, then down the hall where he digs in his pocket.

"We have a deal, Rachel," Manson says, his voice low. "Don't forget it." He pulls out a key, unlocks the door, then pushes me inside.

I stumble, catching myself. Riley's lying on a couch in a small, comfortable bedroom. She snaps up when she sees me.

"Her pussy's wonderful. I can see why you're obsessed." My face burns.

Riley jumps off the couch. "Did you hurt her?" She grabs my arm, yanking me behind her. I turn to see Manson smirking. He crosses his arms. "If making her come over and over counts, then yes."

Riley turns to look at me. There's something in her face

that makes me feel worse. I look down. I just fucked her boyfriend. Against my will, but still.

"Rachel? Look at me."

I do. Her eyes bore into me. In this moment, she looks just like Cali. Protective.

I swallow. "I'm fine."

Manson has a shit-eating grin on his face.

Riley turns back to him, her body relaxed again. "Whatever, Manson, you know I don't care where you stick your dick." She motions at him like she's waving him off. "I'll tell you about Noel if you get me out of this goddamn room."

The room goes utterly still. Riley smiles sweetly at Manson, but I can see the calculating expression in her eyes.

"Let me be specific," Riley crosses her arms. "I'll tell you about him if you give me my freedom back. No more keeping me under lock and key."

"No." Manson's response is immediate.

Riley stiffens slightly. "Yes. And only under those conditions."

"No." Manson turns and slams the door. I hear the lock clicking in place.

"Well." Riley turns back to me and smiles. "He's in a good mood today!"

I look at her, unsure how to respond. Clearly, she's being sarcastic. Right? Because he's not killing either of us, he must be in a good mood?

Riley does a double take, and her voice gets serious. "He hurt you?"

Am I okay? I don't even know. Her concern makes me feel even worse about myself. Her boyfriend, husband, stepbrother, *whatever* just fucked me, and she's being kind? Riley knows how to be kind?

I swallow harshly.

Riley's staring at me. I can feel it, but I don't look at her. She's silent for a minute. "Okay. See, this is why I don't want to be normal. Emotions look disgusting. Go get the shower started."

I move like a robot to the bathroom. I just get the water started when I notice there's a bath, and I turn that on.

Riley pops her head in. "No bath. Shower."

I glance at her in confusion.

"I'm coming in with you, and I don't do baths." She pops back out.

Fuck. She's going to be naked in the shower with me? My brain scrambles. I don't think I've seen her naked. My heart flutters in my chest.

Riley pops back in, completely, stunningly naked. I stare at her, startled. Her body is fit and curvy, her tits looking huge and so much more full than mine. They round out at the bottom and sit perky.

I realize I'm staring at her tits, and I rip my gaze away, my face heating.

Riley chuckles. "You gonna get in with that on?"

"What?" I glance at myself.

"Your clothes, idiot."

I swallow. "No, I'll just wait..."

"Absolutely not." Riley grabs me by my shirt and yanks me toward her, pressing me against her soft breasts. I stiffen, and her voice drops to a demanding one. "Take them off and get in, or I'll pull you in just like this."

My whole body trembles. I feel her body all over my arms and chest.

Riley smirks, and she shoves me back. "Strip."

I do, suddenly feeling self-conscious. Riley steps into the shower, and I try not to look at the way the water cuts down her body, tracing around her curves.

Try and fail.

"Stop lollygagging."

I jump, stepping into the shower as far away from her as I can get.

"Good girl." Riley steps back under the spray, letting it wet her whole head. Her lips are slightly parted, and her chin is tilted up to let the water run down her back.

It's unnecessarily erotic.

I rip my gaze away. What is wrong with me? I'm not gay. Everything that Riley has done to me has been against my will. So I'm not gay.

Right?

"Come here." Riley grabs my arm and yanks me to her so our faces are practically touching. For one, heart stuttering second, I think she's going to kiss me. Then she says, "Cameras."

I blink, the water splashing onto my face and into my eyes.

"Manson set up cameras all through the room."

I try to pull away from her to look, but she pulls me back to her. "Yes, in here too. But he can't hear what we're saying." She waves at the water.

I blink and look up into her dark eyes. All traces of joking are gone, and her gaze bounces between my eyes. "I'm going to bargain with Manson to get me out of this room. But I need your help."

She needs my help? I stare at her. Riley's face is the kind of face I've always wanted: sharp features, clear skin, dark lashes, and plump lips.

I realize I'm staring. "Uh, okay?"

Riley's face softens. "Good. I need you to try and run."

"What?" I pull back from her.

"It'll just be a distraction. I need to make a call. It'll be fast, but I don't want Manson hearing."

I stare at Riley. This could get me killed.

It's like she reads my mind 'cause she pulls me even closer, so now our bodies are completely touching, and her hot skin is all over mine. "I won't let him hurt you." Her gaze darts down to my lips, then back up to my eyes. She licks her lips. "I promise. I just need you to distract him."

Everything buzzes under my skin, and suddenly, the shower feels like it's a million degrees. Riley leans, and as our foreheads touch, it feels like a bucket of cold water is dumped all over me. What am I doing? I'm supposed to be spying on this woman. Getting to know her so I can sell her secrets to her boyfriend in exchange for my life. Not ogling her within an inch of her life and thinking about doing anything she wants just because she asked.

I pull back.

"I...uh." I try to think of a way to back out of this. But there is none. I'm stuck. "Okay," I breathe out softly.

"You're the best." Riley presses her lips to the top of my forehead. It's quick, and then she pulls back. "Has he been feeding you?" She looks me over.

"Yes."

"You look skinny. I have snacks."

I stare at the water pooling around our feet, feeling stupid for the warm feeling I have inside. I know Riley's just manipulating me, but it feels real, and I want to sit in this moment for just a minute longer before I face reality.

Because I know in reality, Riley doesn't care beyond her little game. Manson will use me to get close to her, and then I'll be forgotten.

And against all reason, that hurts.

40

Monster Made of Memories - Citizen Soldier

Manson doesn't come up after our shower or as the night goes on. Rachel and I talk, mainly about the snacks I'm going to demand Manson run out and get, and then it devolves into our favorite foods.

In a turn of events that will shock no one, Rachel has a terrible pallet. I don't think the woman has tried anything new in ten years. It almost makes me want to get her to eat my pussy, just so I can give her something good to eat.

Almost.

I don't let anyone touch me. Ever. Unless it's Manson, and he never gives me a choice, so in a fucked up way, it's still okay. But only for him.

"Are you going to bed?" Rachel looks at me where I'm at on the couch. Her hair is still damp, but she looks relaxed. I realize that we've been having our first normal conversation.

"You can have the bed." I throw one of the pillows over my face.

There's a pause, then she asks, "You sure?"

I turn my head so the cameras can hear it better. "Sure as I know Manson's a dick."

Rachel snorts.

I peek out at her. She's stifling a smirk.

I grin. "Oh, so you do have a sense of humor! I had begun to think it was stuck behind that stick you have up your ass."

Rachel gives me an indignant look, but her eyes are soft. I just wink at her.

"I ought to smother you in your sleep," Rachel grumbles. Suddenly, her eyes snap open. "I didn't mean–"

"Sure you did." I tuck the pillow under my head. "Lucky for you, that just turns me on." I like seeing her like this. Less afraid. I find myself smiling like I do when I'm being dumb and thinking about Manson, and that makes me sit bolt upright.

Oh no.

"You okay?" Rachel looks at me.

"Uh, yeah." No. Bad Riley. Stop thinking about these two. Whatever happened to your badass, 'I'll do it alone' mentality?

There's silence, and then Rachel seems to accept my answer. I hear her shuffling around as she gets ready for bed.

It's quiet for a long time, but it's not a chaotic silence. It's the kind that wraps up the restless anger in my brain and soothes it.

Eventually, I pass out. And when I do, a flashback I didn't remember fills my head.

"Riley!" The voice is gentle and deep. I jump and drop my magnifying glass.

Mom wasn't supposed to leave today. Did she leave?

"Let's play hide and seek."

No.

I stand. I had been so wrapped up in trying to start a fire I hadn't heard any cars pull up.

I glance up. It's one of Noel's friends. He's tall, with a belly and an Oklahoma Sooners shirt on. The man smiles at me. "Animal hide and seek. You remember?"

I do. I don't forget things. I'm smarter than he is.

I glare at him. He just pulls his shirt off and starts growling and throwing his arms around. "Ready or not, here I come."

"What are you doing?" I narrow my eyes.

"I'm a bear. You need to run."

I cross my arms. "No."

Fighting him is a blur. Next thing I know, I'm in Mom and Noel's bed, staring up at the deer head mounted on the wall. There's pain. Lots of pain. Noel's friend is here with me, but I block him out as I stare at a bald patch of skin on the deer.

How did Noel get that? I know he doesn't hunt. This deer had to die to sit dead on some poser's wall.

Anger fills me.

Noel doesn't hunt.

He's a lair. A dirty, dirty liar with dirty, liar friends.

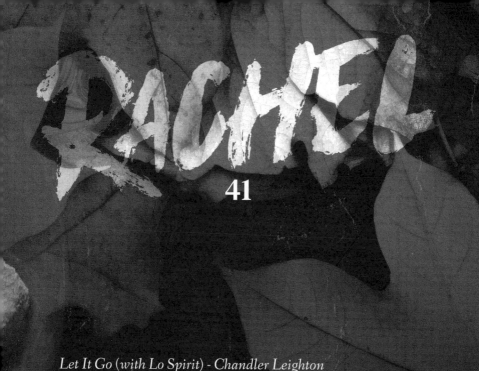

RACHEL

41

Let It Go (with Lo Spirit) - Chandler Leighton

I wake to the sound of whimpers.

I jerk up. The room is dark, and it takes me a second to recognize where I am.

Riley's room.

There's another whimper. It's coming from the couch. I squint. Riley is lying there. Dreaming. Acting like she's in pain.

I swallow. I've had nightmares before. When I had them, my ex used to wake me up, which was both a relief and horrifying. Then, not only did I have to feel the pain, but I had to feel it in front of him while not being able to explain it.

I'm torn, feeling something odd for Riley despite all the things she's done. I realize with a start, that I care.

Riley turns on the couch like she can't get comfortable.

In a moment of weakness, I grab the top blanket and drag it over to her. I lay it softly on her, then creep back to my bed.

The whimpers stop, and Riley sucks in a breath. Then, she bolts up on the couch, her gaze flinging everywhere.

I freeze, not having fully made it back down on the bed. Riley and I make eye contact, and then she glances at the blanket over her.

Her eyes darken, and she glares at me.

I swallow.

"Did you touch me?"

"No, I–"

"Manson!" Riley shouts, startling me. "Let me *fucking* out of here!" She grips her hair, jumping up and pacing.

I'm frozen on the bed. I fucked up. I shouldn't have woken her.

Riley targets the snacks on top of the dresser, shoving them off violently. They crash to the floor.

"I'm gonna kill you, Manson!" She rips her hair again, sucking in heavy breaths. Then, they turn to laughter. She laughs, turning in circles in the room. "Mansooon. I just need a lighter. Just one little lighter."

I see the pain around her eyes despite her laughter. Then, Riley locks eyes with me.

She grins at me, frozen in her spot. Then, she takes a step forward. "No space. I'm stuck."

It sounds like she's pleading with me.

I inch back. "Uh..."

Riley's smile widens.

"You can have the bed." I try to scoot to the other side.

Riley stops, and suddenly, she's staring at me, but she's no longer there. She blinks, then reaches up to rip her hair again. "No bed," she mutters absently. "No beds. Ever. I don't do beds."

Suddenly, her statement sinks into me with brutal clarity.

That was little Riley who just talked to me, not adult Riley. And at this moment, my heart breaks for her.

Riley goes back to pacing.

"It's okay," I say softly, "I don't do armchairs."

Riley yanks her hair again, then looks at me. Something peeks through the blank look in her eyes.

I sink back onto the bed more. "Especially not green ones."

Something flashes in Riley's eyes. She seems to wrestle for a second, holding my gaze like a lifeline. I don't know what she needs from me, but I hold her look. I feel like she's staring deep into my soul, and fear rocks my core. She'll see me deep down. She'll see me and unravel me.

But her gaze is panicked. Like she...needs this.

So I hold it for agonizing seconds as Riley's gaze wrestles in front of me.

Finally, her gaze sinks back to that expressionless one I usually see her wear, but it's less pained. Her eyes have relaxed.

"Didn't know you hated green." She shrugs. "You hear that, Manson? She hates your eyes."

I bark out a laugh.

Riley flashes me a tiny smile, and despite everything, it looks real.

42

HEATHEN - n9neful

I give the women a night. It takes me a whole night not to storm in there and manhandle the information out of them the way I want to.

But that would be impulsive. What's the rush? Riley is mine now. Rachel too.

That fact doesn't keep me from watching the live feeds like they're my heroin and I'm dope sick. I fall asleep with the feed on.

When I wake up, I realize I've slept longer than I meant to. I curse, rubbing the sleep out of my eyes, and I finally allow myself to go to Riley's door.

When I open it, Riley is sitting on the bed...naked.

I stand there, momentarily stunned. I've seen her naked before, but each time, she's just as stunning. She's covered in dark tattoos that trace up her arms, over her collarbones, and all down her thighs. My eyes lock on those toned legs, legs I

263

want to spread open as she fights me. As I look, I lock on the Medusa tattoo on her hip. My eyes narrow, and my stomach clenches.

A Medusa tattoo. When I first saw Riley get it, I thought it was just because it fit her aesthetic.

Riley clears her throat, and I snap my gaze at her. She smiles sweetly at me. "Eyes are up here, Mr. Kennedy."

I shake myself out of my head. I came in here for a reason. "Rachel, let's go." It takes everything in my power not to look down at Riley's tits. Her perfect, round tits that I know are hanging nicely. She's doing this on purpose.

Riley jumps up, and out of the corner of my eye, I catch her tits bounce. "Wait. I want to make a deal."

I clench my jaw. "Rachel, come."

"I'll tell you about Noel if you let me out of this room."

"No." A free Riley is a dangerous Riley—to herself and others.

"Please." She pouts her bottom lip out, which does nothing but make me want to bite it as she cries under me.

Rachel clears her throat and looks at me. Then, she gives Riley a tiny glance.

I stare at Rachel. Is she suggesting that I hear Riley out? How will letting her manipulate me help her love me?

"I'll stay in the house. I just need out of this room."

I stare at Riley, calculating, thinking through every potential problem. There are a lot of them.

Riley frowns. "Fine, I'll just keep my mouth shut then."

I can *feel* Rachel's gaze on me.

I cross my arms. "You can come downstairs to make breakfast."

"Sold." Riley claps her hands.

"You're coming upstairs right after."

"What, afraid I'll charm your dick into letting me go?"

I snap my glare at Riley. Which is a mistake because she just gives me a pretty smile and said dick bobs in response.

"I mean it." I narrow my gaze so I see less of her tits.

"What am I going to do, Manson? You're right here, and you have locks on all the doors. Disappear into thin air? Teleport?" She picks at her nails. Which are perfect.

I just cock my eyebrow. All the doors are padlocked shut, and my windows are nailed down. I've been planning this for a very long time. There's no escape from this house without my permission. But somehow, this is still a bad idea. A very bad idea.

Rachel is standing just outside of reaching distance, so I lean over to grab her arm. "I'll put Rachel away, and then we'll talk."

"Yay!" Riley bounces up and places a kiss on my cheek.

Instantly, all the blood rushes to my dick, and I snap out my free hand, grab Riley by the throat, and yank her to me for a real kiss. As her lips smash into mine, I inhale her sweet scent, and it almost—*almost*—makes me not regret my decision. I yank her away from me. "You still have to talk."

Riley smiles up at me, and her gaze is nothing but trouble. "Of course. Noel—"

"Not here," I cut her off. I won't have my wife's secrets aired in front of everyone. Especially not when she's still naked, and I have her yanked so close to me that she's also touching Rachel. It looks erotic, both of their soft bodies pressed together.

I pull them apart immediately.

Riley crosses her arms and shakes out of my grip. "She can hear what I have to say."

I glare at her. "No. Let's go, Rachel."

"Noel raped me, Manson."

My world slows. As the words sink into the room, there's

deafening silence. I knew this, but hearing her say it makes it horrifyingly real.

"He raped me when I was a kid. A lot."

Rachel is frozen in my grasp.

I clench my jaw and look down at my wife—at her beautiful, soft, stubborn face. I don't see pain in her eyes, but I feel it in my own. In fact, I don't see much in her at all. It's like she's...gone.

And I want her back.

"I don't remember a lot, Manson. But no, yours wasn't the first dick I fucked. Happy?" Riley throws on a fake smile.

Anger fills me. Is that why she thinks I want to know? Does she think that poorly of me?

I snarl, "No. Not happy. Let's go." I yank Rachel with me. I'll put her away, and then I'll deal with Riley.

"Grab some clothes," I snap. No way in hell I can focus with her looking like that.

Halfway down the stairs with Rachel, she trips. I yank her up before she hurls headlong into the bottom step, but her motion has pulled her in front of me. She grips my torso, looking up at me with something like panic in her eyes. "Don't take me back to the basement."

"Let's go." It's hard to see where my next step will fall with her limbs all over me. That, plus Riley's opinion of me, fills me with rage.

"Please!" Rachel just holds me tighter.

I rip her up into my arms, and she starts struggling. "No! Please! I'll be good!"

"Rachel!" Riley snaps, bumping into me as I clear the bottom step. "Chill."

Rachel lets loose a blood-curdling scream, thrashing back and forth. She's not big, but she has surprising strength, and I have to actually hold onto her to keep her from thrashing loose. I cart her through the kitchen and to the top of the stairs, where her limbs hit the doorframe as she thrashes.

"You need help, Manson?" There's a mocking laugh in Riley's tone. "Looks like you're struggling a bit, big boy."

I shove Rachel through the basement doorway, then glare at Riley for a second before Rachel's movement almost causes me to fall down the stairs. She threw clothes on, thank Satan. "Don't go anywhere."

Riley snorts. "Go where? You have a portal in here I don't know about?"

I grunt, carting Rachel the rest of the way. She fights like she's lost her mind until I've chained her up again. My hands shake as I do it.

"Manson, wait." Rachel grabs my arm, and I shake her off, only for her to grab me again.

"We have to talk. About Riley."

"Get off me."

"She has to trust you."

I stare at Rachel, realizing what she's saying. She's covering for Riley. Fear rushes through me, and I start to rush up the stairs.

"She's not running!" Rachel gasps. "You're being reckless! Just listen!"

I slow, halfway to the top of the stairs. I know she can't get out, but some animalistic part of my brain wants to chase her down.

But I'm not fucking reckless. Riley can't go anywhere; this house is locked down.

I turn back to Rachel. "What did you do?"

Rachel bites her lip. "Promise you won't get mad."

"What did you do?" My words come out a growl.

"Riley doesn't trust you." Rachel looks at me like she expects me to jump down on her. She's as far back as the chain will allow. "And she'll never love you if she doesn't trust you."

This is ridiculous. Riley has every reason to trust me. I've done everything for her. I turn to go up the stairs.

"Wait! Think about this."

Rachel looks startled when I snap my gaze to hers. "I have thought about it. It's all I ever think about."

"Then give her space," she pleads. "Whatever Riley's doing, you can track it, right?"

"That depends on what she's doing." I clench my teeth so hard they grind together. I might have to chain both of them up, depending on what Riley's doing.

"I think she's making a call. I don't know, though!"

I pat my back pocket. Sure enough, my phone is missing.

"Wait!" Rachel takes a step toward me as I take one up the steps. "You have to get Riley to trust you."

"How?" I whirl on Rachel. This arrangement is stupid. So far, all I've seen is Rachel getting in the way of my plans.

Rachel swallows. "*You* have to trust *her*." Her voice drops. "Stop controlling every little piece of her life."

Anger washes through me in a hot wave. Not control her? My control is the only thing that's kept Riley safe, out of prison, and with a roof over her head. I'll control every last breath she takes, and she'll thank me for it.

I storm the rest of the way up the steps.

43

EAT SPIT! (feat. Royal & The Serpent) - Slush Puppy

I didn't tell Manson about Noel's friends. I knew what would happen if I did. He'd want to fight my battles for me. He'd want to kill all of them, and they're *mine*. Manson already has Noel. If he hasn't done something to him yet, he will. But those three? They're mine, and I'm the only one who decides how this ends.

But, there is a slight problem. I still don't exactly know who the others were. I have no clue what their last names were. I spent last night racking my brain for their names, but they're still fuzzy memories in my mind. Memories that I don't want to remember.

I wanted to call Noel and ask him, but the more I think about it, the more I know he'll laugh in my face. I could get Manson to stick his prison thugs on him, but that would require Manson knowing what I'm talking to Noel about. And that won't do.

Opening Manson's phone, I realize it's locked. I try a few combinations before trying my birthday. It works.

I go to social media. I had a scam account that was friends with my mom before she died. I was planning on acting like the perfect man and then dumping her, but she was slow to take the bait, and she died before I could finish.

Because, of course, she did.

But I was friends with her and had access to all of her posts, even the private ones from a long time ago.

My hands shake as I scroll. Surely, I can find something on this account. I just don't know how long it's going to take. I don't know if Rachel can buy me that kind of time.

As I'm thinking that, I hear Manson coming up the steps. Fuck. Fuck fuck! I just need this. I need their names. If I can just get their names and a little bit of freedom, maybe the burning, endless rage in my chest will quiet.

Maybe I'll stop remembering.

I clear the apps and toss the phone on the couch as Manson storms into the kitchen. His eyes are livid, and his movements are jerky.

He's out of control.

Despite my frustration, that makes me smile. "Who pissed in your cheerios?"

Manson's beside me in a flash, hand around my throat and slamming me into the wall. "Thought you could get one over on me?"

I chuckle as I try to suck in a breath. "No piss kink then? Shame. And I always thought you were freaky."

"Riley." His grip is so tight I feel the blood rushing in my ears.

"That's my name, don't wear it out." I gasp as his hand spasms.

"What were you doing?"

Manson loosens his grip just enough that I don't pass out completely.

"I was going to call Noel and tell him to go to hell." I smirk.

Manson's head is by my neck, his breath hot in my ear. "He'll never touch you again. I'll kill him. I'll fucking ruin him, Riley. It's over."

Annoyance shoots into me. "Oh, shocking. You're fighting my battles for me."

"Riley." I feel his hand slam into the wall by my head, and it sends a thrill through me. His voice trembles. He's barely in control.

I laugh around the pressure he's putting on my throat. I know poking him is the worst thing to do. There are two parts of me: one that wants to push him until he breaks and another that hates the idea of a world where he actually does give up.

But when I open my mouth, what comes out is, "Did Rachel hit you in the head? All you're saying is Riley, Riley."

Before I know it, I'm on the couch, and Manson drops over me. His hand is back on my throat, and he rips my shorts down. The violence of it shoots pain through me, and I revel in it. The chaos in my brain feels right when he's like this.

"Just fucking...stop fighting me!"

I laugh harshly. "Sure thing, Noel. Oops, sorry, I meant Manson."

If I thought Manson was rough before, it's like he completely lost it. He flips me over, and I hear the crack of his hand before sharp, delicious pain rushes through my ass. His hand cracks down again on the same spot. Over and over until the pain amplifies with each hit. My skin gets hot, and I can feel the force of the strikes in my bones. I can't help but struggle a little.

"Why. Didn't. You. Tell. Me?" He strikes after each hit.

I can't keep the groan of pain down. But it's also accompanied by arousing tingles that rush up and down my whole body. My pussy is soaked.

"Suck my dick," I gasp.

Suddenly, Manson stops. I brace myself, waiting for another hit, and he chuckles. Instead of a hit, his fingernails trace across where he was hitting me, sending another wave of goosebumps over me. It feels fucking amazing.

"What were you doing on my phone?"

"I told you, calling N-"

He hits me so hard I see stars.

I groan, a sassy response hot on my tongue, but Manson switches to my other asscheek, hitting hard and fast, pain lighting up there too.

I struggle to get out from his punishing hand. Manson just laughs, but it's not amused. "Yes, fight me, Riley. Show me just how much it hurts. You can brat until you're blue in the face, but I'll always get my way. Now tell me why you didn't tell me."

I hiss, but he hits me again, and I can feel my skin bruising in a delicious way. Again and again and again, the pain comes. I squirm to find relief, which just makes Manson groan.

I feel my body wanting to submit to him, even while my brain screams that we're in danger. I have to redirect this. "Where's your mask?" I taunt. "Or are you finally brave enough to admit you've been panting after me since we were teens?"

There's a dark chuckle, and it makes goosebumps run across my skin. I'm tempting fate. I know I am. It makes me feel even more alive, sending a thrill through my whole body.

I expect another hit, but it doesn't come. I do everything I can to keep from squirming. Manson has gone deadly silent.

Finally, his fingers run softly across my skin. "Oh, is that what you want?" Suddenly, he flips me over so I'm facing him and drops down over my body. He smiles at me mockingly. "You want me to...how did you say it, pant over you?"

I feel him flex, and his cock nudges against my entrance. I brace, expecting him to slam into me like he always does.

But he doesn't. He just presses in slowly, and as he does, he brushes a strand of hair back from my face.

"Poor Riley. You just want someone to love you?" His gaze is mocking.

"Fuck you," I hiss. Something in my chest tightens. Love is for losers. I hate love.

Manson rocks back gently, then presses back into me, his dick filling me up.

"Oh, Riley." He pants, sneering at me. "Yes, Riley, I love you."

"Stop!" I jerk my hands out from under him and rake them down his back. Manson groans as they break the skin, stiffening in me more. Somehow, when the words come out of Manson's mouth, they sound different. They sound...good.

And I hate that response. Because of all people, Manson has the ability to hurt me. And he's getting way too close for comfort. I growl, "Stop being a pussy and fuck me like you mean it."

"What if this is how I mean it?" Manson snakes a hand down between us to play with my clit. "What if I'm panting after you, Riley?"

"Then I'd say you're weak." The anger is rushing through my body. "And I hate weak."

Manson just laughs. "Say that to me when you're coming all over my dick while I'm worshiping this body."

I rip my nails down on him again, trying to get a reaction, but it just makes his dick twitch in me.

I hate this. I hate this because I could like this. I struggle to get away from him, but that just gets Manson off more. So, I stop fighting.

Two can play this game, dickhead.

Instead of digging into his skin, I relax and massage Manson's back softly. "Oh, Manson," I moan. "Fuck yes."

He looks at me.

I just arch my back into him. "You feel so good." The words send a forbidden thrill through me. Stop it, Riley. We're just playing a game.

Manson looks at me, confused. His face is so perfect, his jawline so strong, and his lips so biteable that I do something impulsive: I grab his face and smash my lips into his.

Manson stiffens. I just deepen the kiss, sucking his tongue into my mouth and nipping it. That seems to wake him up, and he attacks my mouth back. We fight for dominance while our bodies are still softly grinding.

Manson's fingers on my clit are sending pleasure through me. And I hate that. I grind my hips up into him softly and feel his dick twitch again. So he's not as unaffected as he'd like to appear.

I smile into his lips.

"What?" Manson stares down at me, his green eyes searching mine.

"Nothing." I grin at him. I'll get him to come first.

Manson just doubles down, slightly adding pressure and speed to his hand. His dick strokes more upwards, rubbing against my G Spot. Pleasure shoots through me, and I snap my eyes closed.

Manson chuckles. "You're cute. You think you're going to win this game?"

"What game?" But his hand is relentless. I think of anything else. Of the dream I had. Of the way Rachel somehow understood and calmed me down. Of her pretty little face with her blue hair and pale skin.

I feel myself get wetter and moan, trying to buck Manson off.

"Atta girl. Take my dick like a good girl."

"Fuck off," I growl.

"I will. Just as soon as you come." He's still being soft, and I can feel every inch of his muscled body as it lays over me. He's hot, and I hate that I have to admit that. I don't get much of a chance to just feel him when I'm fighting him.

I get wetter, and that makes me mad. I never lose. What is going on?

"Mmm, Riley, you're so perfect. A perfect little wife."

I glare up at him, a mocking retort on my tongue, but I freeze as I see his face. He looks completely serious.

And for the first time, something like fear rushes through me. This whole time, this has been a game between us. A toxic push and pull of mutual hatred. Manson has never said something like that to me before. Was he...being serious when he said that?

He notices me watching him, and then his lips twist up in a mean smirk.

So he was just mocking me.

"Fuck you," I dig my nails into him.

Manson just picks up his pace, and despite everything, I feel my orgasm building. What is fucking wrong with me? I can't keep it from building and building, and I realize I'm not going to be able to stop it.

And what's worse is—I like it. I like everything about Manson, and he won't fucking get out of my head. He's going to break me. He's going to make me weak.

So when I come around Manson's dick, I do the only thing I can think of to keep him as far away as I can.

I moan Noel's name.

MANSON

44

She Keeps Me Up - Nickelback

I lost control. I lost it. I fucking lost it.

I let Riley rile me up, and then I told her she was perfect.

I saw her face when I said that. There was something like disgust or disbelief. Which is about the worst reaction I could get.

I stand stiffly from the couch, running my hands through my hair. Riley's ass is red and bruised. I've never seen her skin so marred. Even now, it makes my dick jerk.

She's marred because I lost control. But despite that, she's no closer to submitting to me. I could probably beat her to death, and she'd still refuse me.

She thought she could hurt me by saying Noel's name, but I'm not threatened by him. But I do think he needs to scream his own name while it's burned into his skin a thousand times over.

Helplessness washes through me. What am I supposed to do? How can I get Riley to see what I see?

Riley has her eyes closed, and she's just breathing softly while my heart races.

Rachel said I needed her to trust me. What does that even look like for us?

Suddenly, an idea fills my head. I could...I'm not sure if she'd like it, but I could try. I have to try. I'm losing her.

"Get up," I demand, my voice husky.

Riley groans.

"Get up," I demand again. I need to leave, and like hell will I go without locking her up.

"Wait, I don't want to go back in that room." Riley groans, covering her eyes.

Too bad. Riley is way too good at disappearing, and as much as I want her to trust me, it won't come at the expense of her safety.

"Let's go."

Riley groans but sits up, and I don't miss the wince of pain. "Please, don't lock me in that room again. I can't breathe." She says that with little to no emotion. It's like, in this moment, she was honest with me.

My chest tightens.

"I just...I can't breathe." She sounds tired.

I clench my jaw. "You have to. I need to sleep, and you can't be free to stab me or run." I don't want to tell her I'm leaving, or she'll try extra hard to run.

Riley rubs her eyes. "Can you put me with Rachel?"

In the basement? Absolutely fucking not. It's not comfortable down there.

"Please?" Riley stands, her voice still just...tired.

I'm caught. I don't like the idea. In fact, I hate it, but

Riley is actually asking for something genuine. I try to dissuade her. "It won't be long."

Riley shakes her head. "Please don't make me."

"I'd have to cuff you."

Riley bites her lip. "Anything but upstairs."

There are no cameras in the basement. I used all of them for upstairs. Is she trying to get out from under my eye?

Riley doesn't push it. Just waits.

I'm going to regret this. "Fine."

There's no celebration this time. No kiss on the forehead. Riley just stands, waiting for me to lead the way.

"Can I get some water first?"

I motion impatiently at the kitchen, watching each movement as she grabs a glass, fills it with water, and then throws it back. While she does that, I grab something from my pocket and then grab an extra pair of cuffs. My feet move like they're in cement despite the fact I know I have every angle covered. Why does this have to be so hard? I can't trust Riley. I won't. Not right now. She's smart and cunning and beautiful and... fuck. Everything I've ever wanted by my side. So why won't she just...be by my side?

Rachel looks surprised to see us, but she doesn't say anything. I crouch down to attach Riley's ankle, but Riley holds out her wrist. "Please. It'll be more comfortable."

I eye her. She eyes me back.

But who am I kidding? I'll give my woman anything she wants that doesn't threaten her safety. I attach Riley's wrist to the same chain Rachel is on, then double-check that it's secure. I check the whole area Riley can reach, then pat both of them down. I slip my item into Riley's back pocket while checking her. Neither of them has anything.

I almost decide not to go. It's not worth it. Riley is behaving too much. But what is she going to do? She's secured to a metal pipe that's bolted to the floor. The chains are thick, and the cuffs are hinged. They're not breakable. And if she does manage to get away, where will she go? She has nothing. I have her girl. There's nowhere I, or the people in my club, can't reach.

And so I leave, setting off on this stupid adventure to win my woman's trust.

WOOF - FKA Rayne

I stashed a paperclip in the glass before Manson came upstairs. After he leaves, I take the clip out of my mouth as Rachel watches. Her eyes widen. "What are you doing?"

"What does it look like?" Manson is leaving. This is my chance.

"I don't think..." Rachel watches as I bend the end of the paperclip and insert it into the keyhole. Manson fucking double-locked them, which means they won't tighten anymore, but it also makes them harder to pick.

Rachel fidgets. "He's going to be mad."

"I'm okay with that." I focus as I work. That time on the couch pushed away some of the bad feelings for a bit, but they're back, buzzing around my head. I can't stop thinking about the mounted deer head on the wall and the bald patch on its fur. I hadn't remembered that. Now I wish I didn't.

"What did he do to you?" Rachel's voice is hesitant. "Manson."

So many things. But for some reason, all I can think about is him fucking me silly and always making sure I come. But there's more than that. He's always been in every detail of my life. So much so that I can't think of a time when he wasn't there. Well, I can, but all of those memories are bad. My life really turned around once he showed up.

I glance at Rachel, realizing I've been thinking about that 'do not think' list. Fuck! I try to cover my ass. "You mean besides being a giant dick and keeping both of us captive?"

Rachel narrows her gaze. It's like she can see through me, so I double down. "That should be enough, little deer. Feeling a bit of Stockholm?"

Rachel crosses her arms. "No. I just...why do you hate him so much?"

I frown. "Where do we start?" Where *do* I start? Shit, my no-no list has me all distracted. I clear my throat. "Manson stood up for my mom. He told me I couldn't kill her."

Rachel frowns.

Okay, yeah, there's the anger again. "He forced me to stay in their home until I was 18. Threatened me with the cops. Has obsessively stalked me, killed my fuck buddies, and told me who *I* can and can't kill. Namely, I can't kill anyone. Even if they deserve it." I fish the clip in deeper. "And he killed my dog."

My hands shake. Remembering Pup leaves a sour taste in my mouth. But, I feel the lock disengage on one side.

I glance up at Rachel, and she's looking at me with her mouth open.

I scoff, turning the paperclip the other way. "That surprises you? So he *is* getting into your head. I knew you were easy to manipulate, but damn."

At this point, I'm not sure if I'm talking to her or to me.

Rachel glares at me.

With some careful maneuvering, I hear the lock click on the other side. I slide my wrist free.

I need to hurry.

At the idea of leaving Rachel alone, I feel a twinge.

"Come with me." The words come out before I can process them.

Rachel's eyes dart to mine. I hold her stare.

"Come with me," I say again, meaning them to sound like a demand, but what comes out sounds more like a...request. An odd feeling fills me. Will she come? And even odder still, why do I want her to come?

What is happening to me?

Rachel holds my gaze with her dark one for so long that my stomach twists. Finally, she opens her mouth, her voice coming out soft, "Riley, I..." she trails off.

I stiffen. That wasn't a yes. My chest tightens, and rage washes over me. She's picking him? Him over me?

Betrayal fills me. Is she really that dumb? I back away.

"Riley, please." Rachel reaches out to me. "If you don't talk to him, you'll be stuck playing this game over and over. Always running!"

I stride over to the crawlspace under the house. My skin is hot. Why did I expect her to be different?

"Please, Riley!" She's pleading now. "Just talk to him."

"He can talk to my lawyer. Once I serve divorce paperwork." I move into the crawlspace, too angry to care about the dust and spiderwebs. There's a faint light coming from the far end of the house, where the opening is. It takes a few good kicks, but I knock it loose and crawl out, ignoring my gut as I leave Rachel behind.

Getting outside is not the elated feeling I expect it to be. It's just...empty.

I glance around to make sure Manson is gone, and when I don't see him, I dart toward the street. My house isn't far, and the morning is cool.

I jog to my house, finding the garage still open and unlocked. Instead of having fun, I'm empty.

I throw things around until I find my old iPad. Unlocking it, I dig into my social media. The farther I dig, the more I remember—things I didn't want to remember. They fill the empty void that's usually filled with anger, taking over my body. It gets so bad that my whole body starts shaking, and I have a hard time scrolling.

But I find them. Those three pieces of shit who stole my childhood. Who stole my humanity.

Sure, I may have been destined to be a heartless cunt since I was born (and don't get me wrong, I fucking love it), but they took without asking. They took my *choice*.

I tell myself I don't care, gathering my Glock and some other items. I wouldn't change who I am now, even if I had a choice.

But some tiny part of me wants to know what it would have been like to love and to be loved back, to feel something other than rage and emptiness.

I have no transportation here, but that's fine. As I walk back toward the road, I have to stop to puke. I'm so full of memories, and I can't get them out.

It's not long before an old farmer drives by, and I pull my half-mask over my nose and steal his truck. He looks shocked to see a gun in a woman's hands, let alone pointed at him.

Whoopsie. Misogyny is gonna cost you a Ram 1500.

As I drive toward my first target's house, my body hums with energy. I almost puke again as forgotten images rush through my head, and I try to shove them out. But it doesn't work. Eventually, the only thing that stops me from thinking about them is Manson's annoying, demanding voice saying I'm being reckless and I'm going to get caught.

As if. It's *me*. I never get caught.

My first target lives near Noel's old place. When I get to his house, a nice two-story red brick, I boot the door in. That action sucks a little bit of adrenaline back into my body. Immediately, a wash of cool air hits me, and I grin under my mask. Cool. I won't sweat my nuts off while stabbing him to death.

"Honey, I'm hooome." I saunter through the nice house. It smells like old people because, of course, it does. He would have aged twenty years since I last saw him.

Reckless. Be careful.

"Ready or not, here I come."

I fire off a round, the sound exploding in my eardrums, removing Manson's annoying voice. Maybe the old man will hear it and get good and scared for me.

I boot my way into the downstairs study, and suddenly, he is there. He's scrambling to get the window open. He's wearing an Oklahoma Sooners shirt and is fat with wispy white hair that doesn't cover his baldness.

I grin as he whirls on me. He gasps, "The fuck?"

I smile. "Not my name. Terrible guess."

"Get out of my house." My target frantically tries to open the window while still looking at me.

"Hmmm." I stop walking towards him and cock my head. "How about no?"

"Nancy!" the man screams.

"Well, that is definitely not my name." I point my gun at his leg and fire a round. He buckles, screaming.

"Gonna guess again?"

The man clutches his knee, screaming.

I roll my eyes. "Nope." I fire another round into his other leg.

I squat in front of him, watching in wonder as the wounds slowly get red with blood. Bullet wounds don't look like they do in the movies, especially from a smaller caliber gun. The entry wound is small and easy to miss. It's the exit wound that'll perk the clit.

If Rachel was here, I could explain all of this to her.

Anger fills me as I think about her. She could have been here to see this with me, but she chose not to. I lean into the rage, letting it take hold of me. It's much better than that empty numbness—the numbness lets the bad thoughts in.

"You remember me?" I sink down to the man's level. He's staring at his legs, eyes wide. He's in shock, probably not even feeling it after the initial fright.

"Let's play a game. You remember animal hide and seek?"

He turns his cloudy eyes up at me.

I grin. "You run and hide. I'll chase. Then we'll see what happens next, hmmm?"

The man makes a choked sound, rage filling his gaze. He tries to stand up but stumbles. I may have taken out some important muscles. Whoopsie.

I turn around, covering my eyes. "One. Two. Three."

I hear nothing behind me, and it annoys me. He's not playing the game. Fucking hell, I wish Rachel were here. I wish she was watching me with those big, pretty eyes full of horror. Horror and admiration.

"Ready or not, here I come." I turn around.

The man hasn't moved. Which just pisses me off. I grab him by the collar, yanking him forward so he falls on his hands. "Crawl, bitch."

That gets a reaction out of him. It's pain. I get a slight dose of pleasure watching him suffer, but it's ruined when he still doesn't move.

I glance around again, trying to imagine Rachel standing by the couch. But it's not doing it for me. I want her here. Now.

I kick the man's head in disgust. He just crumples.

My breathing picks up. This is not what I needed it to be! That shaking is back. Images of what this man did come one after another after another.

I stumble back, beating the side of my head, trying to break them free. They wouldn't be here if I had a distraction. If Rachel was watching, he'd just play my motherfucking game.

What I do from there is a blur. All I see is a lot of blood, and all I hear is a lot of ringing in my ear. The next thing I remember is being back in the car on my way to Manson's.

I won't let her ruin this for me. Rachel doesn't get to decide to just *not* come. She doesn't get to decide anything. She's *mine*, and I'll make her fucking remember. She's coming with me.

46

Dangerous State of Mind - Chri$tian Gate$

I make it to Dad's place. While I'm digging under the tree, I can't keep an odd feeling out of my head that Riley got away.

Impossible. It's impossible. I'm just being obsessive.

My shovel hits something hard. I dig more carefully, unearthing the skeleton.

Trust. I have to get her to trust me. And somehow, I have to trust her back?

I keep digging, carefully removing the skull. It's brown and dirty and frail. Rachel will fix it for me. I'll make her. This is actually disgusting.

What am I even doing?

What if Riley managed to get out? I can check on her without breaking trust.

I whip out my phone, checking her location with the tracker I slipped into her shorts.

What the fuck?

Jesus fucking *Christ*.

My wife is not at home.

My next moves are a blur. I throw everything in the truck and floor it toward her location.

When I find she's moved spots, my entire body is locked up. What happened? What is she doing?

I pull up my scanner for the area Riley's in. It's close to where Noel used to live, but it isn't his house. What is she doing? What could have brought her out there? I don't hear anything on fire traffic, which sends a bolt of relief through me. But when I switch to police, every single muscle I have tightens.

Need more units. Subject is 10-7. Dead.

What in the absolute fuck?

Riley's tracker has her moving away from the house and back to ours. I switch directions, flooring it to intercept her, but she must be fucking flying because by the time I get back, there's a car in the driveway, and Riley is leaning on the porch, covered in blood.

She's acting completely unharmed.

"It's locked." She looks at her nails, which are bloody.

I don't say anything to her. I can't, or I'll kill her right here. I simply unlock the door, and she tosses me a cheeky smile and goes inside herself. She marches straight down to where I want her to go: the basement.

"Rachel!" Riley snaps.

Rachel scrambles to her feet. She's still chained up, right where I left her. So how in the *fuck* did Riley get away?

"Did you think you could just...decide you're in charge?" Riley snatches Rachel up by her neck.

"I didn't—are you hurt?" Rachel looks between Riley, me, and the crawl space. So that's how she got out.

My phone dings.

"Riley," I bark. "Want to explain what *the fuck* you were doing?"

Riley looks manic, shoving her face in Rachel's. "When I say come, you come. When I say jump, you jump? Got it?"

Rachel looks afraid, and my phone dings again.

"Riley." I grab her shoulder and rip her back.

Riley still tries to get at Rachel. "You're mine, Rachel. You got that? You're fucking *mine*."

My phone dings again. "What?" I rip it out of my pocket. It's my cop contact. He's freaking out about something, I see Riley's name, and he sent some video clip.

I tap on it.

The video looks like it's been filmed from inside a bathroom. Then it pans up, and my heart stops.

There's Riley, standing in someone's office with a gun in her hand. She has a mask on, but I know it's her. Her two long braids run down her front, and her leg tattoos are visible under her shorts.

I can feel my heartbeat in my ears, the thump thump thump. In the video, Riley stomps on someone. At least, what used to be someone. All I see is a bloody mess of what used to be a head. Riley is laughing maniacally, crushing the pulp over and over.

For a second, I flash back to my mom.

Fuck, Manson. Focus.

I read the messages. The video has been posted all over social media.

I grip my phone so hard it hurts, and everything comes crashing down around me. This is everything I've tried to protect Riley from, everything I worked so hard to prevent.

"Are you okay?" Rachel's voice cuts through the fog.

I blink up at her. She's staring at me with concern on her face. Even Riley has turned.

"Is everything...okay?" My voice is low and dangerous. "Is it *okay*?"

I take a step forward, and Riley steps in front of Rachel, holding her hand out to block me. "Fuck off, Manson."

"Look." I shove the phone at them and let the video play. They watch in silence, but I can still hear the video. The manic laughter and the squishing sounds of the person's brain as Riley stomped any future she had into the ground. My hand is shaking the whole time, but I don't care.

The video stops, and Riley purses her lips. "I ruined my shoes."

With that one little comment, I lose my mind. I snatch Riley by the shoulders and shove her back until she slams into the basement wall just hard enough that she lets out a breath. She smiles up at me. "What's wrong?"

I grab her by the braids and yank her head back. I see the tears fill her eyes. "Riley." I swallow to keep my voice from shaking. "That's all over social media."

"I wore a mask, dumbass."

"You're recognizable." I give another sharp rip to the braids she branded her murder with. "You're all over the internet, Riley!" My voice gets higher. I'm so out of control right now, and I can't do anything about it.

"Send it to The Hunter's Club. They should accept my application now."

I lose it, my voice a yell, "I can't protect you from this!"

"I didn't ask you to!" Riley is finally screaming it at me. "I didn't fucking ask you to, Manson!"

I can't see straight. She's swirling in front of me.

I let go of her so I don't hurt her and step back, running my hand through my hair and pacing viciously. I can't...I don't know what to do. Riley looked so much like herself in that video; there's no plausible deniability. I can protect her from a lot of things, but when social media gets involved, there are certain things I can't erase from the public mind.

"Let me help." I register the words before I associate them with Rachel. I glance over at her.

"I'm a hairdresser. I can help." She crosses her arms.

I laugh bitterly. A haircut isn't going to solve this problem.

"I'll make her look different. We'll cut her hair off, bleach it, get her some glasses, and we'll erase her old social media accounts." Rachel motions at Riley.

I try to suck in a few breaths.

"You're not cutting my hair," Riley scoffs.

Rachel crosses her arms. "You left it out. So we have to cut it off."

"Fuck. That. You're not touching my hair."

And it's that reaction that changes my mind. Like fuck does Riley get to deny help. Especially when we're trying to save her from herself.

I nod at Rachel. "What do you need?"

Cold - Crossfade

Riley fights all the way up the stairs.

"You don't get to run my life, Manson!"

I'm beyond reasoning with her now. Rachel follows at a safe distance, and when we get to the kitchen, I throw Riley down on a chair. She tries to kick me in the gut, but I dodge it, sitting on top of her and trapping her blood-crusted legs under mine.

Rachel stands in the corner until I wrestle one of Riley's hands down and cuff it to the chair.

Riley screams at me, cussing me out relentlessly and calling me every name in the book. It's only when I get her other hand pinned down that she quiets, panting for breath.

I glance up at Rachel. She nods, approaching hesitantly. "What kind of style do you like?"

"If you touch my hair, I'll end you." Riley thrashes.

I expect Rachel to cower, but she just huffs. "Hair grows

back, Riley." She grabs Riley's two braids and pulls them back, undoing the ends.

"No!" Riley thrashes her head back and forth.

I dart my hand under her jaw, pressing her head back so far she's staring at the ceiling, baring her pretty little neck to me and forcing her to stop moving.

Rachel sighs, running her fingers gently through the braids to unravel them. "Where are your scissors, Manson?"

I glance up at her. They're all locked away. Outside. I mutter that and go get them. When I come back, Riley is glaring at the wall, and Rachel is trying to ask her questions.

"Pixie? Bob? Full shave? Talk to me."

"You can't just control everything I do."

I get ready to lay into her, but before I can, Rachel opens her mouth. "If you'd stop being a fucking child, you'd see he's doing this for your own good."

I freeze, but Rachel's not done. "In this particular moment, Manson's just trying to protect you. So why don't you just accept it and tell me what style you want your hair to be?"

I stare at Rachel. She's all frowns and pursed lips, with her hand on her hip while she glares at Riley. She's...agreeing with me? I know I'm right, but I've spent years with someone who fights me at every turn.

So this? This is different.

"Nothing? Cool, I'll do what I think looks best." Rachel holds out her hand to me, and the tension in my chest loosens. "Scissors."

For a half second, I pause. I'm giving a blade to the woman who, a few days ago, would have done anything to kill us.

Rachel gestures impatiently, then meets my gaze. She

seems to realize what I'm thinking because her face softens. "Just a haircut."

"Just a haircut."

I hand her the scissors, then sit on Riley's legs again. She glares up at me, and I tilt her head back, resting my hand on her neck. I smile down at her. "You're gonna look hot with short hair."

She curls her lip at me but doesn't fight my hold. I trace my thumb up and down her neck, watching as Rachel preps the scissors to make that first cut. I tense, just as Riley does under me.

With a snip, the first cut is done. Rachel works seamlessly from there, cutting, snipping, and giving silent orders to tilt her head one way or another. Which I do, even though Riley isn't fighting anymore.

I move my thumb up and down her neck, deciding Riley needs a neck tattoo. I want it to be my bite mark.

"Do you have any hair stuff?" Rachel asks me.

I shake my head.

"I'm thinking bleach blonde. Anything to make her look as different as we can."

Riley opens her mouth, but I glare down at her. "As different as possible, got it."

Riley arches a brow but says nothing.

"I don't have any of that box dye."

"Then you'll have to go get it." Rachel snips and cuts, taking Riley's hair from elbow length to a long pixie cut. I like it. It suits her face well.

I don't want to go. Not right after this. I don't want to leave them alone.

"Or I can get it." Rachel shrugs. "Doubt that's the better option for you."

I snort. I may trust her when I'm here, but definitely not

alone. She could lead the cops right back here. I have a lot of them in my pocket, but not all of them.

"Fine." I stand. "It won't be long. Don't get any ideas."

Riley groans. "Yes, Dad."

"I don't want to hear another word from you." I uncuff her and haul her up.

"Another word?" She smiles sweetly.

I swear to god, I'm going to kill this woman.

But the infuriating thing is, I won't.

My biggest flaw is that I will always pick Riley. Always. And I've been the only one to do that her whole life.

But as I glance over at the woman beside her, I wonder if maybe I'm not the only one anymore.

"Upstairs." I bring both of them to the locked room I have. "I'll be back in twenty minutes. Try not to kill anyone else."

RILEY

48

I Wish a Bitch Would - Delilah Bon

I'm fuming.

And when I fume, someone usually ends up dead.

Manson locked us in the room, and I've been counting down the minutes since he's been gone. Not only does my head feel oddly lighter, but my entire body is buzzing on this strange sort of high. It's like a rage high, and it makes me want to laugh every time Rachel looks at me funny.

She tries to shove me in the shower, which I accept only because I want to say something to her. When the water is on and steaming, I jump under it with all my clothes on, yanking Rachel after me.

"Riley!"

"Rachel," I mock, slamming her into the shower wall. "Oh, hello, little deer. I think you forgot some rules."

She struggles under me, her soft body writhing, which

307

only turns me on. I tighten my fist in her clothes. "I make an order, and you follow it. Got it?"

"Riley, I–"

"What is it with you two and your incessant need to wear out my name?" I curl my lip at the thought of how close she is to Manson. Like they're best buds now. "You're coming with me."

Rachel turns her pretty eyes on me. "Where?" she spits. "We're stuck here."

I cock my head. "Are we, Rachel? Or are you just saying that because you want to kiss Manson's ass again?"

Rachel glares at me. "There's a difference between ass kissing and common fucking sense! Your hair had to go!"

I bark a laugh. "This isn't about my hair, Rachel. So here's how this is going to go. I'm going to leave. You're going to follow me. No questions asked."

"What?" She blinks falling water out of her eyes.

"I just said no questions asked." I shove away from her.

"No, you can explain to me what we're doing." Rachel follows after me. "Tell me what you're doing, or you're just as bad as Manson!"

I snort, getting out of the shower. I'm dripping wet, but I need to get this buzzing out of my system. Killing that man didn't help, and I can only assume it's because the other two are still breathing.

Not for long.

I march out into the bedroom. It's been just long enough that if Manson is going to town, he's in the middle of nowhere, with spotty service. I cover up the cameras so he can't see what I'm doing.

For a fleeting second, I want him to see it. I want him to see and stop me. To wrap me up in those strong arms and get rid of all the chaos floating in my head.

But that would mean Manson would win, and he could look down on me and pity me. I think if I could be afraid of anything, it would be that.

Rachel follows me, wrapping up in a towel as I glance out the window and then estimate the spacing of the studs in the wall. Her eyes get wide as I turn and donkey-kick the drywall.

It breaks with the first kick.

Rachel sucks in a breath but says nothing. I turn and rip out chunks of the drywall, yanking on the insulation and ripping it out with my hands. Thankfully, the studs are two feet across, so there will be no problem squeezing between them.

A flashback fills my mind, and then I remember the taste of the grape popsicle. Those were always my favorite.

I dry heave.

"That'll hurt later," Rachel deadpans.

I hope it fucking does.

I turn to kick through the remaining wall. This one is harder, with the siding also holding it in. But the taste of grape flavoring fills my mouth, and I want anything other than that taste. I kick harder and harder, over and over.

"You got it," Rachel's voice is bored.

I glance around. Sure enough, there's a hole to the outside.

Elation fills me. Manson will not win.

"Let's go." I motion at Rachel.

She crosses her arms. "This is the second story."

"Yeah, and while we're stating facts, the sky is blue."

"Not always."

"Jesus, Rachel," I whirl on her. "You're coming with me, even if I have to throw you out of here."

She shakes her head. "Why do you hate Manson, Riley?"

Not this right now. I can't fucking do this. I start toward her.

"Let me get dressed!" She moves to the dresser and throws me a change of clothes. "Here. If we're going to murder someone, at least don't wear the same clothes you wore to the last one, for the love of God."

I glare at her.

She gets dressed quickly, and I frown at her, but I also switch out my clothes. She picks out pants, which is an abomination, but she glares at my tattoos. She also makes me switch shoes, so thank god Manson is a maniac planner and has multiple outfits and choices in this room.

When she's standing beside me at the hole, she mutters, "You hate Manson because he gives you no choice, but you do the same thing for me." She turns her angry gaze on me. "So fuck you, Riley Kennedy. Fuck you."

RACHEL

49

Cacao and Cocaine - Sofia Isella

I've had it with these two. Absolutely had it. They're the most stubborn, blind people on this planet. Stubborn, blind, and dangerous. And I'm forced to go along with it.

After we dropped out of the wall, Riley grabbed a truck key from the bushes in the front yard and put me in a truck I know she doesn't own. And because I'm pissed, I do the only thing I can do—I cross my arms, face away from her, giving her the silent treatment.

My head is a confusing place. Despite everything, it was hot to watch a soaked Riley literally break through a wall while claiming me. Her nipples were visible through her shirt, and her eyes were so angry they made me wet.

And that's when I decided I needed therapy. Lots and lots of fucking therapy. In fact, I don't think I should ever leave the office.

"Who are we killing now?" I ask it harshly. It's meant to

distract me from thoughts of Riley's nipples. To remind me that she's absolutely insane. That we're most likely on our way to murder someone.

Riley doesn't answer me for a while, which does great at pissing me off. But when she does speak, I immediately swallow. "My green armchair, Rachel."

I glance over at her. She still looks pissed. At least, I think she's pissed. She's frowning and looking straight ahead. Then, she says softly, "At least, one of them."

There was more than one? Against my will, my throat tightens.

Riley glances over at me, and she looks like she's going to be sick. "Talk to me, Rachel. I need a distraction."

The vulnerable look in her eyes is probably manipulation. I don't know enough about people to tell. But it tugs at me anyway, and I glower. "What do you want to talk about?"

"Anything. Anything, please, just something."

She's gripping the steering wheel so tight her fingers are white.

"I, uh...how do you like your hair?"

I wince. That was smooth. But I think the cut suits her face. Her jaw cuts out in a pretty line and is much more visible now, and I think I did a good job, considering my scissors were dull as fuck, and her hair was coated in blood.

Riley laughs roughly. "If you ever do that again, I'll kill you. You know that, right?"

"I know." I stare out the window. Manson's going to be so upset that we're gone. He left at my suggestion. "You'll have to beat Manson to it."

"You mean your buddy?" Riley glares at me.

"He's not my buddy." I shake my head.

"Sure he isn't."

"Listen. I'm just trying to survive, okay?"

"I told you I'd keep you safe. What part of that did you not believe?"

I glance over at her. She looks back at me before glancing back at the road. Her voice gets so low I barely hear it. "I couldn't keep myself safe. But now...now I can at least keep you safe."

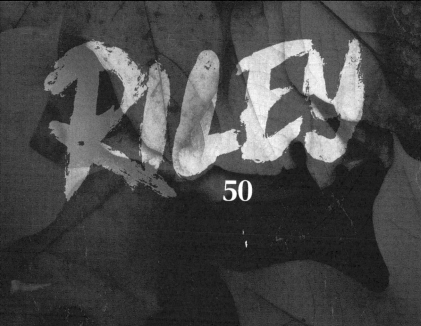

50

A GOOD DAY TO DIE - *Arankai*

When we get close, Rachel starts asking all kinds of questions about where we're going and who we're getting. At first, it pisses me off, and I snap at her that I don't need more judgment. She just waves me off. "Planning, Riley. We're planning."

I stare at her. She's just going to...go along with it?

Rachel looks at me expectantly. "Riley. What kind of house is it?" She looks earnest. "And do we have masks?"

I blink. "It's not a house. It's an assisted living home."

Rachel's eyes shutter for a second, then she's back. "Well. How convenient. I've spent a lot of time in those."

She's overthinking this, but I realize that her talking has pushed the sick feeling to the back of my mind.

"Right." She picks at her nails. "So there's cameras everywhere, but not in the rooms. There will be medical masks we can wear at the front door. But..." she trails off. "We aren't family or on their visitor's list."

I shrug. "Sure we are. We're his nieces."

She darts a look at me. "I don't have an unc..." She catches my drift a little late.

I smile. She's cute. "Leave the lying to me, sweety. I'll get us in there."

Turns out, I don't need to lie. We just follow behind a woman going into the building. She gives us a quick glance and lets us in.

No one expects women to be killers. Whoops. That'll cost you a life.

Rachel made me wear my other mask in addition to the medical one she grabbed for me. I roll my eyes, but I humor her.

She's cute when she gets huffy.

She also grabs us medical gloves from a nurse's cart and forces me to put them on. Fucking bustling around like a mother hen. This isn't my first murder.

It's my third. No thanks to Manson. He can be my fucking fourth.

My next target is sleeping in his room when we get there. Rachel shuts the door softly behind us, and the smell of rancid breath is locked in the room with us. It's a small, dark room.

Rachel crosses her arms, leaning against the door and muttering, "There is no way we're not going to get caught."

I laugh, pecking her forehead through my masks. "Come here."

"No." She's stiff. "Please. Just do what you're going to do and...let's go."

"Now now." I grab her hand and pull her with me into the dark room. "How else are you going to learn?"

"Learn?" She hisses. "I don't need to learn–" but she stops talking as I round the bed of the man. I look down on his face, and suddenly, I see him over me with a grotesque sneer on his face. I'm frozen for a second, caught in the memory.

The smell of bad breath breaks me out of it. "Come here," I demand roughly.

I don't hear Rachel obey, but I can't take my eyes off the man. He's so frail now. Why didn't I kill him back then? Why didn't I stand up for myself?

A small hand slides into mine and squeezes. I look down, and Rachel is staring at the man. Her face is pale, making her dark lashes stand out against her creamy skin. In this moment, in the dim light, she's so stunningly beautiful it almost takes my breath away.

I stand there, staring at her until she glances up at me.

My heart squeezes, and I suck in a breath, looking away. What the hell was that...thing squeezing my chest?

I glance around. I need to focus, and I need something to keep him quiet. I find socks in his drawer and stuff them into his open mouth.

The man stirs, coughing.

I wink at Rachel, who is still standing close, pulling a knife out of my back pocket. "Want to see what a dick looks like away from the body?"

I lean down into the man's face. He's sputtering awake, and I yank the covers and then his pants down. Seeing his body fills me with disgust. I should have killed this disgusting piece of shit back when I had a chance.

The man fights me, but he's old and confused. I slice his dick off with a few saws. It's hard to get a hold of since it's so small and shriveled.

That's when the screams start. And they sound so, so

good. I turn with the dick, grinning at Rachel. She blinks slowly. I start to wave it in her face, just to get a good reaction out of her, when I drop it.

Fucking hell.

I bend down to get it, and as I glance back up, I see the man swinging a large item at Rachel's head. She doesn't see it; she's just watching me with the dick in my hands with a horrified expression.

I dart back up in time to catch the blow on my shoulder. The impact rocks through me, and rage lights inside me. This fuck was trying to hit my woman?

I think the fuck not. My vision goes blurry with more anger than I've felt all day. I whirl, ripping the thing—a Bible —out of the man's hand. He tries to stop me, but there is no stopping me now. I raise it up and beat him down with it, hitting first his head, then his arms, then anything I can reach. All I see is hit after hit after hit. I want to see him bleed. I want to see him suffer. No one touches my woman.

There's a tiny weight on my back, and I realize Rachel's yelling in my ear. "Riley! Riley stop. Riley, please."

I heave in a breath enough to make sure he isn't going to move, then dare a glance at her.

"He's dead. Please, let's go," she pleads.

I stare at her, then back at him. I can still recognize him. I haven't done enough.

"Riley!" She rips at me again. "The more blood there is, the harder it'll be to get away. Please!" She sounds desperate.

I catch her face in my hands, forcing her to look at me. "I won't let you get caught. It's okay."

"Then please, let's go." She looks up at me with the biggest eyes. She looks so vulnerable and pretty.

"Fine." I drop another masked kiss on her forehead. "Whatever the little deer wants."

But as we walk away, I can't help but feel there's something still missing from this one. My chest feels...empty.

Is it because there's still one more kill? Because Noel's still out there?

It's been awfully quiet. There's no bossy voice in my ear telling me what to do. No annoyed looks coming from across the room. No silent force watching my back. No strong mountain keeping me safe.

I shake my head. That's ridiculous. I can't be wanting Manson, right?

Right. It's just that I have one more kill. One more, and then my heart will stop turning flips in my chest, and finally, *finally,* I'll be safe.

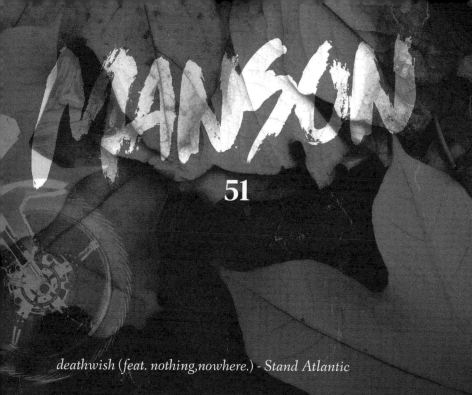

51

deathwish (feat. nothing,nowhere.) - Stand Atlantic

It didn't take me long to see that Riley had covered all the cameras. Which is never a good thing.

What the hell is she still trying to do? Why is she so frantic to leave? Clearly, I've missed something. Something important.

So I do what I've been avoiding this whole time. I make a call to the jail.

It doesn't take long to get the information I wanted, and that information makes me pull over to the side of the road and empty my stomach of everything that was in it.

I missed it. Somehow, I missed it. For years, I pushed her, held her down, and forced her to submit. I knew everything I could know about my wife, but I somehow missed this.

I couldn't keep her safe. It doesn't matter that it happened before I knew her. I couldn't avenge her.

And now she's trying to do it alone. Unprepared.

I find the locations of the other two men. I don't know which one she's picking next, but I go for the closest one.

I pull into town, drive around for a bit, and then find them just outside town, parked at a roadside stop, eating McDonald's chicken nuggets. Or, Rachel is. Riley's just watching her with an unreadable expression.

I don't yell. I don't shout or throw them over my shoulder. I'm numb.

The significance of how badly I failed hits me. I'm usually numb when I'm not around Riley, but this sort of numbness is so much deeper. It's like my whole brain is empty.

I couldn't protect the one woman I've been obsessed with my whole life. The woman who always has something interesting to say. The woman who never gives in to me. The woman who always makes me mad.

But I can't even get mad now. There's just...nothing there.

I just sit next to them on the tailgate. Rachel offers me a chicken nugget, and I take it.

We're all silent, just watching the wind whip over the harvested field. Watching the sun as it gets close to setting.

I don't want to talk to her. My chest tightens at the thought. Will she mock me? Laugh at me like she always does?

Fuck it. I failed her and, by proxy, myself.

I know she won't listen to me. She never has, but I feel like I have to at least say it. Finally, I open my mouth. "The day you tried to kill your mom, there were cameras recording your every move."

A bird flies across the sky, slow and unhurried. Riley says nothing.

"I would have bought the cops out for you, Riley. But I

knew there would eventually be a day I wouldn't be able to do that, and I wanted you to learn how to do it right."

The wind whips the warm smell of baked grasses into our faces.

"Everything I've done, I did to protect you. I kept you from the life I lived because I didn't want you to be..." I trail off as I squint at the setting sun. "Me."

The silence is heavy. It sits heavily on my shoulders, pressing down so I can't breathe.

I jump off the truck's tailgate and move to mine. My boots in the gravel are the only sound. When I get what I need from my truck, I walk it over, leaving it on the spot I was sitting in.

"I never killed Pup, Riley. I did kill the neighbor who killed him, though. And I won't apologize for that."

I stare at the skull on the tailgate in the setting sun. I don't look at Riley. Because I know if I do, I'll grab her up and take away her choice. History will just repeat itself, and I'll lose my woman completely. The last few days with her shoving me out have been some of the worst of my life. So I do the hardest thing I've ever done.

"Meet me at home, wife."

And then, I turn and walk away.

RACHEL

52

sorry im a haunted house - Savage Ga$p, KAMAARA

We don't go home. Riley is completely silent at our next stop. She makes me wait in the car, but I hand her the gloves and my medical mask. She takes them without a word.

I'm exhausted and overstimulated, so I sit there, staring at the dash.

Riley protected me. She got in the way of a blow that was meant for me. And damn if that didn't make my whole entire body feel warm. For the first time since I was a kid, I felt...safe.

I swallow around the lump in my throat.

When Riley comes back, I don't even question it when she dumps a limp body in the back of the truck.

We drive back in silence. I don't miss the fact that Riley has brought the skull up to the front seat.

"I'll clean that for you."

Riley just nods.

"You know that's not a dog...right?" Am I missing something?

Riley just gives me a look. She looks off, and I stiffen.

She goes back to looking at the road.

Oh fuck. I overstepped.

As I stew in the silence, I realize that Riley and Manson had the conversation I've been needing them to have the whole time. I can tell they're going to work things out. It'll take a bit, but they'll work things out.

Which, I realize with horrifying clarity, makes me obsolete.

They don't need me anymore.

MANSUN

53

Heavenly Bodies - Arankai

Meet me in the backyard. 10 mins

54

Barbie & Ken - Scene Queen, Set it Off

I check the phone that I stole from my third mark. It's been nine minutes, and Manson hasn't responded to my message. Which, I suppose, is only fair. I had never responded to his all those years ago.

"Fuck." I put the phone back in my pocket, strangely unsettled. I can't even deny that I care about him responding to me.

Fuck me running. I care.

I pace back and forth, and Rachel gives me a look. "You okay?" She's been quiet all evening. I assume she's just tired. I have to remember she's new to killing. But it'll be okay. I'll get her used to it.

"I'm fine." There's still no text. I wring my hands. Clearly, I'm dying. I fucking care if Manson Kennedy leaves me on read.

Someone take me out. And not on a date. I will never

recover from this.

The sun is completely down now, but I turned on the maze, and all the lights are flickering, and the animated voices are cackling: *Ready or not, here I come.* The scarecrow at the front of the maze looks down on us in a manic glare.

I set my mark loose in the maze after I gave him some acid and cut his Achilles. I don't think he'll be going far, but I'm not antsy to test that.

That emptiness is starting to surround me. It feels like I've dropped something and I can't find the last piece. I *hate* that feeling. I fucking hate it.

I'm about to turn around and give up when I see headlights cut into the lot. Against my will, my stupid heart picks up, racing in my chest.

It's hard to see in the dim light with the lights pointed right at me, but as the vehicle stops, I squint. I see the door open, and then a tall figure jumps out.

The figure stalks toward us with all the good-naturedness of a lion.

Yep. That's him. All angry and pissed and fucking *him.*

I grin. Oh fuck it all to hell; warmth is tingling across my skin. I look over at Rachel.

She's giving me a look that I can't quite interpret and don't have a chance to before Manson's presence is there, big and heavy and somehow loud, despite not saying anything.

He stops right in front of me, tattooed arms crossed, staring down at me.

I lift an eyebrow, knowing it's killing him that he has no idea why he's here. I let him sweat for a second, watching the pulse pounding in his neck.

Finally, Manson's eyes flash, and he growls, "Where at?"

"What?" I flash him a tiny smile.

He grinds his teeth. "Where do you need the hole? I'm assuming that's why you called me? To dig it for you?"

Oh, he thinks I kept him out of the fun. I put on a bored look, examining my fingernails. "Well, considering he can still climb out of it, it's probably gonna need to be deep. So maybe out behind the field."

There's silence for a second.

Manson's voice gets dangerous. "Riley. Is he still alive?"

"Winner winner, chicken dinner." I throw a look at Rachel. "I'll get chicken *nuggets* for you, bambi."

"Where at?" Manson's hand is around my throat before I can blink.

I grin. There's the man I hate so much. "Somewhere in here. You took long enough to get here, so I don't know exactly–"

"Riley!" Manson shakes me, and I moan. The way he handles me is raw power and sex and everything that gets me off. I glance at him to find his green eyes pinned on mine. They're usually dead, but right now, I see a flash of conflict. He squeezes harder, making the edges of my vision darken.

"You drive me crazy, you know that, little pain?" Then he leans down and kisses me. It's a deep kiss, harsh and demanding. He works my mouth open, then bites down on my tongue so hard I try to jerk away. He just yanks me closer, growling into my mouth and pressing so hard my lips burn. It's like he's trying to brand me as his.

I pant through my nose until he finally lets me up for air. When he does, he snaps his gaze to the side.

"You." His body jerks, and I stumble toward him. Before I know it, he's yanked Rachel to my side with his other free hand. "You let her do this?"

Rachel sucks in a breath.

I open my mouth to defend her, but she speaks up first. "If you can't tell Riley what to do, how do you expect it to work for me?"

I jerk to get out of Manson's grip so I can deck him before he hits my woman, but he just throws his head back and laughs. The laugh is deep, throaty, and the first time I've heard it in...forever.

I just stare at him. Is he okay?

Manson lets us go and pulls a gun from the back of his waistband. For a brief second, I think he's going to use it on Rachel, but he just checks that it's loaded and keeps it pointed at the ground. "Whoever finds him gets him."

He glances at Rachel, then pulls a knife out of his pocket and, to my complete shock, gives it to her. "Use this on either of us, and I'll braid your intestines while you're still alive." He winks at her, then turns back to me. "I should get a head start since I'm at a disadvantage."

I almost have to shove my mouth shut. Who is this Manson? Where's the lecturing? The bitching?

He just looks at me. "Oh, don't worry. I have a lot to say when this is done, and you're going to sit and listen to every word while Rachel dyes your hair whatever fucking color it takes to undo this shit."

I swallow. He looks just like the Manson I've always known. The annoying brother, the overbearing fucking dick, and the man who killed my dog. But...he didn't. He killed the person who did, and that brings a warmth to my chest that I didn't think my dead heart was capable of feeling.

As I look at him, Manson rolls his eyes and shoves past me. "Finders keepers, Riley."

I snap out of it, darting after him. "You break it, you buy it! I broke it; it's mine."

Manson just shoves me out of the way, making me stumble into the corn. Oh, this fucker wants to be a dick? I jump up, grinning, and chase after him.

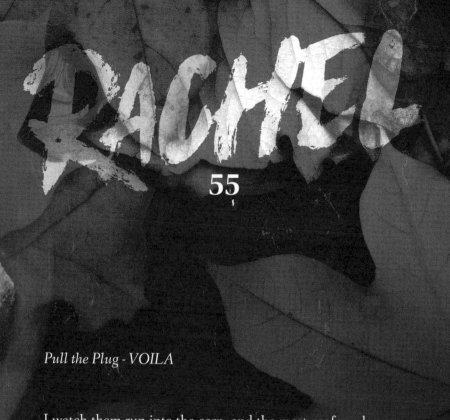

55

Pull the Plug - VOILA

I watch them run into the corn, and the most profound sense of loneliness washes over me. I see the love those two look at each other with. Well, it's not love. It's a fucked up mix of possession, protectiveness, hate, and loyalty.

And I want it.

And if that doesn't scare the living piss out of me, I don't know what will. Fucking hell, get me into a therapist. Right fucking now. Because I'm feeling left out of a murderous duo.

Despite myself, I find my feet following them. I'm gliding on my tiptoes, and I shuck my shoes off and keep going. I feel the earth under my toes, just like I wanted to do when I first came to this maze.

I should go. I absolutely should go. Run and not look back. They won't want me. They have each other. That's why they needed me all along, right?

But I'm still running over the earth, following them. I cut

out of the maze into the rows of uncut corn. The dry leaves are whispering in the hot wind, and I smell the acidic dirt.

I hear shouts and veer toward them.

I'll run. I will. I just need to see this last one out.

For my papa's sake.

There's a scream close by, and I slow, peeking around. There are no lights in this part of the field, but my eyes have adjusted.

There's a crash of corn and a bloodcurdling scream. It's followed by a gleeful laugh. It's Riley.

"What's my name, little pincushion?"

"I found him first."

There's another scream, and I inch closer. I see them then. Manson and Riley stand around a man on the ground. He's gripping his side, heaving for breath.

Riley kicks him. "I asked you a question."

"Riley," the man pants.

I see the flash of her teeth as she grins. "Wooow. Better than Sooners."

I watch as Manson and Riley stalk around him like predators. They look completely in their element—powerful, unfeeling, and dangerous.

Even though I know them, it makes a shiver run down my spine. Which makes my pussy wet.

The man tries to crawl away, and Manson steps quietly on his hand, making him moan. "My wife was talking to you. It's rude to walk away."

Riley's grin widens as she stares down at the man. "You're pretty bad at hide and seek, fuckhead. Which is ironic 'cause it was your idea to play."

He moans, and she jerks her hand down toward him. I notice the flash of a blade as she pulls it back toward her. She stabbed him.

She looks so wild like this. So powerful and...free. And I fucking love it. It makes my stomach do flip-flops. I realize with a start that she looks like everything I wanted when I was a kid. Both of them do. Someone to protect me. Someone to be the confidence I needed.

Suddenly, Riley looks up. She looks around her like she's looking for something. Her dark eyes pierce the corn.

My body tenses. I should run. I should go now before she catches me.

But against all reason, I don't.

Riley's gaze locks with mine. Instantly, the lines on her face relax.

Manson drives a kick into the man's ribs as he tries to run. "Where's Rachel?"

The energy in Riley's gaze is electric. I feel the connection run up and down my arms, making goosebumps run over my skin. Eye contact has always been hard. Scary. But with Riley? It's fireworks. Still scary, but there's a thrill to it.

Riley holds my gaze as she smirks. "I'm sure she's around."

Manson glances up, right at me. Slowly, his mouth quirks up in an evil smile.

Manson and Riley go back and forth, taking turns toying with the man. They work seamlessly as a team, working to maneuver him between them and stringing him along. I know they could kill him quickly, but they don't.

My throat tightens. I can't take my eyes away. It's like a beautiful ballet. Their bodies are lithe and powerful. They both make my stomach do flips. Even Riley. Especially Riley.

So maybe I'm a *little* gay. Or maybe a lot gay. I'm not sure it even matters anymore.

As I watch them torture a man, my chest tightens as multiple emotions swim through me. I struggle with myself for a minute. It's not the torture that's confusing. Suddenly, it hits me that it's sadness I'm feeling.

I never got to get my justice. It was ripped from me in the most undramatic, slow way possible. I always used to tell myself I didn't care. That at least he was gone, and that's all that mattered. But maybe I do care.

I care enough that Riley getting her justice makes my throat tighten in something that's a mix of sad but mostly something happy.

I swallow down the tears.

The man stops moving after a while. I know he isn't dead yet 'cause they've now begun a competition to see who can wake him up.

That's when I know I need to go. It'll be over soon, and then they won't be distracted. I need to be gone. They won't bother much to chase me down. They know I won't say a word. I know what they're capable of. Fuck, Manson knows where my mom lives.

But beyond that, I wouldn't say a word anyway. It's gotta be Stockholm, but I get it. I really get it. Riley's just hurt, and Manson tries to protect her. She doesn't deserve to be in jail. I don't want her to be in jail. Either of them.

I take a step back, and my chest tightens. The dirt digs between my toes, grounding me.

I take a deep breath. I can do this.

I turn, and I run.

The only place I have to go is back to my house. I find my shoes at the edge of the maze and run. It's a long way back to town, but I don't want to steal their car and give them another reason to chase after me. So, I run until someone picks me up and drives me back home.

Every second I'm gone, my body feels tight. I feel tight. When I make it back to my house, my front door isn't locked, and when I open it, I find pieces of the door jamb on the floor. It must have been from when they took me the first time.

I shut it behind me, even though it's meaningless. Dawn is just starting to poke through, casting meager light into the house. My Halloween decor is still up, and all it makes me think about is Riley.

No. Fuck. Bad. I have to forget her. Forget either of them existed and go back to being me.

My throat is tight again. I'm both extremely wired and bone-achingly exhausted. I check my bedside table, finding just two sleeping pills left in my bottle. I'm about to take them when my eyes lock on the mouse skull sitting on the table.

I stop. My eyes well up with tears, and this time, some of them spill over.

No! Fuck, no.

I pop the last two pills in my mouth and fall into bed, trying my best to keep the rest of the sobs locked in. I got what I wanted. Right? I'm alive, and I'm home. Everything I could have ever wanted. Right?

It's quiet in here. So quiet. There's no passion, no battle of wills, no nothing. That used to be a comforting thing. But now, all I feel is empty and unsettled.

This isn't right. I can't possibly want two serial killers. It's just the Stockholm. I'll get over it in what...a day? A week? A few weeks?

It feels like an eternity. I toss on my bed, suddenly bitter. How dare they do this to me?

How fucking dare they? I slip into a fitful sleep.

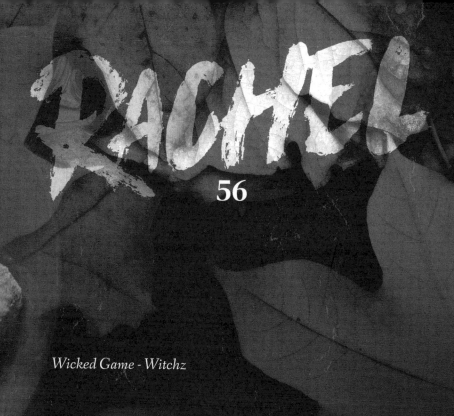

56

Wicked Game - Witchz

When I wake up, something isn't right. I'm groggy, and I feel like...I'm sitting up.

I shake my head, looking around. It's dark, and I'm in the back of a car.

"Oh, our little intrigue is awake."

The grumbly voice makes realization come crashing in.

It's Manson.

I scramble upright as I meet his gaze in the rearview mirror. Only, this time, he has the same mask and helmet on as when I first met him. He looks cold and harsh, his eyes barely glinting behind the mask.

There's movement to my right, and I look over and see Riley there. She's back in her cop uniform, with the half mask over her mouth.

I squeeze my eyes shut. They came to kill me. To kill me because I ran.

And that thought makes me mad.

"You thought you could get away, Rachel?" Riley's voice is soft. It's the deceptively soft sound, where she lulls you into complacency, then pounces. It makes goosebumps prickle across my skin, and the blood rush to my pussy.

Fucking hell! I shouldn't be getting turned on right before I die.

We pull into Riley's place, and the sight hits me with unexpected nostalgia and then anger. I'm nothing more than one of their marks. And after I caught feelings? How embarrassing.

Manson pulls up to the back door and then jumps out of the car. He pops my door open. "You have thirty seconds to run." His voice is slightly muffled, and it comes out lower than normal.

I give him my meanest death glare. He gives it right back, looking down through the mask like he might just pound me into the car right here. I realize again just how big of a person he is.

So I run. I dart into the house and shut and lock the door. Manson doesn't come here much, and Riley spends all her time in the barn, so I have at least a partial chance. As I scramble through the hall, I dart to the kitchen to look for weapons.

I'm shivering in anger.

How dare they do this to me? Treat me like this?

As I dig through drawers, I find a knife. Gripping it, my vision clouds over with tears, and my hand shakes.

Get it together, Rachel.

I know this house is trapped, so I dart carefully up the stairs and to the one room I know is safe. Riley's room.

A deafening bang comes from downstairs, and I stifle a

scream. Whirling, I back into the wall and face the door, the knife still in my hand.

I glance down at it, heaving for breath. I don't think I can use this on them. Either one of them. Even the idea of swinging it at them makes me sick.

There's another bang, and then I hear racing footsteps.

"Ready or not, here we come."

"Move, dickhead. She's mine."

There's scrambling, and my heart races. My hand shakes, and I feel sick. I can't kill them. I can't.

What sounds like a gunshot goes off, followed by Riley's laughter. It's a belly laugh, and I realize that Riley sounds...happy.

It makes my stomach flutter.

But I hear multiple footsteps on the stairs, and I stiffen before the door is booted open.

I scream, darting to the corner. Manson and Riley shoulder in, their masked faces immediately turning to me.

"Rach," Riley cocks her head, the edges of her eyes crinkling. "You're kinda bad at hiding."

I hold out the knife, hands shaking so bad I know they see it. "Fuck you, Riley."

She laughs. "And to think, I used to think you were meek. Come here." She darts at me, and I jump onto the bed to get away from her. But that only puts me closer to Manson.

"Don't! Get away!" I wave it at him. "I'll stab you!" As soon as the words are out, they sound like a lie, even to me.

"He'll just get off on it. Don't waste your time." Riley pounces on me, dragging me down into the bed.

I scream, dropping the knife, only for Manson to sweep it up and away from me. Riley pins me to the bed, dropping her hips on mine and trapping my wrists under hers. She heaves for breath, looking down at me. "Got you."

"Get off me!" I scream, bucking my hips, but she's strong. And that only sends a jolt of sensation to my pussy. I'm trapped.

And fuck, I like it. All the emotions bubble up in me and boil in my chest. Only this time, I feel my eyes welling with tears that I can't stop. Soon, they come rolling down my cheeks against my will. I squeeze my eyes shut, trying to control my breathing.

"Oh, crying already?" I feel Riley's masked face nudge the side of my head, nestling into my hair. "We're just getting started."

I catch a whiff of her shampoo, the one I used to get the blood out of her hair, and for some odd reason, it just makes me cry harder.

"Rachel." Riley groans, grinding into me. "You know I'm a sadist, right? This only gets me off more."

But I can't stop. Horrible, ugly sobs are taking over my body, and there's nothing I can do about it.

Because I found the strength and the protection I've always wanted, and now it's going to be ripped from me.

"It's not fucking fair!" I try to rip my hands out from under Riley, managing to get one partially loose before she snatches it up again.

Suddenly, Riley is shoved off me, and Manson is there. I scramble to get away, but he just drops his weight over me. He's bigger and much heavier, and it's like I'm being suffocated under a blanket of water. His mask falls into my face. All the weight is pressing into me evenly, and suddenly, all I can focus on is my breathing because there's nothing else I can do—in and out and in and out.

"Hey! I found her first."

"Give her a minute." I hear Manson's rumble.

I suck in breath after breath, trying to come up with

something to say, but I can't. I find myself relaxing into him, getting one last taste of what it's like to be with them before I can't anymore.

Finally, Manson shifts, and when he does, I feel that he's hard. He lets off just enough that I can see both of them. Both have taken off their masks, and they're staring at me with those dead eyes.

My face burns. Why do they have to look at me?

"Rachel," Manson's voice is low and unhurried. "You ran."

I squeeze my eyes shut. Here is where they kill me. This is it. They'll kill me because I defied them.

But both of them are silent. They're silent for so long. I only know they're still there by Manson's body on me and Riley's soft breaths on my skin.

"Just kill me and get it over with," I mutter.

Riley snorts.

I snap my gaze open. She wants to mock me? I open my mouth to yell at her, and her eyes spark in excitement.

I snap my mouth shut.

"Oh, come on, bambi. Play with me," she pouts.

"Play with you?" I sputter. "Play with you? Really? After all this time that you've been playing with me? With my life and my..." I stop. I was about to say my heart, and that would sound horrendously stupid.

Riley opens her mouth, but Manson growls, "Feelings, Riley. Play nice."

Play nice? Play fucking nice? My face burns with embarrassment, and I buck into him. I want to get away. Have to get away. I can feel their eyes burning into me, seeing me, seeing my struggle, and I hate it. I fucking hate it. I struggle until I'm panting. Manson hasn't even budged.

"Yeah, he sucks like that." Riley looks at her nails. "If you want something, he'll lean in extra hard. Feel free to kick him in the nuts for me."

I just stare at her. She picks at her index finger. "Now you've got me picking at my nails, bambi. Gonna have to get you to kick that habit so I can kick mine."

I blink. What in the ever-living hell is going on?

"Are you...going to kill me?" I can't keep the question back any longer.

Riley and Manson share a look. Riley's pretty eyes lock back on mine. "Uh, no? What the hell, Rachel? You thought we were going to kill you?"

My heart starts racing again, and I glance between the two of them. "Isn't that what you've been saying this whole time?" I can't help the screech in my voice.

"Well, I mean, yeah, we're gonna fuck you within an inch of your life, but we won't actually kill you, Rachel."

I still can't understand. They aren't going to kill me?

Manson leans up a little more. Just enough to trap both of my hands in his one and trail the other down my chest. He runs a finger down to my breasts, turning one in circles around my nipple.

"Why?" I gasp.

Riley cocks her head. "Well, to start, you're mine. Why would I want to get rid of something I've worked so hard to keep alive?"

"Ours," Manson growls, and a shiver runs through me.

"Well, she's more mine 'cause you tried to kill her more often."

Manson snorts. "If I was actually trying, she'd be dead, Riley."

I blink at both of them. Manson's finger is causing delicious tingles to run through me and distracting me.

"And," Riley snaps her gaze back to me, "I *want* to keep you."

I swallow. She wants this? There's no way.

"What Riley means to say," Manson keeps messing with my nipple, softly twisting, flicking, and teasing, "if she had any cognitive empathy, is that she likes you."

I'm completely frozen. Riley...likes me?

"You're stuck now." Riley snakes her hand around to mess with my other nipple. "If you ever try to leave, I'll end you."

"You're really bad at this." Manson shakes his head at Riley.

"So are you, dickhead. So we're even."

Both of their fingers are driving me mad. I arch my back to get away from the pressure, but they just follow me. Manson chuckles. "Yeah, keep struggling. Just like that." He rocks his dick against my leg.

"Fuck yeah, Rachel. You look so good helpless." Riley gets up, and as she does, Manson flips us. I gasp, suddenly on top of him, looking down. He arches into me, his hands gripping my arms, keeping us pinned even in this position. He grins at me. "Ready?"

"Ready?" I repeat, feeling hands on my shorts, and they're ripped down. I cry out, turning to see Riley has come back. She's grinning at me with something in her hand. It's small and plastic, and it's a...strap-on?

"We're both gonna stuff you full. So full you stop questioning who you belong to."

I jump, trying to scramble away. Manson takes advantage of me being up and rips my shorts the rest of the way off, inching his down as well.

"Both?" I squeak. I don't know how they're both gonna fit. The strap-on seemed relatively small, but I know Manson is big. I have no idea how this is going to work.

"Shhh." Manson guides me back on him, so I'm on his dick. He grinds me up against it. "It'll feel good."

"Good? I've never–" Manson lifts me, effortlessly holding me right above him.

"Hmm, Manson. Looking a little...fired up here." I see Riley's hand grab his dick and pump.

Manson's grip on me tightens just slightly. "Put it in."

"So hard already. You look like you're going to come."

I feel tingly and worked up seeing Riley tease Manson right below me.

"Riley." There's a bark of darkness in his voice. "Put it in. Now."

"Shesh." I jump as I feel her tease his dick along my opening, shooting sensation through me. "Just trying to save you from embarrassing yourself."

The tip of his dick slips inside me, and I already know he's going to feel how wet I am. Sure enough, he flashes those green eyes at me, and the corner of his mouth kicks up. Then, in one movement, he impales me on his dick.

Pleasure and pain shoot through me, and I suck in a breath. Holy shit. Manson holds me still, eyes closed, breathing heavily.

Riley chuckles. "Called it. Don't come now, or she'll think you're a bad lay."

"She knows that's not true." Manson moves one hand from my arm to play with my clit. "Isn't that right, Rachel?"

I glance at Riley, and she lifts an eyebrow as if to say: now's your chance.

I don't answer, and Manson just pumps into me once, forcing a breath of air out of me. "That's okay. We'll just repeat the last time then. See if we can beat our last record."

His touch and his dick inside me are already making me feel so fucking good. I hear a snap behind me, and Riley has strapped her dildo on and is coating it in lube.

Fear rushes through me. "Where, what–"

"Shhh." She presses into my back, tracing her hand down me. "Don't encourage me, bambi. I'm trying to be nice." Her fingers trace down to my asshole, where she feathers them against my rim.

I clench, and Manson moans. The feeling isn't unpleasant, just different.

"That's right. We're going to do what we want with our body, and you're going to be a good girl and let us." Riley's voice is husky, and Manson slowly starts pumping into me.

My body erupts in goosebumps. They keep saying they own me, and I hate how hot it sounds. It touches something deep down inside me. Something that wants to let them do whatever they want.

Riley's finger presses into my ass, and I hiss, sucking in a breath. But she doesn't stop, just pumps it in and out. "Nasty girl. You look so good riding him and me at the same time."

I groan. The stimulation on my clit, my G-spot, and my ass is overwhelming. Riley doesn't give me much time and adds a second finger. This time, it stretches a little more, and I grunt, causing her to give a throaty moan.

Manson locks eyes with me. His gaze is unsettling in its perception, and I look away. It's like he can see all the way down to my soul—like he can see the lonely, scared, hurt girl who got swooped up by two tornados of power and possessiveness. It's like he can see how much I want them. And that scares the shit out of me.

I gasp when I feel the tip of Riley's strap-on against my ass.

"Easy." Manson strokes my arm gently. "Relax and let us in."

Riley presses in, and I jump, trying to get away. Manson just presses me back down. "No, no. Let us in, Rachel."

The stretch is painful and feels weird, and I'm clenching down, trying to keep the sensations down.

"The tip is in, relax." Riley snakes a hand around to where Manson's stroking my clit. I feel their hands war for a second, then Riley's takes over. She immediately rolls my clit in her fingers, making a jolt of pleasure run through me.

"There you go, good girl." Her voice is the same calming, rich tone that I remember from the first time I met her. Manson's hand moves up to my tits, grabbing a nipple and playing with it. Despite the pain in my ass, his touch is gentle, and a shiver of shame washes through me as I enjoy his touch. But I lean into the bite of pain as Riley rocks slowly into me. The sensations wash together in a blissful wave, crashing over my body in warm tingles.

"Good girl. Good lord, you're taking both of us. What a good little slut." I feel Riley grind up behind me, her breath heavy in my ear.

Manson picks up his pace, thrusting into me from below. "So...tight."

Riley's fingers and Manson's fingers, and both of them inside me, are winding me up faster than I've ever felt. Everything is tense and pleasurable at the same time, and it all builds in my chest until I let out a low moan.

Manson's dick jerks and Riley groans. They build me slowly until I'm on the edge of wild pleasure, and then, with a pinch of Riley's fingers, she shoves me over the edge. I come, moaning, losing myself to the pleasure exploding in me. Losing myself to them. The pleasure washes over me in waves, and I just...let go.

As soon as I come down off the high, both Riley and Manson pick up the pace. It's overwhelming and overstimulating with a bite of pain in the best way possible. I throw my head back, coming again.

"That's it, what a nasty girl." Riley's voice is husky. "Come all over Manson's dick while I own your pretty little ass."

They fuck me through that orgasm, then another and another. The stimulation quickly gets to be too much, and I squirm, trying to get away.

"Fuck," Manson pants out, holding me still. "Yes, just like that."

They work me higher and higher until the pain blends with the pleasure, and I can't tell the difference anymore. The letdown of the emotions from thinking they were going to kill me hits me all at once, and I think a few tears escape.

Vaguely, I hear Manson demand, "Come, Riley."

"You first."

There's some shuffling, then we're on our sides, and Manson's hand is banded over me, reaching between us to Riley's pussy. My head is buzzing with the mix of orgasms, but I hear Riley groan and feel Manson moving.

"Fuck...you," she breathes, her whole body stiffening. As soon as she stiffens, Manson comes, his dick jerking in me, feeling so tight with the dildo up my ass.

We all lay there for a minute, gasping, sucking in air. It takes me a while to come down from the fuzzy feeling. For some reason, all I can think about is we're on a bed. We're on a bed, and Riley seems okay.

After a few more minutes, Riley groans and rolls out of bed. "I'm starving."

Manson just moves to bury his nose in my hair.

"I'll make some food." I hear her pad out of the room and move downstairs.

I shift. I should probably get up.

Manson holds me still. When he talks, his voice is gruff, "Just so you know, I want you here too."

I try to pull back to look at him, but he just holds me harder, holding me still. "I like you. You're logical and even-headed. You're also good for Riley. You ground her, and that's something I've been trying to do for a long time."

I swallow.

"You also help me. With her. I think we'd make a good team, Rachel Hiebert."

This all feels too good to be true. "Are you lying?" The words slip out before I can stop them.

Manson chuckles, the sound coming from deep in his chest. "Deadly serious."

Still, I hesitate.

"Gonna have to tell me what's going on inside your head. I'm better than Riley, but still not great. I don't feel what you feel, Rachel."

I swallow. There are so many emotions turning around in my chest right now. Fear, hope, vulnerability, with more and more coming in, and trying to decide which ones he wants to hear about makes me feel like I'm in one of those wind machines trying to grab money, but it keeps slipping out of my hands. Which one does he care about? Why is he asking? Finally, I say, "I...don't know."

Manson just holds me.

"Rachel!" Riley shouts up the stairs. "How many chicken nuggets?"

I jump in surprise. I don't know. There are too many decisions and too many sensations going on right now.

I open my mouth, "I'm scared, Manson. What if this goes wrong?" What if they break my heart?

"Okay, I'll do ten!" I hear her clattering in the kitchen.

Manson strokes my hair. "Well, we aren't scared. Let's just take it one day at a time, hmm? None of this will be easy, Rachel. That's not what we're asking. We're asking to do it together."

Together.

I want that. I pick at my nails, letting all of the emotions in my chest filter out through that repetitive motion. Over and over and over. Pick, pick, pick until I feel quiet enough to take a deep breath.

Then, I make what might possibly be the stupidest decision I've ever made. My voice comes out quietly, "Okay. Together."

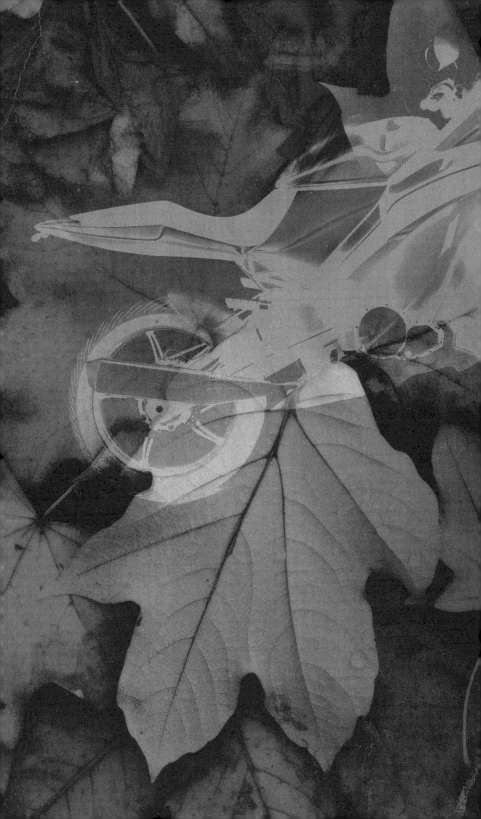

57

Alkaline - Sleep Token

"You think I care? Give them my fucking number." I hang up the phone. I've been trying to track down Rachel's friend Cali, and I've finally got her pinned down. Only Wyatt is being a royal pain in the dick about it.

It's been a week since Riley's angry murder spree, and we brought Rachel back. I had to burn the truck Riley stole. She threw a fit about it, so I had to promise to buy her the same make and model.

It's been a disaster trying to keep the cops off Riley's ass. An expensive disaster. Thankfully, the only murder with any evidence was the first one. And DNA records can be "misplaced" when you have enough money and the right connections. Her image is still all over social media, but with her mask, a lack of DNA evidence, and our lawyer's heavy involvement, there isn't much to go on besides speculation. And if you're rich enough, speculation never lands you in jail.

My phone buzzes in my hand. It's an unknown number. Well, that was fast.

I find Rachel in the barn with Riley. They've been spending a lot of time together out here. It's mostly silent, each of them working on their respective projects. Rachel hasn't gone back to her house except to bring all her skulls to Riley's garage. I offered to get them, but she told me she'd 'cut my balls off' if I messed with her system. So Riley and I just went with her and watched as she carefully packed them up to bring back. It took hours. Rachel insisted she could do it herself, but we aren't letting her out of our sight. Not until we're good and sure she won't spook.

"Rachel. Phone." I hand it to her.

Surprised, she looks up from her buckets of chemicals with some bones inside. "Who is it?"

I shrug.

She looks like she doesn't want to take it, but she does. "Hello?"

There's a beat of silence, and then Rachel jumps upright. "Oh my god. Cali?" There's another beat of silence, and then she lets out a squeal and moves to the other side of the barn.

Riley throws me a look. "Cali?" Riley has short silver hair now, and I think it suits her. It's hot, and it just makes me want to fuck her now more than ever.

I reach out to wrap my arm around Riley's shoulder, but she ducks away from me, brandishing the knife she was using to skin a deer. "You found Cali?"

I hold up my hands. "Yes. And?"

Riley's face draws more into a scowl. "You mean, the Cali with whom she was in love with? That Cali? The one who is actually still living?"

I cock my head. "She was in love with her?"

Riley throws up her hands. "For the love of god. Where is she so I can kill her?"

I grin, darting in to snatch the knife away from Riley. "No sharp objects while we fight. I want to stay alive." I toss it onto her workbench and wrap my arms around her.

"Let me go!" Riley struggles, but I just hold her tighter. "You mean the Cali who's on lockdown so much that I now owe Wyatt a huge favor for a simple phone call?"

"Oh?" Riley perks up. She loves any time I talk about The Hunter's Club, which still pisses me off. I don't want her to have anything to do with them. It's not safe.

"I don't think you have anything to worry about. I've seen the way Rachel looks at you." I rest my chin on her head. Riley is stiff for a second, then slowly relaxes. She's been lighter since everything happened. Less angry. And it feels like the band that was perpetually around my chest has loosened.

Of course, I told her what I was doing with Noel. I expected her to fight me on it, but she just requested to talk to my jail contact to put in a few requests of her own. He will live a very long and very excruciating time in prison. I've seen to that.

Rachel returns after a few minutes, face bright.

Riley has been trying to play it cool, but she can't stop fidgeting. So I've kept her in my arms.

"How is she? Still breathing?"

"Yeah, she's great." Rachel hands me the phone, then glances at the ground, her voice soft. "Thank you for that."

Riley growls, "Good. More fun for me then."

"Riley," I shake my head. "No more killing."

She gives me the most annoyed look, and I shrug. "Not this one. Wyatt would actually kill both of us, and that sounds like way too much work." I don't mention that she made it into The Hunter's Club. I figure she'll find out sooner or later. I'd rather it be later. My gut is already twisting at the thought of protecting her during a brutal group hunt where the hunters are in just as much danger as the hunted.

Riley rolls her eyes. "I'm better than him."

Rachel snorts.

Riley turns her gaze on Rachel. "Want to repeat that, bambi?"

Rachel continues with her bucket and bones. "That's naive."

My eyebrows shoot up, and I let out a loud laugh.

Rachel glances between both of us, confused. "What's so funny? She's saying she's better than the head of an organized crime club, but she only has four bodies under her belt? And one of them was on camera?"

Oh, bless her factual little heart; she's only digging her hole deeper. My grin just widens.

Riley tries to get out of my arms. "Again, little doe?"

Rachel realizes her mistake and pales. "Uh...I mean..."

"Here's how this is gonna go." Riley's voice lowers. "You're gonna run. I'm gonna catch you. Then I'm gonna teach that pretty little mouth a lesson, yeah?"

Rachel squeaks and looks at me. As if I'm going to protect her. I laugh again. "Better get going, or she'll catch you pretty quick." I know Riley won't actually hurt her. I see the lack of any real anger in her. It's just their fun game.

I let go of Riley, and she growls, "Ready or not, here I come."

Epilogue

Halloween (feat. Nicolle Galyon) - Walker Hayes

Two months later

"Jesus, Rachel."

The unexpected voice makes me jump. I look up from where I've been walking the riverbed, looking for Riley. I don't see her until she clears her throat. I look up. She's in a tree stand right over me, rifle held facing up.

She cocks a dark eyebrow. "So much for not coming into my area, hmmm?"

Shit. I was supposed to be walking the woods quite a ways away. But I got caught up in this stream and kept finding skeletons of mice, muskrats, and even a deer, so I followed it.

I grimace. "Sorry."

She shakes her head, but there's a small smile. "Come here."

I frown, looking up at her on the small platform.

"Come up here." She motions.

I walk to the base of the tree. "I don't think there'll be room."

"I'll make room. Up here, now." There's demand in her tone, so I drop my bag and climb up the ladder. It's rickety, and I feel it moving with every step. But when I get to the top, Riley has made just enough room for both of us to stand.

I feel the stand shift, and I grip onto her, brushing her chest. Immediately, I let go of her, trying to make space. "Sorry."

I expect her to freak out, but she just looks at me with those dark, expressionless eyes. "Again."

"What?" I look at her, thoroughly confused.

"Touch me," she says quietly.

I freeze.

Riley chuckles softly, then grabs my hands. She yanks me closer to her, and as I tip into her, she smashes her mouth to mine in a kiss. The press of her soft, full lips to mine makes the blood rush to my pussy. Riley kisses me harder, tracing her tongue along the seam of my lips until I open to her. I sneak my tongue out to meet hers, and she groans into my mouth, melting into me and pulling me closer. She nips and sucks and licks, worshiping me with her mouth. I can feel the press of her lips shoot sensation all the way through me.

Riley pulls back for a breath, a slight smirk on her lips. I blink, also breathing heavily, only to notice that my hands are on her tits. Where she's placed them.

I try to yank them back, but she keeps them there. "Touch me."

"Riley, I..."

"I want to try it." She looks at me, her dark eyes remaining the same. I see no anger or pain in them. Her tits are soft and pillowy and feel so fucking good under my hands. I can tell she isn't wearing a bra, and it just makes my cheeks flame hotter. I pull my hands away just enough to trace them around. When Riley feels what I'm doing, she lets go of my hands completely, letting me explore. I trace soft circles around them, feeling their fullness even under her shirt. She's so soft and perfect and just...everything. I feel my pussy getting wet.

"That's pretty gay for a straight girl."

My gaze darts to hers, and there's a twinkle in her eye.

I shake my head and open my mouth to say something, but Riley lifts her shirt in one go. "Uh uh. If that mouth's gonna open, it's gonna be to suck titties and nothing else."

I stare at her perfect breasts, then at her eyes.

"I'm good, Rachel. You feel good." Her pupils are wide. "Now suck."

I lean down, anticipation buzzing along my skin. For a second, unsureness fills me. I don't know how to suck a titty or make it feel good.

"Here." Riley's hands snake behind my head, and she pulls me to her, lining me up with her nipple. "Lick."

Tentatively, I stick my tongue out and swipe it across her nipple. I see the nipple pebble, and Riley lets out a soft breath. "Again."

So I do. Riley's reaction is everything. She grips my hair tighter, pulling me closer. So I close my lips around her nipple and suck. Her breast is soft, but her nipple is hard, and I roll it around in my mouth. Riley groans, falling back against the tree. I stumble into her, and she catches me, breathless. I look into her eyes, and it doesn't fill me with discomfort. Just a sense of...peace.

Riley grins at me. "That was hot."

My face flushes, and I pull back. "Was it...okay?"

"Yeah," Riley's voice is soft, and she brushes a piece of hair out of my face. "Because it was you."

Warmth runs through me, and I blush again.

We stay there for a while longer, just looking at the woods, soaking in the peace and each other, and then Riley takes me home. Well, to Riley's barn. We spend most of our time there, with Riley working on hides and butchering and me organizing and making a space for myself. Riley is chaotic at best, and things get scattered everywhere. Plus, the barn is old and full of junk. So, I've had my hands full sorting and organizing to my heart's content. It's peaceful in the best way.

I am muddy from the stream, so I head to my room and start changing my clothes. I've made a room for us out of an old stall. I've turned it into a giant bed of sorts. There are mattresses and pillows all over the floor, fairy lights strung up in crisscrosses across the top of the stall, and fake ivy and leaves all over the walls. Every available wall space is hung with shelves for my skulls, but it's still not enough, so I just keep my favorites in here. Pup is here too, right by the head of our bed. I'm pretty proud of how white I got the bones. Oh, and there's also spell ingredients everywhere. Riley collects the most random things and leaves them all over the place. The chaos bothers me, but it seems to make her happy. So I leave them.

I get into my dry clothes and sigh. I haven't decided if I want to go back to work yet. Manson insists he can get me my job back if I want it, but part of me loves the silence and peace of hanging out here. And I'm not ready to face the emptiness of my old place. Not that I think they'd let me go alone. Neither likes to let me out of their sight. They breathed down my fucking neck when I got my skulls so much that I nearly dropped my snakes and raccoons, bumping into them.

I glare at the wall, just thinking about it. I'd have skinned them alive if they made me break anything.

Riley's been hunting a lot more recently. Manson decided to move all the bodies of the people he dumped here for Riley to dispose of. Said there's too much heat on us right now. He's having Riley bury the carcasses of the deer she gets over the spots the people used to be, just in case the cadaver dogs are let loose on our property. In addition to hunting, Riley has been disappearing at odd hours and coming back with random deer mounts. There are beginning to be so many of them that I've had to devote an entire stall to their housing. She never wants me to display them, and when I ask, all she'll say is: at least it's not murder.

I hear a commotion at the door, then Manson's voice says, "Goddamn it! Riley, come get your dogs."

Riley's coyote pups yip. I grin and step out of the room. The two pups howl and jump up on Manson, who brushes them off with a look. They love him and immediately follow him whenever he's around. He hates it.

"Printer, Toothbrush, down." Riley halfheartedly waves at the pups, then gets back to packing her bag. Riley brought them home after one of our hunting missions. She found them without a mother and brought them back to the barn. She insisted they were dogs.

They are not. But Manson humors her, so I do too. She also insisted on naming them the most random things, and secretly, I'm here for it.

"Rachel, I have something for you," Manson says. He drops the bag he's been holding and pulls out a bone. It looks like some kind of...deer femur.

He hands it to me with a proud smirk on his face.

Manson has been bringing me back random bones he finds while he's out...digging up Riley's bodies and whatnot.

"It's not human." Manson shoves it at me.

Well, I know that. I smirk and take it. I only collect the cool bones, like skulls and sometimes the spines. That is until Manson started gifting me with them. Now, they all seem kinda cool to me.

"Thanks," I smile.

Manson turns back to his pack. "Oh, and something else." He pulls something small out. It's a...vial of some liquid. With a needle attached.

I frown.

"Birth control," Manson explains.

Riley turns to look at it, then at me. "Manson." Riley lifts an eyebrow. "She doesn't need birth control; you're fixed."

Manson just motions at me. "Come here."

I most definitely do not want to go near that needle. I look between them. Riley mouths something at me, and Manson shoots her a glare.

I couldn't tell what she said. Riley shakes her head, then stage whispers, "Tracker."

Manson sighs loudly. "Fine, it's a tracker. Come here."

"What? I don't want a tracker." I take a step back.

He just raises an eyebrow. "You're mine now, and I need to know where you are at all times."

Riley looks at the vial, then back at me. She grins, and before I know it, she's snatched me up and put me on her workbench. "It's all you," she gloats. "Loser."

Manson comes around to my other side, and both of them trap me in. "Oh, I already got you, Riley."

Riley snaps her gaze to him. Manson just shrugs. It takes a second, then Riley's eyes widen, and she pats her body down. "Where?"

Manson just shrugs again.

"Where, Manson?"

He just smirks. "Guess you'll have to find out. Your turn, Rachel."

Riley rips off her shirt, patting herself down with exaggerated motions. "Manson, I swear to god I'll kill you."

He just laughs. "Bring it on, little pain."

I inch off the table. I know what running will do. I know they'll hunt me down and force me to take it. But it's become our little fucked up game of hide and seek. The push and pull between all of us is dynamic, scary, exciting, and kind of everything I didn't realize I was missing in life. I know things will be hard living with these two. They already have been, but these are two of the most stubborn people I've met in my life. When there's a problem, they dig into it until it's addressed.

I've fallen for two serial killers.

And I wouldn't have it any other way.

Ready or Not is part of an interconnected standalone series. Cali's story can be found in Wanna Play a Game? *Wyatt's story will be the next to be released!*

AUTHOR'S NOTE

Hello my nasties, you made it. Writing fucked up books for you guys is my favorite. If you want to keep in touch or up to date on the Alina May universe, please follow me on socials and join my Facebook group! Please, don't be shy!

Tiktok: Alina_may_author
    Instagram: Alina_may_author
    Facebook: Alina May's Book Babes

ACKNOWLEDGEMENTS

Alex and Sarah, ya'll are the goat. Like, seriously, thank you so much for all your help with this book. Core memories were made as we created it and I love you so much. To my other betas, Laurelyn, Charlotte, and Amanda, and to my sensitivity reader Paige, you guys are my backbone. I couldn't do this without you and I'm so grateful for you! Also, to my editor and PA Taylor, I love you to pieces. Thank you for always being the absolute best and keeping my chaos to an organized medium.

Does anyone ever read these? If so, secret gold star for you. You nosey bastard LOL. It's okay, I'm the same way.

Made in the USA
Monee, IL
10 October 2024

67609450R00214